"*Journey of the Dead* is Estleman's most provocative book, with the strongest visual imagery and the most complex characters."
—*Amarillo Globe-News*

"This is a Western novel that also is a work of literature. Loren D. Estleman can do that."
—*San Antonio Express-News* on *Journey of the Dead*

Praise for Loren D. Estleman's Acclaimed *Billy Gashade*

"*Billy Gashade* . . . is a work of American literature."
—Dee Brown, author of *Bury My Heart at Wounded Knee*

"His entire story is a song, lyrical and alive with biting wit, drama, and the grace of a fine tale well told. . . . Rousing and entertaining."
—*Publishers Weekly* (starred review)

"*Billy Gashade* is at once a lively coming-of-age story and an annotated pastiche of American history." —*The New York Times*

"Estleman seizes the reader's attention and never relinquishes it. He is as addictive as morphine in that one's craving is never satisfied for long, but always returns, hungering for that next novel. And the next. But for the time being, savor this one, for it's vintage work by the master of his trade." —*Amarillo Globe-News*

"A brilliant creation. The dialogue is magical, the prose poetic, the characters earthy and real." —*El Paso Herald-Post*

"Estleman rivals the finest American novelists with his gritty vision and keen ear." —*The Washington Post Book World*

"Loren D. Estleman has written a number of impressive novels, but his latest, *Billy Gashade,* rises above them all."
—Associated Press

BY LOREN D. ESTLEMAN FROM TOM DOHERTY ASSOCIATES

City of Widows

The High Rocks

Billy Gashade

Stamping Ground

Journey of the Dead

Aces & Eights

Jitterbug

JOURNEY

of the

DEAD

Loren D. Estleman

A TOM DOHERTY ASSOCIATES BOOK *New York*

This is a work of fiction. All of the characters and events portrayed in this novel are either fictitious or are used fictitiously.

JOURNEY OF THE DEAD

Copyright © 1998 by Loren D. Estleman

A Forge Book
Published by Tom Doherty Associates, LLC
175 Fifth Avenue
New York, NY 10010

Forge® is a registered trademark of Tom Doherty Associates, LLC

ISBN: 0-812-54916-3
Library of Congress Card Catalog Number: 97-34381

First edition: April 1998
First mass market edition: July 1999

Printed in the United States of America

0 9 8 7 6 5 4 3 2 1

In Memoriam
Gordon D. Shirreffs
(1914–1996)
Más allá!

*Pity for him who one day looks upon
his inward sphinx and questions it. He is lost.*
—Rubén Darío

LEAD

Chapter One

The Coming of the Long Man

The desert is an amphitheater. Eternal in its architecture, infallible in its silence, it marks the disturbed pebble, the broken blade of feathergrass in never-decreasing reverberations to its outer edge. At a distance of fifty miles the click of an iron shoe against sandstone is as the scrape of one's own fork on the plate before him. This is how I became aware of the long man the moment he crossed into old Mexico.

The way along La Jornada del Muerto was hazardous and harsh, but the long man knew it like a lover. Peace after all was a fugitive concept. A war had torn him from his birthplace in Alabama, a different kind of war had transformed him from a hunter of buffalo into a hunter of men, and jeopardy was a state of being. He had a wife and a daughter, but they were aberrant to the Life, a respite rather than an addendum. Home was a place to gather strength and copulate and obtain fresh horses. It lacked the substance of heat and hardpack and the things with thorns and stings. He lived along the Journey of the Dead.

At night the day's heat drained away between the loose grains of sand that made up the desert floor. The long man's breath made jets of gray in the dry blood of dawn; those of the saddle horse and packhorse smoked thickly around their muzzles and condensed into drops that stung their eyes and made them blink. In the long shadows the long man wore a blanket of Hopi manufacture across his shoulders. As the sun grew yellow, the weight of the coarse weave lay heavily upon him, and he rolled it tight and lashed it behind his cantle. The sun's rays made blue pools atop distant rises, but he was not fooled by them, nor did they force him to drink from his canteen, although they made him thirst. He had more than water enough to reach his destination, but even a rich man did not spend his money promiscuously. He would drink when he rested.

In the stonehammer heat of midday he sat in the shade he created by stretching the Hopi blanket between a pair of boulders and two mesquite branches thrust into the sand. There he drank from his canteen, ate one of the pemmican cakes his wife had made for him, and dozed until the shadows stretched. Then he mounted and rode until darkness made the ground treacherous. He did not drink but that he fed water to the horses first from the cup of his hands. He did not make a fire lest the beacon attract the attention of Apaches. He lay wrapped in the Hopi with his hand around the oiled walnut handle of his big long-barreled Colt's revolver, and rose stiff and cold in the tarnished light reflected from below the horizon on the bellies of the clouds to resume his pilgrimage.

On the forenoon of the third day he entered the village.

He had found it more by instinct than direction, the instructions he received from farmers and beggars he had encountered along the road having been delivered in a mulch of bastard Spanish, Yaqui Indian, and fragments of the spoken from the language of the hieroglyphs in the ruins of Tenotchtitlán; and what he had managed to understand was inaccurate. The four directions are as one to the snail who starts and finishes his existence within a handful of miles, yet he is either too polite or too fearful of the consequences of silence not to make some show of knowing the way for the turtle who pauses to inquire.

The village meant little more to him than the desert. Indeed, its features were more like the bleak memory one carried away from that country than the country itself, which seldom failed to surprise even the seasoned traveler with the variety of its shades of umber and saffron and terra-cotta, and after a brief rain with the glory of its blossoms. The squat earthen huts, the wrinkled brown men in their bleached cotton and the widows in their faded weeds, the flies humming soporifically around sides of meat slung from hooks in front of the butcher's like drunks singing, might have belonged to any of a hundred communities sprung up like cottonwoods wherever water trickled down from the yellow-ocher mountains. The desert hammered everything to sameness.

This village, at least, boasted a bath house, the only one between El Paso del Norte and Mexico City. The Aztec Baths shared a building with Juan Morales the barber, and after his haircut and shave the long man stripped to his red raw skin and soaked away the hard crust of sweat and sand like a salt rind while the old woman brushed his brown wool suit and boiled his white shirt in corn water and pressed it with a flatiron until it was as level and stiff as paper. When he emerged from the water, glowing all over and plum-colored in his armpits and private parts, he toweled off vigorously, put on clean long johns, dressed, and combed his thick black hair and smoothed his trailing moustaches before a mirror with an iron frame.

He smelled like a French king. The scent, heavy with crushed violets and lime water and oil of oleander, came from the bottles in Juan Morales' barbershop, where they had increased in potency from long disuse; but it could not entirely eradicate the long man's own smell, of woodsmoke and black powder and harnesses left out in the weather. It was his principal distinguishing feature after his great height, which in the time before he could afford tailoring had obliged him to stitch pieces of hide to the bottoms of his ready-made trousers to cover his long legs. He had never worn garters to gather the material of his shirtsleeves.

The path to the place he sought, and which had brought him all this way into a foreign country, was worn hollow and led through a stand of quaking aspen whose shade was as black and as cool as a subterranean lake. It ended at the base of a rock wall, natural and without features, with a ladder made from ironwood branches lashed together with sinew leaning against the face. This he climbed, the sun cruel upon his shoulders, the air parching his lungs, to the deep ledge at the ladder's summit. There the warm moist air struck his face like the breath of a large friendly dog.

The mirages of the desert could not deceive him, but the green grotto where stood my hut caused him to shut his eyes tight to clear his head of phantasms. Yet when he opened them again the grotto remained. Green in Durango is as gold in the cup of a blind beggar, and the story is yet told of the Spanish priest, his skull caved in and his hamstrings slashed by Apaches, who crawled upon the bloody stumps of his knees for thirty miles across that region that he might collapse and die with his face in the reeds that grew along the bank of the Rio Mezquital, in the time before the first Dutchman set buckled foot upon Manhattan. Had those yellow-green reeds ventured to show themselves upon my rock, I should have plucked them up and flung them over the ledge. Bushes of coriander, wandering vines of basil, forests of mariposa, rows of mandrake and ginseng, and half a hundred more varieties of herbs, spices, roots, and creeping ivy grew in profusion underfoot and wound up the aspen poles that supported the lattice overhead, from which hung black moss in bunches and chokecherry tendrils. Here was every shade and tint of green, from cerecloth black to fiery chartreuse, blinding bright; a botanical garden of wondrous diversity contained within a few square yards of weather-battered stone. There was not another like it between Tres Marias and the Gulf of Mexico. The air was drunken with leafy scent and as heavy as the atmosphere in a rain forest.

Opposite the ladder, nearly invisible in the deep shade, was the entrance to my workshop and home, a trapezoidal opening in an adobe hut of Pueblo Indian origin with walls three feet thick, which from a distance appeared as nothing more than a hollow in the rock scooped by eons of erosion. On his way there the long man trod upon the black soil that covered the rock, soft as pine needles, and ducked beneath a flowering bough that sagged from the lattice.

His stature compelled him to bow his head to clear the lintel and afterward stand with shoulders rounded and his hat off to avoid colliding with the objects that hung from the beams. He stood unspeaking while he waited for his eyes to adjust to the dimness within.

When they had, he still did not speak or look in my direction, but wandered the room, examining with a browser's interest the globes, astrolabes, books bound in decomposing calfskin, and apothecary jars crowding the plane table and shelves, the stuffed crow perched on the lintel over the doorway, the hard varnished shell of the armadillo suspended by rawhide from the center beam of the ceiling. He squinted at the calligraphy on the labels attached to the jars, trying to make out the foreign words, picked up the skull of a prairie dog, registering surprise that it weighed little more than air, smelled the unfamiliar odors that I myself had ceased to smell, of dessicated herbs and she-wolf urine and the exhalations of the athanor. He would know from instinct that these odors were as old as the building itself, permeating the adobe when the clay was yet damp, in the time of the trouble with the Indians up in New Mexico two hundred years before. Such things cannot be manufactured.

At last he came up to where I sat on my tall stool before the chimney, grinding yellow beetles in a mortar. His eyes took in the table in front of me with its litter of retorts, iron tongs, wooden scoops, clumps of borax, ampullae, and my grandfather's bellows, spliced and patched all over so that scarcely a square inch of the original apparatus survived. He cleared his throat loudly and shouted, in dreadful Spanish:

"You are the one the villagers call El Viejo?"

"I am," said I in English, without looking up from my pestle. "It is not necessary to raise your voice. I am not deaf. Merely old."

He hesitated, then dropped his tone. "You speak good American for a Mexican."

"I speak good English for an Englishman. And I am not Mexican. I am Spanish."

"I don't see the difference."

"You would if you came here from Castile with my great-grandfather in 1556."

"Sorry to give offense," he said. "I'm a stranger here. An old woman in Socorro told me you're the man to see when things need fixing that a doctor won't touch. I expected you'd be Indian."

His accent was gentle, dusted but lightly with the dry grit of the Southwest. There was nothing in it of the high honking bray of the Yankee. He had through all remained a Southerner, and he was genuinely apologetic. This too cannot be manufactured.

I laid aside my chore and studied him. The hat in his hand was a new Stetson, blocked into the Texas pinch, with a brown leather sweatband to which clung a number of cut hairs. His thinker's face was long with sorrow. To his vest was pinned a five-pointed star in a shield, nickel-plated, without engraving.

He was perhaps thirty, but his soul was older even than mine.

"What is the name of the old woman you spoke to in Socorro?" I asked.

"Epiphania Ruiz. She's a hunchback."

"I remember her. I treated her for epilepsy when she was a child. Her father was a stonecutter in this village."

"It wasn't her. She's eighty if she's a day."

"She is older than that. It was in the last year of the old century."

"That'd make you right around a hundred."

"It would. It does."

He said nothing, too polite to express disbelief.

"It is no great personal feat to live a long time," I said.

"It is in my work."

I folded my hands in the lap of my apron. "I am not a shaman, although I have learned much from their society that has helped me to subsist in this country. You saw my herb garden on your way to my door. Does it impress you that I have succeeded in making things grow on this bare rock where the rain comes once in three years?"

"I know a piece about growing things. I was raised on a plantation."

"For ten years I employed Yaquis to carry soil by the basket up the naked face of the rock. Nothing grew the first five years.

During each of the next four, the plants reached a height of a sixteenth of an inch, then turned white and died. It was then that I sought out a shaman one-third my age and acquired the secret that has allowed me to harvest my own herbs for seventy-three years. I continue to employ a boy to bring water each day, and once each month to carry and spread horse manure, compost, and some other substance that he refuses to identify for anyone but another Yaqui. To know some things it is not enough even to be born in a place to generations born there. One must also share blood."

"Do you sell the herbs?"

"No. I am not a merchant."

"What do you pay the boy with?"

"Instruction works two ways."

He nodded, as if he understood. "You were born here?"

"It is the only home I have ever known. I have never traveled more than twenty miles from this spot."

"You missed a lot."

"Only things of small consequence. This village is the only source of water between Durango City and the Rio Nazas. Travelers stop here often, and they bring with them the news of the world. In time everything that matters finds its way to my rock."

"I didn't mean to say it's all bad. Missing things."

I saw then that the sorrow in his face came from behind it, and that his eyes were but the surface of a black pool whose depth was impossible to sound. They were the eyes of my grandfather in a painting made by my father from memory at my request, upon the occasion of my father's one hundredth birthday. My grandfather was slain in his ninety-seventh year by the Pueblo Indians in Santa Fe. They pierced his eyes with the lancet he used to bleed lizards and poured molten silver from his own athanor into the sockets, then threw him off a cliff. His third wife fled to this place with my father, who was then in swaddles. He was an alchemist, like his father and grandfather, who left Castile to avoid the inquisitors. We have all sought the secret of the Philosopher's Stone. What we have learned from our failures has been of greater value than what most seekers learn from their successes.

I asked the long man what had brought him so many days from Socorro.

"I ain't from Socorro. I was just riding through. I'm sheriff up in Lincoln County."

I had heard of this place, and of its troubles. Men who had no need of additional wealth had coveted the same piece of ground, and had employed other men to slay one another until one side or the other had lost too many men to defend their part of the ground. Both sides had claimed the protection of the laws they violated.

I said, "I cannot help you to apprehend fugitives from your justice. It is not the kind of knowledge I possess or pursue."

"I ain't looking to find anyone. I'm looking to get rid of something."

"A sickness?"

"Dreams." He circled the brim of his hat through his long nervous fingers. "I want you to give me something to stop the dreams."

Chapter Two

Badgers, Buffalo, and Bad Men

The long man's name was Pat Garrett. Born in Alabama, he had moved with his parents to an eighteen-hundred-acre plantation in Louisiana at the age of three, where he developed a man's hard muscles chopping apart the clods of red earth with a hoe and sharpened his eye plucking squirrels out of hickory trees with a boy's single-shot rifle. What reading and writing skills he ever had he acquired squirming on an axe-hewn bench in the single room of a log schoolhouse on the edge of a bayou alive with mosquitoes and cottonmouth snakes. Throughout his life he associated figures and words on paper with physical misery; his sheriff's account-books were a chaos, his stock tallies an affront to the rules of arithmetic. He acquired a reputation for not paying his debts because he couldn't be bothered to keep track of sums.

Religion he looked upon as scarcely less confounding. When he was ten, Pat put on a white sheet and allowed himself to be tipped backward into the spring behind the Baptist church by a minister who wore a plug hat with his gown to cover the scar from a scalp wound he received during the Seminole War. The veteran lost his grip and nearly drowned him in the roiling ice-shard waters. Pat dated his lifelong agnosticism from the moment he was hauled spluttering from the ropy mud, his eyes and nostrils burning hotter than his faith. God was a hard old cob to work for if He existed, and although Pat had known some as hard, they paid better wages on the average and gave him Sunday.

That same summer, he set himself to rid the plantation of a badger that stole from its burrow in the black of night to carry off his mother's laying hens. After tracking the thief to its hole, Pat walked around spreading the tall grass with his boots until he found its hidden exit. This he plugged with a small boulder, then made himself comfortable a few yards from the remaining hole, intending to shoot the badger when it made its appearance under the half-moon. All night he waited, and at sunup went back to the house to learn that another hen had been taken. He returned to the burrow, but found the boulder undisturbed. For another hour he searched, finally discovering a third hole beneath a ledge of shale. He jammed another rock under the ledge, and that evening he again took up his vigil.

Past midnight a bank of clouds rolled in and erased the moon. Pat crept closer to the burrow, fixing his eyes upon the entrance while his pupils expanded, sorting the empty black of the hole from the shallow blackness that surrounded it. Things scurried through the grass, too small to be the badger. Crickets stitched. Somewhere off in the void, a pair of great wings pounded, followed by a short sharp squeal of pain and terror, then silence, filled quickly by the noise of the crickets.

At length something shifted in the blackness of the burrow. A pale muzzle emerged, paused, and lifted to sniff the air. Very slowly a shadowy bulk separated itself from the deeper darkness. A pair of tiny black eyes glittered in a shaft of starlight leaking through a hole in the clouds. Pat, who had applied whitewash to the front sight of his rifle, aimed at the center of the bulk and fired. The hen-stealing ceased.

The Civil War fell heavily upon Louisiana. Glowering, monkey-faced men in kepi caps rode through the cotton, their horses' iron shoes chopping the plants to pieces. In the winter they built fires to drive out the damp and left them smoldering when they broke camp, to flare up before the first wind and burn down the crop. Peace was worse. Conquered by Northern shot and steel, infested by small-eyed Yankees in derby hats and side-whiskers, ridden over by sour veterans with pillowcases on their heads and lynching ropes slung from the horns of their saddles, the land bled and mortified. Carpetbaggers confiscated Garrett cotton. Pat's father John, in debt and drinking, quarreled with a Union sympathizer on the courthouse steps, fumbled a ball-and-percussion Colt's revolver from under the waistband of his trousers, and discharged a chamber into the Yankee's belly. The muzzle flash caught the man's flannel shirt afire, and Pat, who witnessed the confrontation, would forever afterward associate the stench of burning cloth with violence.

The wound infected and the man died twenty-one days later raving of gangrene. John Garrett died soon after of drink and regret and self-loathing. The plantation was seized and sold. On a sodden January morning in 1869, Pat Garrett, aged eighteen, hauled his six feet and five inches into the saddle of a broken-down gray and rode to Texas.

He put in a season working a cotton field in Dallas County, then threw down his hoe forever to take up the reins of a cow pony. He helped drive a herd of longhorns from Eagle Lake to Denison, then signed on with another outfit to ride the line through the winter. There he rounded up strays that had drifted off the range ahead of the icy winds and shared the dugout line shack with a legion of field mice and a high-smelling cow-puncher named Doob. Doob spat tobacco into the stewpot as he stirred it over the fire and every three or four weeks put on a fresh shirt without removing the old one first. When Pat reflected aloud that he would never need a calendar so long as he could keep track of time by counting the shirts his partner was wearing, Doob came at him with a skillet. Pat unholstered his father's Colt's from the nail in the wall where it hung and squeezed the trigger point-blank. It misfired, but Doob put the skillet away. They finished out the winter without further incident. However, Doob was a talker, and Pat Garrett became known as a man with his father's hot temper. This together with his great height marked him as someone to walk around.

In a saloon in Fort Worth hung with skins and a buffalo head the size of a cast-iron bathtub over the beer pulls, Pat got into his cups during poker and delivered a lecture to his fellow players on the various grades of cotton, and how a farmer not overburdened with scruples might deceive a potential buyer into paying a premium price for a substandard crop. Among his listeners was a rangy fellow three or four years Pat's senior, who spoke like a Georgia cracker and invited him for a drink at the bar when Pat went bust. The man's name was Skelton Glenn. He told Pat he had spent time in Louisiana himself, where he'd accumulated a knowledge of the cotton trade that had enabled him to establish a profitable plantation in Texas after he mustered out of the Confederacy, and to recognize another expert when he heard one.

"I'll spare you the rest," Pat said. "I've had my life's portion of farming. I'm a cowman and a first-class horse breaker."

"I guessed that from the look of you. I'm in cattle myself. Year before last I ran longhorns to Florida, then came back last year with a remuda. I cleared eight thousand."

Pat sipped at his whiskey carefully to avoid getting drops in his beard. He'd grown a nice one since leaving Louisiana, full and black and stiff as quills. "You hiring?" he asked.

"No, I'm looking for a partner."

"Sorry, Mr. Skelton. I don't have a penny to invest in cattle or horses."

"Skelton's my Christian name. There's no mister about it. What's got you spooked, Indians or rustlers?"

"Neither. Both. My skin's mine to do with as I damn well please, but I don't favor letting my savings ride on critters so dumb they'll follow anybody anywhere, rustlers and Indians included."

Glenn grinned. "You had me going there. I was afraid you was smart."

"Well, I'm innocent of that." Pat's teeth showed briefly in his whiskers.

"I'm getting out of the cattle business, horses too. I could be a rich man if I stayed in, but that ain't why I come West."

Pat said nothing.

"Ever hunt buff?" Glenn asked.

"I never did."

"Money in it."

"I thought that wasn't why you come West."

"It ain't. That don't mean it's against my religion. It's something different is what it is. Buff's free for the taking, and you don't have to bring back nothing but the hides. They're fetching top dollar in Fort Griffin."

"I hear it's dirty work."

"None dirtier, nor hotter in summer nor colder in winter nor worse for bugs and rotten grub. I said it was different from cattle work, not better. I figure a man who'd trade cotton farming for fifteen and found and all the alkali he can swallow is a natural for buffalo hunting."

They had another drink apiece and shook hands on the deal. Pat and Glenn, a Kentucky friend of Glenn's named Luther

Duke, and Joe Briscoe, an affable youth Pat had taken up with in Fort Worth, piloted a buckboard over three hundred miles of Texas to Fort Griffin, where Pat bought a '73 Winchester carbine with a brass receiver, called the Yellow Boy, and the others selected big-bore Sharps rifles. They bought a thousand cartridges, eight hundred pounds of lead and six kegs of powder for reloading, bacon, beans, coffee, tobacco, and liquor, and corn for the horses. They picked up two saddle horses at thirty apiece and a pair of skinners named Buck and Grundy for wages and struck out for the buffalo range.

At first Pat took to the hunting. Reading the trail excited him as nothing had since he'd staked out and shot the badger, and he was a crack shot and a natural stalker, who with the wind in his face could down a hundred buffalo in a stand before the herd caught on and stampeded. Soon, however, the experience palled. There was little hunting involved on a plain that was often black with their quarry, and the shooting itself was little more than butchery. A parade of thunderheads marched down the Double Mountains and across the tabletop land, saturating everything and making campfires difficult. Everyone developed a rash. Partners and employees sniped at one another. Fistfights broke out.

Young Joe Briscoe was Irish Catholic and serious about it, each night before retiring and each morning after rising, he kissed the tiny crucifix he wore on a chain around his neck. Pat, who normally kept his lack of faith to himself, was wet and irritable, and his clammy underclothes put him in mind of his near-drowning in the name of God's mercy. One morning he muttered something about "that damned dumb Irish Christer," and Briscoe charged. Pat, who had nearly a foot on his attacker, merely knocked him down. Briscoe sprang back up, only to be put down again. Pat knocked him down twice more, and then

Briscoe scooped up the axe the party used to chop wood and split carcasses and swung it at Pat's head. Pat ducked and dived for his Winchester. It didn't misfire.

The authorities in Fort Griffin heard the facts and decided not to pursue charges. However, the incident soured Skelton Glenn's opinion of his partner, who had insisted upon bringing along the inexperienced Briscoe despite Glenn's objections. The party sold its hides in Fort Griffin, divided the proceeds, and went in five separate directions.

Pat lived for a time on his profits, then found work in Fort Sumner, New Mexico Territory, on a ranch owned by Pete Maxwell, the son of the late cattle baron Lucien Maxwell. There the vaqueros, thick-waisted and low to the ground, made jokes about the gringo's ridiculous height while their women admired his Southern good manners and custom-made clothes, an extravagance he allowed himself in an area where the trousers in the mercantiles ran out of material two inches above his boot-tops. In 1877 he met, courted, and married Juanita Gutiérrez, the daughter of a freighter. She quickly became pregnant and died of a hemorrhage. After the funeral, Pat strode away from his friends' soft words, mounted the tall bay he had asked Pete Maxwell for in lieu of his wages, and rode up into the bluffs of the Llano Estacado. What he did in that naked, wind-scraped country he never told anyone, but when he returned months later to Fort Sumner, he had shed his beard. His eyes were as hard as bedrock, and although his temper was noticeably under better control, in times of trial the muscles in his jaw were observed to stand out like train couplings. He was leaner than ever; his cheeks were gaunt, the joints of his arms and legs visible beneath his clothes. From any distance he looked like a prairie wolf strung from the overhang of a hider's cabin.

Cattle work no longer interested him. He took a room in Fort

Sumner, his first home in any sort of town, and stepped behind the bar of Beaver Smith's saloon, where he kept track of territorial activities through information supplied by the thirsty transients shedding the dust from their clothes at the brass rail. There he refilled their glasses from a measured bottle, listened to their reports, and kept his opinions to himself.

Most of the news came drifting in from Lincoln County to the west, where an Irishman named Murphy, backed by Jim Dolan's political machine in Santa Fe, established a general store in the city of Lincoln. A lawyer named McSween then opened a competing enterprise with financial help from two ranchers, big-eared, whipsaw-lean John Chisum and John Henry Tunstall, a young Englishman. The tendency of Tunstall and Chisum cowhands to "throw a wide loop" around unbranded strays, a common practice and largely overlooked, enabled William Brady, the Lincoln County sheriff and a stolid Dolan man, to issue warrants. One was sworn out against a slight, garrulous, buck-toothed youth who worked for Tunstall. His wanted condition drove young Billy Bonney to do most of his drinking and gambling across the county line in Smith's saloon.

Pat, who liked poker almost as much as he favored tracking and shooting game, took time out from behind the bar frequently to sit at Bonney's table. The pair got on, and when they broke for drinks, the spectacle of long tall Pat and little Billy standing side by side at the rail, observed in the mirror behind the bottles, moved the smaller man to laughter. Billy's mirth was infectious; Pat, who had lived long enough with grief, joined in.

Billy Bonney loved cards. His hands were small and slender and he liked the feel of the waxed pasteboards between his fingers, the way they skidded off the sensitive tips. He took to calling Pat "Big Casino," one of his favorite poker terms. Pat in turn called Billy "Little Casino." Fort Sumner was Billy's vacation place. He kept company there with Paulita Maxwell, Pete's daughter, and visited the Mexican bordellos on the other side of the Pecos when Paulita had the curse. Whenever things in Lincoln became too lively even for Billy, he could always go to Fort Sumner to rest and drink and fornicate and gamble and share gossip. Billy loved a salty story about people he knew as much as any ranch wife, and he knew more about what went on behind the arched doors of the whitewashed adobes in Santa Fe and Albuquerque than anyone else in the territory.

Then in February 1878, deputies sworn in by Sheriff Brady ambushed and killed John Henry Tunstall on a canyon road, and Billy stopped coming to Fort Sumner. On April 1, six men crouching inside a corral fired rifles through holes drilled in the adobe wall and cut down Sheriff Brady and a deputy named Hindman on Lincoln's main street in naked daylight. Witnesses recognized Billy Bonney's Irish green hatband among the killers.

A murder warrant was issued from the governor's office for Billy's arrest. To serve it, a successor had to be chosen for Sheriff Brady. Pat listened to the political talk in Beaver Smith's saloon, then untied his apron, crossed the county line, and threw his Texas hat into the ring.

Chapter Three

Long John

In January 1880, Pat Garrett married Apolinaria Gutiérrez, the sister of his dead wife. A small, otter-eyed woman, she wore her blue-black hair in ebony combs atop her head during the ceremony to lessen the difference in their height, but at all other times allowed it to spill to her shoulders in a glittering fall. She had no English, and Pat's Spanish was bad; when they fought, she threw china and he slammed doors. They loved each other completely.

Her father, the freighter, bought them a small house in Lincoln. It was a pleasant adobe, built flush to the ground with the warm pinkish hue of the native clay showing through the whitewash in a way that pleased the new sheriff. Riding in the rain and the heat, he looked forward to settling his angular body into the depressions in the big horsehair chair by the kiva fireplace, when he wasn't attending a hanging or riding down yet another rumor about Billy Bonney's whereabouts. Apolinaria decorated the rooms with bright rugs and wooden crucifixes and embroidered the couple's initials in blue and silver thread on the fine linens in their bedroom. There was always a pot of strong Mexican coffee boiling on the stove in the kitchen.

The Mexicans in Lincoln enjoyed their sheriff. Like Pete Maxwell's vaqueros they coined rhymes about the way he towered over them in the street, looking like a great stoop-shouldered crane, and grinned when during their fandangos he could not keep his big feet from bouncing to the music of the drums and trumpets and tambourines even when he sat. They called him Juan Largo, Long John, and asked to see his big long-barreled Army Colt's, which he had purchased from a gunsmith in Fort Sumner to replace his father's cumbersome ball-and-percussion Navy of Civil War manufacture. Pistols were expensive everywhere. The machete was the weapon of preference locally; many of the civil disturbances Pat was called upon to investigate involved beheadings.

Some of the crimes over which he had jurisdiction shocked him. The Mexican temperament was a bed of smoldering coals, fanned into white flames by a sudden crosswind or splash of the raw tequila that could not be drunk except through a crust of salt to cure the stomach lining. When the hot wind blew up from Chihuahua, withering the poor corn crop that supported them, the men drank, the women's tongues grew sharp, and the children whimpered and howled because their bellies were empty. One blistering July night, an unemployed ranch hand named Manuel hacked up his wife, his boy and girl and a neighbor boy who was visiting, and took off for the Sierra Capitan aboard a razor-backed burro without provisions or even a canteen of water. Pat examined the scene in the little adobe hut, went out to throw up his coffee and corn cakes, and mounted up to follow the unshod tracks. After two hours he spotted the burro grazing, and a few hundred yards away discovered Manuel's body, seated with his back against a piñon tree and his bowels in his lap. He had let open his belly with the machete he had used on the others. Because he could not be buried in the churchyard with his family and the neighbor boy, he was dumped into a hole in the desert. A few days later his body was dug up and devoured by scavengers. Some blamed the digging on coyotes, but Pat suspected Manuel's brother-in-law, a Yaqui who had fought for Juarez and fled Mexico when he had failed to foment another revolution against Porfirio Diaz. It was a harsh land, more brutal in its way on those who lived upon it than the war had been in Louisiana.

Pat was not often in Lincoln. When he was not dining with John Chisum, who complained between courses about the Mexican squatters he was obliged to burn out and run off his range, he was in Santa Fe discussing with Governor Wallace the wisdom of issuing pardons absolving the participants of all responsibility for crimes committed during the war in Lincoln County, and whether Bonney's shootout with federal troops during the siege on McSween's general store made him eligible for reprieve at the territorial level. The latter question went unresolved, condemning the Lincoln County sheriff to scour town and territory for Bonney.

The young hellion knew the country better than most natives. New Mexicans reveled in his audacity, distrusted authority, and delighted in sharing the details of his exploits, magnifying them for the sake of the story and shifting the locations to confound the law. Now he was in Las Cruces dealing three-card monte, bewildering even hardened gamblers with the swiftness of his slender hands and long, delicate fingers; two days later he was in Roswell, one hundred sixty miles away, shooting the epaulets off a cavalry lieutenant who favored luring outlaws to Santa Fe under the promise of pardon, then trying and hanging them. The same night he was in Fort Sumner, sharing a bottle of mescal with Pete Maxwell and galloping his daughter. Pat followed up the rumors that sounded most logical, and more often than not found himself sitting in a chair in some flyblown cantina still warm from Bonney. He had a sense for looking in the exact right place, and for being exactly twenty-four hours late each time. This stimulated rather than frustrated the long man. It excited him to come so close to the man he sought, and he knew Billy well enough to be certain that he would one day linger too long in one place.

That happened on a bitterly cold night in December, when word reached Pat in Puerto de Luna that Bonney and a group of his confederates, among them Charlie Bowdre and Tom O'Folliard, were camped outside nearby Fort Sumner. Pat, who disliked ambushes in open country, where there were as many escape routes as there were directions, apprehended a Mexican named Juan Gallegos, who was sympathetic to Bonney, and offered to blow his head out from under his sombrero if he did not agree to tell Bonney that Pat and his deputies were pulling out of Fort Sumner bound for Roswell. Gallegos, badly frightened by Pat's show of temper, carried the message, and came back to report that Bonney and his crew were on their way into town to celebrate.

On the east side of the plaza stood an adobe missionary hospital, abandoned for years, with its roof fallen in and holes in the walls big enough to sling an armadillo through. Charlie Bowdre's wife lived there, and Pat calculated it would be Bonney's first stop. He seized the building, locking up Señora Bowdre and a number of Mexicans who might warn Bonney in one of the rooms and stationing a guard with them to keep them quiet. Pat dispatched Barney Mason and others to block the most likely path of retreat, and with Lon Chambers took up a position in the darkness under the overhang of the front porch behind a tangle of hanging harnesses. As the moon rose round and white, glaring off the snow on the ground and turning the adobe bone-white against the hard machined edge of the shadows, Pat swore he caught a whiff of sorrel blossoms, which he had neither smelled nor seen since leaving Louisiana. He decided it was the memory of a scent. It had filled his nostrils when he'd waited out the badger that had stolen his mother's hens. Then as now he had crouched in darkness, gripping a rifle, while the minutes crept past like small creatures in the grass. His fingers stuck to the metal of the Winchester's receiver when he touched it, like that of an iron pump handle in the cold.

He sensed the sound before he heard it. He turned his right ear, numb now, crosswise to the wind that skinned around the edge of the building, squealing through the spaces between the roof and the posts that supported it. There was another high-pitched sound below it: someone whistling between his teeth. Pat knew the refrain. "Darling, we are growing older." Silver threads among the gold. Billy Bonney's favorite. He whistled it when he raked in his poker winnings, sang it when he was drunk, in a light, untrained tenor, as pure as any boy's in a church choir.

Now came a creak, as of stiff saddle leather or a hoof crushing untrod snow. Lon Chambers, invisible in the shadows at the opposite end of the porch, heard it, too; he hissed between his teeth. Pat made no noise in response. Bonney had ears like an owl.

Ghostly silent, like a line of ships against a foggy backdrop, six horses and riders slid from darkness into the moonlit ribbon of road, strung out, the men hunched in the thick vapor steaming from their mounts' nostrils, headed for the old hospital. Pat recognized Billy Bonney's green hatband on the sombrero of the man in front.

A dozen yards shy of the building, Bonney reined his horse's head around suddenly and trotted to the back of the line. Pat swore beneath his breath; the youth had seen or sensed something, and was conferring with one of his friends about fleeing.

"Halt!" barked Pat; and again, "alto!"

The rider who was now in front straightened up suddenly in his saddle. His horse's head was under the porch roof. Pat saw moonlight reflecting off its blaze face, felt the mist of its spent breath condensing on the back of his hand where it gripped the forepiece of his carbine; the tiny droplets twitched and crawled like ants. The man clawed at his bulky overcoat. Lon Chambers and Pat fired simultaneously, their muzzle flashes splintering the shadows. Afterward Pat would swear he'd heard the slugs striking the horseman, like meathooks chunking into a side of beef. That old homicidal stench of burning cloth shriveled the hairs inside Pat's nostrils. The horse spun, whether in its own panic or its rider's no one knew, and clattered back down the road. Now Pat and Chambers swung their guns on the others. Reports crackled and snapped in the frozen air; spurts of blue and orange flame destroyed Pat's night vision, yet he continued firing and levering fresh shells into the Yellow Boy's barrel. Barney Mason and the men Pat had stationed down the road joined in, catching the riders in a ferocious crossfire. Billows of pewter-colored smoke drifted across the road and collected under the porch roof. Sulphur stung Pat's eyes and scratched his throat.

The horsemen bolted from the road in two directions, shouting and quirting their reins across their mounts' withers. The night swallowed them. One rider remained, slumped in his saddle with his back to the hospital: the man Pat and Chambers had shot at point-blank range. Slowly, leaning far out to one side, he turned his horse in Pat's direction. One arm hung lifeless. The moonlight reflecting off the snow glittered on the fresh dark stains on his coat and shirt. Pat recognized the beardless face beneath the slouch hat. Tom O'Folliard had often accompanied Billy Bonney during his visits to Beaver Smith's saloon at the time of the war in Lincoln County.

"Don't shoot, Garrett," he called out. "I'm killed."

A figure came loping the rider's way from the shadows down the road, carrying a rifle. "Take your medicine, old boy." It was Barney Mason's voice. "Take your medicine."

Pat cupped a hand around his mouth and shouted. "Back off, Barney! He can pull a trigger yet." To O'Folliard: "Throw up your hands, Tom."

"Pat, I ain't got the sand to throw up breakfast." The words were slurred.

Pat and the others came forward then, helped O'Folliard out of his saddle, and carried him into the hospital, where he died forty-five minutes later, begging for someone to put a bullet through his head and finish the pain.

The tracking began. The sheriff, who never felt more alive than when he was on the scent, acknowledged neither fatigue nor the cold that froze his companions to the marrow. At times the hoofprints they followed were obliterated by the wind-driven snow; hours would be lost while they quartered the countryside trying to pick up the trail. At times Pat led by instinct alone. Then a freshly broken tree limb or a black hole in a frozen stream where a hoof had gone through would appear, and they picked up the pace. At Lake Ranch, acting upon a hunch, the posse surrounded a house, but it turned out to be empty. They pushed on.

After three miles they encountered a lone rider. Pat called for him to throw up his hands. When he obeyed, Pat rode up and recognized Emmanuel Brazil, an old friend who worked at the Wilcox Ranch nearby, a sometime stopping-place of Bonney's. Brazil reported that the gang had pulled out of the ranch several hours before, and with the posse retraced his steps to where a trail of fresh tracks led away from the road.

"What's that way?" Lon Chambers inquired.

Pat said, "Stinking Springs." To Brazil: "Alejandro Perea used to have a house there."

"It's still standing."

The riders came upon the old shack in the iron cold of predawn. A cramped, bare-bones structure built of native pine with a slant roof and no door, it stood against a backdrop of rolling foothills dotted with aspen. A thin curl of smoke twisted up from the stovepipe. Three horses were tethered to the roof-beams that projected from the front of the house.

"They've either lost two men or two horses," whispered Chambers.

Pat flicked frost from his moustaches. "They've not lost either. If I know Billy, he's got two horses inside."

"What do we do, start blasting?"

"Only if they start to leave. We'll surround the place, then wait for first light. Fire when I raise my gun."

"No call to surrender?"

"Billy ain't the surrendering kind. It's my intention to kill him the second he pokes out his head. The rest will throw down their arms then."

"I heard you was soft on Bonney. I reckon I heard wrong."

Pat swung down from his bay. "You might have noticed Bonney's friends don't fare much better than his enemies."

The posse fanned out, silently in the fluffy snow. Pat tethered his horse to an aspen rubbed raw by mule deer and cleared himself a resting place in the snow with a boot. Then he stretched out on his stomach. The ground sloped down to the shack from a treefall across which he rested the barrel of his Winchester. Before leaving Fort Sumner he had thought to dab whitewash on the front sight, but the snow gleamed with an illumination all its own. If Billy were to show his face at a window, Pat could have shot him between the eyes as easily as at noon.

The shadows east of the shack had begun to grow grainy before false dawn when someone stirred inside the doorless entrance. Pat worked the stiffness out of his fingers and drew a bead at doorknob level. A man in a loose canvas coat and broad-brimmed sombrero came out carrying a nosebag. Pat strained to make out the color of the man's hatband. It looked black. In daylight it might be green.

The long man rose to his knees, bringing the Yellow Boy to his shoulder. The chugging of shots from all sides drowned out the sound of his own. The tethered horses reared, squealed, and jerked at their reins, releasing a shower of dirt and dust from the projecting rafters. The man in the entrance stumbled, dropped the nosebag, and pitched backward into the shack. Slugs chopped at the boards on either side; one gonged off something made of iron inside, a stove or a skillet. The guns went silent then, as if a bell had been rung.

"Garrett, that you?"

Lon Chambers broke cover and duckwalked Pat's way. "Who's that, Bonney?"

Pat shook his head. He cupped a hand around his mouth. "Is that Billie Wilson?"

"It is. You sure killed Charlie."

"Charlie Bowdre?"

"None other, though he's breathing yet. You boys got him through the lungs and gut and I don't know what all. He's bleeding like a leaky bucket."

"Tell Charlie I'm sure sorry. I thought he was Bonney."

"Tell him yourself, Garrett. He's coming out."

There was a scuffle inside, and then the wounded man plunged out into the snow, hands out from his sides with a big pistol dangling by its trigger guard from his right forefinger. His canvas coat hung open, his shirt dark and drenched.

Chambers lifted his rifle. Pat laid a hand on the barrel, deflecting his aim. "Don't waste your shot, Lon."

The face beneath the big sombrero was young and pale and glistened in the light reflecting off the snow. He spotted Pat at the top of the slope and lurched that way, sinking in up to his knees and gesturing with his free hand in the direction of the shack.

"I wish," he said. "I wish—Lord, Pat, I'm killed." He fell on his face in front of the treefall.

"Billy Bonney, you in there?" called the long man.

"Why don't you come down and take a look for yourself, Big Casino?"

"That's him," Chambers said. "Goddamn."

"How you fixed in there, Billy?"

"Pretty well, though we got no wood for breakfast."

"Come out and get some, then. Be a little sociable."

"Can't do it, Pat. Business is too confining. No time to run around."

While Bonney was speaking, an arm bent around the door frame. A hand closed around the reins of the horse tethered closest to the door.

"Sheriff," Chambers said.

"I see it." Pat drew a bead on the back of the horse's head and fired. The animal threw up its head and heeled over, blockading the entrance.

"Nice shooting, Sheriff."

Pat said nothing. He worked the lever twice and shot through the reins holding the other two horses. They reared and cantered away, slowing and stopping at the edge of the little clearing to nuzzle through the snow for grass.

That ended the conversation. Pat sent Chambers to the Wilcox Ranch for provisions and spread his blanket on the ground, settling in for a long siege. When the wagon came in the afternoon, the posse built a large fire and began cooking. The sharp smell of hot grease from the beef and chickens rode the smoke in the direction of the shack.

"God*damn,* don't that meat smell good," Chambers said. "I ain't et since Fort Sumner."

Pat said, "It ain't for us."

Twenty minutes later, a rifle barrel nudged out through a window with no glass in it. A dirty white handkerchief fluttered from the muzzle.

"Tell your boys to hold their fire, Pat. We're coming out."

Pat and the others disarmed Bonney, Wilson, Tom Pickett, and Charlie Rudabaugh; fed them, bound their wrists and ankles, and loaded them in the wagon with Charlie Bowdre's corpse wrapped in a blanket. Pat rode alongside on the way to Las Vegas.

Billy Bonney stared at the corpse. "I sure will miss old Charlie. We was fixing to homestead as soon as we stole enough cows."

"I heard that," said Pat.

"Tom O'Folliard's dead too, I guess."

"Dead as King George." The long man rode a little farther. "What spooked you outside the hospital? I was about to plug you when you turned around and rode back."

The young outlaw showed his big teeth. "I wanted a chew of tobacco bad. Wilson had some that was good, and he was in the rear. I went back after tobacco."

"Too bad for Tom."

"Tom didn't chew. I guess you could say it was tobacco killed old Tom."

"I mean, too bad he missed tomorrow. Charlie too."

"What's tomorrow?"

"Christmas Day."

"Well, well." Bonney stared down at his bound wrists. "I didn't have time to get them nothing anyways."

Barney Mason rode up from the rear. "I was you, Billy boy, I wouldn't shop for Easter, neither. You're fixed to hang in Lincoln for Brady and Hindman."

"Oh, I'll see Easter. Just like the Lord."

Chapter Four

Midnight in Fort Sumner

And did he see Easter?" I inquired.

The long man looked up quickly from the swept stone floor of my hut; not so much as if he'd forgotten I was there as in surprise to find he wasn't still on the road to Las Vegas, New Mexico Territory, talking with Billy Bonney.

"He saw it," he said then. "Independence Day, too, though not by much. He killed two of my best deputies in the Lincoln County courthouse, stole a horse, and rode away with about a hundred folks looking on. Coroner counted thirty-six buckshot holes in Bob Olinger's body."

Bonney's recapture became a condition of Pat's continued employment as sheriff.

Incredibly, or so it seemed to Governor Wallace, Pat's rivals for county office, and many of the outspoken citizens of Lincoln (some of whom had watched from windows and boardwalks while the territory's most notorious outlaw stepped calmly into leather and steered his pilfered horse around Deputy Olinger's butchered body in the street), the long man appeared to do nothing for nearly three months. He replaced the hinges on all the doors in his house, strung fence along his western property line, oiled all his harnesses, and whitewashed the barn. Apolinaria had recently given birth to his daughter, Ida, and he bought a goat for the milk, only to learn that it was a disagree-able animal that tried at every opportunity to disembowel him with its horns. After one particularly close incident, Pat went into the house, came out carrying his ten-gauge Stevens shot-gun, and blasted the nanny as surely as Bonney had blasted Olinger. Since then he had entertained a hatred for all goats more intense than any he managed to work up for the slayer of his two most dependable men.

Meanwhile, newspapers and gossipmongers who at the end of 1880 had celebrated Pat Garrett's abilities as the most popular lawman on the great frontier had swung the light of their ad-miration to the audacious Billy Bonney, who as before was re-ported to be working his outlaw wizardry from Mexico City to the Panhandle of Texas. Sheriff Garrett's lackadaisical attitude toward his duties obliterated his former celebrity; rumor sug-gested Wallace was considering replacing him with John W. Poe, a stock regulator and sometime deputy U.S. marshal, or Charles Siringo, a cowboy up in White Oaks with law-enforcement ambitions. Pat replaced some broken tiles on his roof and said nothing.

Frustrated with the sheriff's inaction, on April 30 the gover-nor issued a proclamation:

BILLY THE KID
$500 REWARD

I will pay $500 to any person or persons who capture William Bonney, alias the Kid, and deliver him to any sheriff of New Mexico. Satisfactory proofs of identity will be required.

I read the notice, printed on brown newsprint disintegrating at the folds, which the long man produced from a soft stubbled cowhide wallet stitched with leather cord. He had cut it from the Lincoln newspaper and still carried it in hopes of collecting the reward.

"Billy the Kid?" said I.

"I don't know where Wallace got that." He refolded the cutting and returned it to its place as gently as if it were the five hundred itself. "I never heard no one call Billy that to his face, nor heard him referred to that way before the governor did. Now I almost never hear him called nothing else."

Since Bonney's escape, Pat had taken the single step of posting a letter to Emmanuel Brazil, his man in Fort Sumner. Early in July Brazil wrote back: While the governor, the newspapers, and those pundits who gathered in cantinas and found their opinions in glasses and bottles had been after Pat to scour Arizona and Texas and old Mexico, the fugitive had not left the territory. He had been seen coming and going in Fort Sumner, where blossomed Paulita Maxwell, the fairest flower of his young life.

This was the news the long man had been waiting for. He wrote again, asking Brazil to meet him and his party at the mouth of Tayban Arroyo, five miles south of Fort Sumner, one hour after sundown July 13.

In White Oaks, Pat met with John Poe across a linen-covered table in the dining room of the hotel where Poe was put up by the Canadian River Cattle Association. A thickset former cowboy with pomade in his hair and a weakness for Norfolk jackets and striped ascots, the young man had spent months tracking down and stringing up rustlers for the association, which had recommended him to the Lincoln County sheriff as a dependable detective and mankiller, who also held a commission as a deputy United States marshal. He had the cleanest fingernails

Pat had ever seen; pared, pink, and polished, they flashed like pearls as he prised open an enormous pile of steaming clams on the plate in front of him.

"Bonney's gone from New Mexico," Poe said, chewing the rubbery meat. "Even he isn't reckless enough to hang back with a price on his head and every peace officer between Taos and the border carrying his reader in his vest pocket. But I'll ride with you to Tayban. Things have not been various enough around here to suit me."

In Lincoln, Pat and Poe collected Thomas K. "Tip" McKinney, short of stature, mild of feature, and the most amiable and obedient of Pat's deputies, who took off his hat, scratched his crown, said he doubted Bonney was anywhere within five hundred miles of the territory, and went to get his saddle. Since the deaths of deputies Olinger and J. W. Bell, Lincoln had gotten to be as quiet as White Oaks, and McKinney was inclined to fiddle-foot. The three set out for Tayban Arroyo.

When, two hours after dark on the night of July 13, Brazil had failed to show up, Pat asked Poe if he knew anyone in Fort Sumner.

The deputy marshal screwed a cheroot into the ground with the heel of his boot. "No, I'm a stranger in this country. Want me to ride in and sniff around?"

"Give it some slack. Fort Sumner's mostly Mexicans. They'd take the devil's side over the government's, and they're brought up to hate the devil."

Poe swung aboard his piebald. The moon shone on his pale barbered face. "You think Bonney got wind of what Brazil was about and killed him?"

"I doubt it. Billy don't kill in anger. Mostly it's for something to do."

"Them greasers don't know one date from another unless there's a fiesta attached." Tip McKinney grinned.

Pat slid a mesquite branch into the campfire. The flames gobbled the dry wood. "Showed the white feather, more than likely. You never can tell when Billy might get bored."

Poe returned the following night. His brow was congested and the cords showed in his neck. "You called those Mexicans right," he said, spreading his palms in front of the fire. "They all forget their English when they see me coming."

"You didn't tip your hand?" Pat asked.

"Credit me for something better than a fool. I am just not Mexican enough for their high standards."

"Is he there?"

"If he's not, that's one suspicious son of a bitch of a town for no good purpose."

"You *are* a stranger here," Tip said.

Pat untethered the bay. "We'll go in and talk to Pete Maxwell. He never did make his peace with Billy sniffing around Paulita."

Tip said, "Pete's half Mexican."

"We'll just talk to the American half." He stepped into leather.

Pete Maxwell's house, modest for the dwelling of a successful rancher, was a single-story adobe, built in the territorial style over brick, with a gray puckered pine porch running its length. The three visitors dismounted, tied up at a log fence, and started across a green orchard separating them from the house. A sudden Gatling burst of laughter stopped Pat, who threw out a long arm to stay his companions. In a patch of mottled moonlight scattering through tree branches, a group of men in sombreros were seated on the ground a hundred yards distant, passing around a bottle and conversing in rapid Spanish. As the trio watched, one of them rose unsteadily, vaulted the fence near the house, and walked down the shallow slope to a smaller building nearby.

"Know him?" Poe asked Pat.

"Let's go in another way and avoid these fellows."

They retreated to where they had left the horses and walked around the orchard. In front of Maxwell's porch, Pat said, "I'll go in and talk to Pete. You can watch out here."

Tip blew on his hands. "I wouldn't turn down a swallow or two of tequila. These summer desert nights are colder than Montana in winter."

"I'll bring you out a bottle. Pete ain't much for crowds."

A row of doors provided access to all the rooms from the outside, in the old Spanish style. Pat went to the one that led into Maxwell's bedroom and let himself in without knocking. A slab of icy blue moonlight lay like a stone on the floor by the bed. The sheets were humped and motionless in the reflected light. Pat crossed the room noiselessly and sat on the edge of the feather mattress near the head.

"Pete, it's Pat Garrett."

The man in the bed did not move or acknowledge that he'd heard. His breathing was shallow, and Pat saw the gleam of an open eye.

"Que hora es?" said Maxwell then, and switched to English. "What's the time?"

"I don't know. Past midnight."

"You're too quiet, Pat. You always was too quiet for a cowhand, always slipping up behind folks. I near winged you once, just so's you'd drag a foot."

"Seen Billy, Pete?"

There was a long silence, as if Maxwell had drifted off to

sleep. But Pat could see his eye gleaming. "Here and there," he said then.

"I ain't interested in there."

"He's been about, all right. I can't say if he's left yet."

"Can't or won't?"

"Don't ride me, Pat. I gave you work when no one else would."

"The work's different now."

"A whole heap's different."

"Quien es?"

The question was a hiss, louder than the footfalls of the man who had sprung through the open door from the porch outside. A slight figure, this, bareheaded and shirtless, with his galluses dangling and his feet clad in stockings only. Pat, whose instincts had not been blunted by life in civilization, looked quickly at the man's hands. He held a knife in his left. His right was empty.

The newcomer was blind in the darkness beyond the slab of moonlight. He crept toward the bed. "Who is it, Pete?"

Pete Maxwell sat up. "That's him!"

Here the long man fell silent.

I waited, seated upon my wooden stool, while the flames in the athanor lunged at the few crumbs of charcoal that remained. "And was it him?" I asked at length.

The long man nodded, not looking at me. "It was him, all right. Tip and Poe didn't know him, and when he asked them out front who they was in Mexican, they thought he was one of Pete's vaqueros and let him pass. Some folks claim now it wasn't him, but some imposter, and that Billy's raising hell down in Mexico or some such place. But I heard him, and I seen that long jaw and them big teeth clamping his bottom lip like a prairie dog's. When Pete said, 'That's him,' Billy come up from his crouch and pointed that Bowie square at me there in the darkness.

" 'Quien es?' he said. 'Quien es?' "

"I swung up my Colt's and shot him and rolled off the bed and shot again. I wasted that second ball."

"And the first?" I asked.

"It caught him just above the heart. He was dead as Pharaoh when he hit the floor."

"I have a question."

I waited until he looked at me. It took a long time, although not so long when measured against the hours I had lived.

"When Pete Maxwell said, 'That's him,' " I began.

He nodded, anticipating the rest but too polite not to let me finish.

"Was he talking to you or Bonney?"

The long man smoothed his moustaches. They were as even as the legs of a machine-made table. "I don't know," he said. "I don't reckon Billy knows neither."

" 'Knows'?" I asked.

Chapter Five

Phantasms of the Night

Billy Bonney had been dead one year. In the time between, his fame had spread like black Spanish moss beyond the boundaries of Lincoln County and the territory of New Mexico. He was written of as far east as New York City, where newspaper accounts of his youthful exploits (he was said to be but twenty-one at the time of his death) had inspired a number of fabulists to embellish upon that which had already been invented. Stamped in syrupy ink upon coarse brown paper, his edda whirled off steam-driven cylinders through carniverous trimmers and piled page upon sawtooth page like igneous and aqueous; these were pressed between bright paper covers and shipped to train stations and mercantiles across the continent, whence they invaded the libraries of civilized homes on the Hudson River and the saddle pockets of cowboys not much older than Bonney. Lanky youths in chaparajos and hook-heeled boots mouthed the unfamiliar words by the light of campfires and lanterns from the grasslands of Nebraska, as flat as a scraping stone, to those same fluted canyons into which Bonney had fled to elude Pat Garrett along the Journey of the Dead. In death, Billy Bonney had acquired both a legend and a nombre de guerra that he had scarcely known in life. As Billy the Kid, his name was spoken in places whose very existence he himself had not suspected.

Pat Garrett acquired notoriety in equal measure. The body had scarcely begun to stiffen in its grave when Pat found himself writing a book.

His collaborator, Ash Upson, was thick-built and fifty, with fingers permanently stained purple, who bore a close, if debauched, resemblance to the novelist Alexandre Dumas. He was a former New York newspaperman who had come west to establish journals in Albuquerque, Las Vegas, and Mesilla. Weary of newspapers, he now ran the post office in Roswell and served as justice of the peace and notary public while selling desert acreage to gullible transplanted Easterners on the side. He drank pure grain alcohol when he could get it, trade whiskey when he could not, and while in his cups was given to questioning sacred beliefs with an edgy persistency that had cost him most of his friends. He wrote with the skill of Arthur Conan Doyle and possessed the poetic vision of Lord Byron, along with most of the latter's social indiscretions. Pat liked him on sight. He pistol-whipped red-faced saloon rats who proposed to string up the drunken journalist for smashing their icons in discourse, carried him home when he could no longer stand without the bar for support, and on whoozy mornings poured thick hot Spanish grind down his throat in time to open the post office lest Washington City move to revoke Roswell's charter. On his side, Upson paid no attention to Pat's needling humor and held his tongue and kept his distance when the sheriff's temper was short. They were fellow unbelievers, bonded by the common religion of their lack of faith.

Whose idea the book was, neither could say. Pat, whose first political campaign had taught him to track the course of popular opinion as surely as a fugitive's line of retreat, sensed early that Billy's posthumous reputation might surpass his own on this side of the pale, and chose to press the advantage of hindsight. Upson, who when he cut himself while trimming his goatee bled purple ink, was not so much the public servant and private pariah he had abandoned his instinct for a story with legs. They met through the summer in Pat's house, Upson's bottle-strewn room above J. C. Lea's general store in Roswell, and the Lincoln County courthouse where Billy had slipped his manacles and slaughtered Olinger and Bell, Pat reminiscing and at times rationalizing, while Upson scribbled with a chewed stub of yellow pencil on folds of tattered newsprint. They passed the bottle and suggested substitutions where Pat's memory failed him and Upson's knowledge stumbled into one of its alcohol-eroded holes. At length, when the manhunter had exhausted his investment capital, Upson locked himself away and under the influence of his hundred-proof inspiration weaved a scarlet tapestry of point-blank duels, harrowing escapes, and breath-snatching midnight rides on the backs of lathered steeds to fill in the blanks in Bonney's past. The physical manifestations of his muse included a chipped marble bust of Homer that had come with him all the way from New York and a greasy stack of paperbound Buffalo Bill novels written by Ned Buntline.

The book was published in April 1882 by the New Mexican Printing and Publishing Company. A tinted lithograph made from the only known photograph of Billy Bonney, standing with his Winchester propped on its buttstock at his side, decorated the paper wraps. The legend on the front read: *The Authentic Life of Billy, the Kid, the Noted Desperado of the Southwest, Whose Deeds of Daring Have Made His Name a Terror in New Mexico, Arizona, and Northern Mexico. A Faithful and Interesting Narrative by Pat F. Garrett, Sheriff of Lincoln County, New Mexico, by Whom He Was Finally Hunted Down & Captured by Killing Him.*

The slim volume sold for about as long as it took the average reader to digest the title.

Upson, publishing veteran that he was, sought refuge behind the writers' scarred but dependable breastwork of poor distribution and inadequate advertising. Pat, who assumed books were like harnesses and either walked out of the stores or grew cobwebs in the back room according to their merits and deficiencies, wondered if the book would have found more readers if the ending were different. Upson called him an ignorant heathen and started an angry letter to New Mexican Printing and Publishing, but got too drunk to finish it. Pat carried him home.

Restless, the long man decided not to seek reelection as sheriff. He endorsed John Poe for his successor. His former deputy's predilection for red-wheeled buggies over saddle horses and his ability with a ledger, whose narrow-ruled columns Pat just made a mess of with nicotine thumbprints and blobs of ink, seemed best suited to the clerkly duties that the office had begun to assume. The sheriffs of the future, he thought, would wear pinchnose spectacles and only carry pistols on ceremonial occasions.

Despite the disappointing sales, the announcement that Sheriff Garrett had written a book increased his standing as Bonney's killer. When two vacancies appeared on the New Mexico Territorial Council, Pat made known his intention to run for one of them. If manhunters were obsolete, he proposed to lay down his cartridge belt and don a wing collar.

It was at about this time that the dreams began.

One night—one vaulted, star-scattered night in the endlessly turning wheel that is New Mexico in late summer—Pat Garrett arrived home stinking of horse from ten days of riding in search of votes, certain that his bones had torn loose from his tendons and that he was dragging them behind him like scrap iron in a gunnysack. His wife had retired hours before; not having left home on the best of marital terms, he was unwilling to wake her. He poured himself a tall whiskey and stretched his long legs toward the fire. The big shabby leather armchair was suited uniquely to his own physical imperfections, the piñon flames in the kiva fireplace were warm and danced mesmerically, like the Aurora Borealis atop the table rocks along the High Road to Taos, filled with fandango figures and visions from the pueblos in Socorro where the long man had chewed peyote and waited for news of Billy. Very soon he dozed.

His sleep, light in times of peace, was in periods of stress so close to waking that he could afterward recount everything that had happened in his presence when others had thought him safely under. Now he started awake at the squeak of a light footfall on the pine floor, or so he was certain at the time, so vivid were the details of the room and what he heard there.

"Apolinaria?" said he, raising his chin from his chest; for he thought that his wife had entered the room.

"Well, Big Casino," came a voice in response.

Pat was on his feet in an instant, clawing at his belt for the big Colt's in its scabbard. He wore neither, as he had not thought he'd need a weapon to hunt for votes. For one terrible, sphincter-tightening moment, he felt as if he stood naked on a needle rock, a target in the moonlight. Only one person in this world had ever addressed him by the name he had just heard, and in his state of exhaustion the long man had forgotten that person was dead.

"Billy?"

This time there was no response. The room was filled with shadows, much like another room he remembered in another house, and though they stirred in the crawling light from the hearth they were empty. They moved in, enveloping him like a Navajo blanket and warming the blood in his veins.

He knew then he had dreamt. He did not suffer physical hardship so well in his thirties as he had when he was an over-

grown boy in chaparajos, and the quest for political support in
the bunkhouses and barrios of that vast territory had proven
fully as frustrating as the hunt for Billy Bonney, with tracks
harder to follow. Dissipation and strong spirits had made fissures
in the walls that enclosed the present, allowing a shade from the
past to slip through. To satisfy his manhunter's instincts he circled the room, poking at the dark corners with the toes of his
boots and tapping at the panes in the windows to make sure
none had fallen out. Then he undressed and went to bed, sliding carefully between the crisp linen sheets to avoid waking
Apolinaria.

"Quien es?"

Now he sat up rifle-straight, and again reached for a phantom
weapon. An exclamation escaped him, startling his wife awake,
her hair in her eyes.

And for an instant he saw.

Saw a pale half-naked figure, translucent in the moonlight
shining through the window upon the whitewashed wall facing
the bed, approaching in leather breeches only; saw the hairless
cylinder of his torso and the slack jaw beneath the band of
shadow covering the top half of his face; saw the prominent
front teeth, as large as dove's eggs, in the mouth that opened to
repeat the question:

"Quien es?"

Who is it?

Saw the blade in the intruder's hand, shining like cold fire. . . .

And then the figure was gone, evaporated in midstride as
completely as the stain of breath upon glass.

Pat did not tell his wife about the apparition. He explained
merely that he had been awakened by a nightmare whose details
he could not remember. Apolinaria was Mexican and supersti-

tious. If he told her he had seen Billy Bonney, she would insist upon bringing the local padre to the house to make the sign of the cross and pronounce three long and tiresome exorcisms in border Latin, and Pat could not abide this particular padre, who considered him an infidel. He turned over, but he did not sleep for hours. Bonney had looked exactly as he had that night in Fort Sumner, and asked the very question he had had upon his lips when he died. The scene had not been so real even when the long man had set it down for publication.

It had seemed to him, too, that there had been an element of threat in Billy's approach holding the big knife. Paulita Maxwell had told Pat, among tears and wishes that his soul would rot in hell, that Bonney had gone straight from her bed to her father's house that night to carve a slab from a side of beef Pete Maxwell kept in a cold box on the porch; but upon the occasion of this dream, if dream it was, Pat had felt that the blade was intended for him. If so, this was a vindictive shade, more so even than the youth who had lain in wait to slay the men who had butchered John Tunstall.

Since that night, Pat Garrett had dreamt of Billy Bonney dozens of times: at home, in the gaudy and flyblown hotel rooms along the electioneering circuit, lying on the ground beside a fire, sitting upright in a day coach on the A.T.&S.F.; wherever bone-weariness overcame his fear of the phantasms of the night and he slid into slumber. Sometimes his tormentor was fully dressed in the Spanish costumes he favored, complete with the green band. More often he appeared as he had died, fresh from sex and holding a shaft of moonlight in the shape of a bowie. On occasion he recognized Pat and addressed him as Big Casino, showing his big front teeth in that idiot's grin that had finessed so many into thinking him slow and weak, so many dead by his hand. Other times he did not know him. Pat would start awake with the smell of Billy's semen and his own sweat in his nostrils, chilled to the core.

The long man could not say which Bonney he found more unsettling, the swaggering dandy or the sleep-fuddled lamb trotting all unknowing to the slaughter. Chiefly he feared that if the dreams continued he would soon be as mad as those excursionists from Rhode Island and New Hampshire who struck out across the Jornada del Muerto with heads uncovered, their brains frying in the sun like tortillas.

I listened without interruption to the narrative of the man from New Mexico. He was an individual on the cusp: When his account touched upon his public life, he spoke in elongated, windy phrases, invoking politicians' fustian with the stiff, uncomfortable gait of a backwoodsman trying on his first tailcoat. Only when his subject became personal did he subside into the shambling speech and broken accents of the plantation youth, the western drifter, the laconic lawman. At these times I rather liked him.

Insofar as a man of my cloth could ever enjoy the person of a supplicant, and an Anglo-Saxon into the bargain.

At last he fell silent. Sunlight dappling through the leaves outside lay across his narrow face in the path from the window like patches on an adobe wall.

"No other words passed between you?" I asked.

He shook his head. "Just them. He calls to me, or he wants to know who I am. That's it."

"I don't suppose you've tried talking back."

"No. Maybe I'm loco, but I ain't so loco as to try talking to a dead man."

"And yet who among us possesses the wisdom of the dead?" I stepped down from the tall stool and crossed the room, aware that with each step I eradicated a measure of whatever polite belief he held that I had passed the century mark. It had only been since my ninetieth year that I had given up my daily climb down the ladder that led from my rock to the desert floor, leaving the harvest of toads to the boy who brought my water. From a high shelf I brought down an apothecary jar, ancient in the time of my grandfather, and removed its glass lid to sniff at its contents. They smelled of dust and putrefaction. I replaced the lid.

"Do you know grams?" said I.

"I sure don't."

"A teaspoon will answer, or a quarter of a jigger if you haven't a spoon. Heat that amount over a low flame until it liquefies. Swallow it then, just before retiring. The dreams should stop."

He peered at the label. "That Mexican?"

"Latin. You wouldn't understand it even if you could translate it. My people have used it as a nostrum against phantasms since before Christ."

"It smells it." He wrinkled his nose and clamped down the lid. "Come back if the dreams continue."

"Ain't you got any more faith in your medicine than that?"

"One day it will be gone. The same is not always true of a ghost's patience."

"I don't believe in ghosts any more than I believe in God or the Devil," he said.

I folded my hands. "Perhaps if you live to be as old as I you will not be so certain about the Devil."

"How much?" He produced a drawstring pouch from the pocket of his trousers.

"I have no need of money. The villagers provide me with food and I have no reason to leave my rock."

"What, then?"

"Bring me wisdom."

He bounced the pouch on his palm. The coins shifted and clanked like hollow bones. He smiled then, as slowly as shadows lengthening. "That's a stiff bargain, seeing as I got so little to spare."

"Your store is abysmal," I agreed. The smile withered. "Still, it is the medium of exchange here. I honor no other."

"Just what kind of wisdom are you wanting?"

"You will recognize it. When the dreams stop."

He put away the pouch and tugged on his big hat, growing with the gesture. At the door he looked back. His long solemn face clouded with thought. "I'm kind of a long time paying my debts. It's a failing."

"I shall be here," I said. "I am always here."

He left my shop. He remained in my thoughts.

The nostrum is but a sleeping draught, distilled from poppies and wormwood, with oil of creosote to bind. It was first composed by my great-great-grandfather, alchemical master to King Philip II, to send that ruler to the black depths below the level where dwelt the demons that gnawed at him in the dark. In return, my clever ancestor was granted the whole of Durango, of which the rock upon which stands my simple workshop is all that remains. My great-great-grandfather was a quack, a detestable puffer who worked his bellows to no good purpose but his own exalted station. He was drawn and quartered when his crystal failed to reveal the Armada's destruction. But his nostrum has its uses.

IRON

Chapter Six

Generations

Clay to iron, iron to steel. All substances are transmutable to base metal, and all metals save one transmute to the stuff of which the earth was formed. Heat and corruption are the agents of change. Quicksilver is the first to liquefy, at minus thirty-nine degrees Fahrenheit. Tin, cadmium, bismuth, thallium, lead, and zinc melt at less than red heat; antimony, calcium, and aluminum, at more. Silver, copper, and gold—trackless gold, the blessed Mary of elements—require a cherry-red heat to alter their outward shape; iron, nickel, and cobalt a white flame. Platinum, iridium, rhodium, vanadium, ruthenium, and osmium are the most intractable, demanding the intense, world-generating heat of the oxyhydrogen blowpipe, the voltaic arc—indeed, the athanor, the alchemical furnace from which poured forth the stuff of life like milk from a pap. All these things I had transformed in the womb of the chimney upon my rock in the desert.

Iron to rust, rust to clay. Oxidation and time transmute as surely as heat. This process I had not the life to follow to its finish, nor had my father nor my grandfather nor my great-grandfather, nor all the chain completed. The passing down of notes from generation to generation did not answer, for the very corruption that was under observation destroyed the record, unless one squandered the little time he had transcribing what has already been written. Sulphuric acid hastened the timetable, but distorted the effect, like turning up the flame beneath a spitted hog to expedite dinner, incinerating the meat and making it inedible. A beast in a cage will not behave as it does in the wild. Time is the enemy as well as the agent.

Quicksilver to silver; elusive. Maddening. It is brittle, it is liquid. It is neither of these long enough to scrutinize and assign to a category. It is a woman in the prime of her beauty and treachery, glittering just within reach and then spinning upon its heel and fleeing before one's grasp, to turn again at the top of the next hill, flashing its eyes and laughing. It courses through the Devil's veins, it is the nimbus about the head of Christ. It may be the Philosopher's Stone. It may be fool's gold. It has consumed the lives and studies of more alchemists than all the other elements combined. We know nothing more of its true nature than we knew in the beginning. We bypass it in the service of time at the risk of losing our way forever.

Silver to gold; unlikely. Silver putrefies before the naked eye, turning black like a potato and then dissolving in a despicable foam, like hydrophobic spittle. It is a charlatan, like my great-great-grandfather, and its glory is brief. Its metamorphosis is in retreat from the blessed goal rather than toward it.

Lead is the basest of metals. It changes not, except to become even more like itself. It is an unwashed old man, malleable by force but resistant in its obese spirit. Its filth comes off upon one's hands. It knows no conscience and once smelted, will weight a fishhook or form the snout of a bullet. Moreover, it is poisonous. Its venom leeches forth to work slowly and undetectably, and by the time it is discovered it has blackened the blood and bagged in the liver, transmuted its victim to lead. It is a loathsome gray tongue in a dead mouth. It is to gold what the lowest pit-brained ape is to the dignity of man.

But if clay to iron and clay to gold, why not iron to gold? The orange cast iron assumes is encouraging, but then like all things it disintegrates short of the state, like Galahad in possession of the Grail. Its failure is noble, but in the end, it is no better than false silver or amoral lead.

Nor was I; nor am I yet. In the time after the departure of the long man, villagers and strangers came to my rock with their complaints, shouting at the top of their lungs to make themselves heard as my eardrums thickened with callus. I slept at a level close to waking, I shrank in stature, my joints swelled and pained me when the monsoons came. I lay round-eyed on my pallet, wondering (when I should have been reflecting upon the day's experiments) who was crueler, the Pueblo Indians who blinded and tortured my grandfather before they put an end to him or this eternal millstoning time, that ground a man small and smaller until he was fine enough to fall between the wheels. The son of the boy who carried water to my garden when I gave up that chore, a father now himself, assisted me when I could not apprentice myself, recording the lengthening list of failures in the yellow leaves of my notebook when I was unable to hold a pen, and gathering the coals to feed the athanor when my back would not bend. But my eyes were keen, and my mind was as a thing honed by the wisdom that came my way in small quantities, like grit on a whetstone. Tin to bronze, bronze to brass. The books I had read rotted on their shelves, like oranges that had surrendered their juices and whose seeds were barren. Increasingly I felt an urgency to uncover the secret of the stone. I had no grandchildren, no children. My wife and infant son had perished of a plague borne upon the wind from the field of the bloated dead of Chapultepec. Another wife had flung herself from the rock upon being told that she could never return to her ancestral home in Mexico City. I had considered training the boy who brought water, then rejected it. The mysticism was too deeply entrenched in his people, he would never succeed in laying aside the old gods in the service of pure reason.

The thick and braided vine with roots in the court of Carolus Magnus ended with me. There would be none to work the bellows when I relinquished the handles; no hand would take up my pestle when I set it down at last. I who sought to live in three centuries would close a way of life that was already ancient when the pyramids of Egypt rose from the quarries.

Antimony and arsenic. The first is medicinal, the other deadly. It was an ancestor of mine who discovered the health-preserving properties of antimony, by accident; for all things not directly applicable to the production of gold are serendipitous. How many of my forebears may have found the opposite to be true of arsenic will never be known, for they died before they could record the fact. We perish in flame, we die from poison, we wear out our lives in the quest. Like the metals themselves, rapid and slow oxidation is our fate.

Iron to rust, rust to clay. Gold to gold. Not for personal wealth, never that, but for the benefit of knowledge, and of man's mastery of the natural world. Gold to gold. Gold did not oxidize; of all the metals it was the only one to break the circle. There was the lock that fit the key.

But where the key? Not in the red lead of cadmium, nor patrician-white platinum, that self-deluded metal that thought itself gold's superior. Not copper, nor zinc. Certainly not molybdenum, forged in fire and generations removed from the earth. Tungsten, manganese, palladium, the alloys and amalgams— disappointments all. My notebook, my larder filled, but it did not nourish.

In a seizure of pique I threw my grains of ore into the fire. They ignited, sending sparks up the flue. Their essence rode the smoke to freedom and then, heavier, settled to the desert surface, beginning the long slow return to the womb that bore them.

As would I.

These things I heard; for a lone village in a naked desert draws travelers as spring water draws the creatures that fly and the beasts that crawl, and wisdom is the coin of my tiny realm.

John W. Poe, Pat Garrett's friend and deputy during the final days of the hunt for Billy Bonney, swept Lincoln County in the sheriff's election, bringing eastern-style efficiency to the office. Pat's splotched, thumb-smeared entries in the ledger gave way to Poe's tidy, two-colored calligraphy between the columns. Instead of Pat's tall horse, the whirring red wheels of Poe's buggy announced that the sheriff was on his rounds. With oiled charm and blue-eyed promises he siphoned gold from the big ranchers and silver from merchants and pennies from bean-snappers into a treasury that had rattled like a dry gourd before the hackle-raising efforts of his predecessor. There were those who said that Pat used the territorial cache as his personal bank account, drawing from it willy-nilly to buy supplies and fresh horses and pay his mercenaries as he scoured the country for Bonney. Others grumbled that much of the money never got to the treasury. Bonney himself had been overheard to say that if John Chisum would pay him what he was paying Pat to prevent Bonney from rustling cows and horses, he would leave off rustling cows and horses. Sic transit gloria.

None of this was lost on the newspapers. Ink and press oil and bales of newsprint are not bought with deeds of glory, but with advertising. Hordes of money in Santa Fe meant roads and reservoirs, and roads and reservoirs drew pilgrims, who bought lumber and farm implements and seed corn from general merchandisers, who bought quarter-pages and fillers to hawk their stock. Pat Garrett had no use for roads or reservoirs. Pat Garrett spent money on cartridges and scaffolds. Pat Garrett punched holes in bandits in the dark and crowed about it in books. A pilgrim with his nose buried in a nickel novel had no time to read a newspaper and learn of the many wonderful items that can be procured for a fraction at the Great Plains Emporium.

The editor of the *Rio Grande Republican* tagged Pat, who had declared his Democratic candidacy for membership in the New Mexico Territorial Council against D. M. Easton and John A. Miller—endorsers both of his campaign for sheriff—"Ungrateful Garrett," called him an "illiterate man," and opined that "the newspaper notoriety he received from his success in killing Billy the Kid has upset his brain." Many of the same sentiments appeared in a later issue in the form of a letter to the editor signed *X*.

Pat, trusting his reading skills hardly more than the opposition press, passed the letters column across the breakfast table to Apolinaria to read to him aloud. His brow darkened and the points of his moustaches met beneath his lower lip as she mouthed the difficult English words. Before she finished, he stood up from his chair, upsetting it, and reached for his cartridge belt and holster dangling from the coat peg beside the door.

His wife asked him what he was planning to do.

"I found Billy Bonney," he said. "I'll find *X*."

"Where will you look?"

"That pleader Roberts in Lincoln's had a hard-on against me ever since Billy jumped jail while I was out of town. I'll start there."

"You did not sleep last night."

This was the coded statement Apolinaria used whenever Pat

was about to commit a foolhardy act. On this morning it was literally true; despite taking a double dose of the nostrum the night before, he had dreamt again of Billy, and awakened smelling the stench of spent powder. Unwilling to take up the dream where he had left off, he had stayed awake, reglazing a windowpane that had been threatening to fall out of its frame. This, and the fact that his wife had gone to their daughter's crib and unbuttoned her blouse to let the child feed, made him reach instead for his hat.

"I'll go see Ash."

"Buy flour." She sat down, cradling the infant to her breast.

Pat found Ash Upson sober behind the counter of the general store in Roswell. The journalist-merchant-realty salesman's hair was brushed back, his moustaches trimmed, and his chin scraped. As soon as he recognized Pat he said, "I read it. You on your way to blow a hole through the Republican son of a bitch, or are you on your way back?"

"I don't do that kind of thing any more, Ash. I'm running for office."

"You mean like Garfield."

"I got pigs to feed. You going to help me write a letter or not?"

Upson sat down at the rolltop in the back corner and opened a drawer. "Go feed your pigs. I'll bring it around for you to sign."

The letter, when it appeared in the *Republican* late in September, was a marvel of the ghostwriter's art, which was the ability to state a case with journalistic eloquence while preserving a sufficient imperfection of style to sustain the premise that it had been penned by the man whose signature appeared at the bottom. It continued for several columns, sniping at X's accusations with the patience of young Pat waiting out the chicken-stealing badger on his father's plantation, laying out the planks in his political platform, and effectively transforming the opposition newspaper into a conduit for his campaign message. Upson even found opportunity to indulge his good-humored contempt for his friend's deficiency in letters: "If this be true, I claim that it is more my misfortune than my fault, and I must say it does not look very generous for *X* to blame me for faults over which I have no control." He was rather more satisfied with the result than he had been with *The Authentic Life of Billy the Kid*, in which he had had to put up with contributions from the man who was there. After posting it he celebrated by going on a bat, and found himself four days later in Toyah, a hide-smelling town with the bark still on it on the Texas Pacific right-of-way; a place he never visited when he was temperate. He knew he'd bought himself another week in Purgatory whenever he woke up in Toyah.

The *Republican* editor, an old campaigner with a taste for peppermints and snuff and an eye for a distinctive style, was not taken in by the letter. He had read the putative Garrett book and was familiar with Upson's New Mexico newspapers—a number of which he had occasionally pilfered items from to fill out his own columns, in a tradition that went back to the respective editors of the *Sodom Intelligencer* and the *Gomorrah Gazette*—and recognized the bibulous Easterner's pet phrases when they crossed his desk. Nor was he diverted by this bald attempt to use his journal for a Democratic shinplaster. He had voted with the Party of Lincoln since the beginning, supported abolition when Free Staters were strung from the trees like May ribbons, and had twice been forced to seek cover when some supporter of the old Confederacy fired a dissenting editorial through his plate-glass window. However, he was a newspaperman first, and not unaware of the fact that Pat Garrett's name sold papers. He typeset and printed the letter without comment or editing.

Ash Upson remained proud of the letter throughout the remainder of his days, quoting from it from memory long after it had been interred in the bound back numbers of the *Rio Grande Republican* and all who read it had forgotten it, along with everything else about Garrett save that he had killed Billy Bonney. Whenever he and Pat fell out, he would grumble over his cups that it might have influenced the election had Pat heeded his advice and gone down to old Mexico to hunt lions until after all the ballots were counted.

While the issue containing the letter was going to press, Pat encountered W. M. Roberts, whom he considered the man responsible for the *X* letter, in J. A. LaRue's dry goods store in Lincoln, where the attorney took delivery on his monthly shipment of General Gordon cigars from Denver. The long man inquired, with the kind of diplomacy more associated with a sheriff than a politician, if Roberts was *X*. Roberts denied the accusation vehemently, maintaining that he had better things to do with his time. Pat seemed satisfied, but when the two were out on the street in front of the store, Pat said that if he was not *X*, he certainly knew who was, and if he didn't come forward with the man's identity, Pat would know Roberts was in bed with Easton and Miller and the *Republican*.

"You have my answer," said the attorney. "If you try to make it anything else, I'll call you a goddamned liar."

Pat said nothing. At this point, Roberts selected a General Gordon from the box, snipped off the end with a clipper attached to his platinum watch chain, and struck a match on a porch post. The flame found twin reflections in the long man's dark eyes.

The former sheriff of Lincoln County unholstered the long-barreled Colt .45 he had used to subdue Billy Bonney and opened two deep gashes in Roberts' head with the heavy butt.

The lawyer fell into a swoon, His cigar rolled to a stop in the thick dust on the street.

Later, Pat asked Ash Upson if he thought Roberts would prefer charges.

Upson, still recovering from Toyah, held up his coffee cup for Apolinaria to refill. "I wouldn't concern myself," he said. "They'll hang you in the *Republican.*"

No legal action followed the incident. Pat carried Lincoln County in the election, thanks mainly to John Chisum and his ranch hands. He lost in all the rest.

Chapter Seven

Texas Fever

The years passed, slowly in the desert, like gilas on their pale bellies, and for many of them I heard nothing of Pat Garrett. I concluded from this that his passage was quiet. It is the fate of the alchemist to be wrong more often than he is right.

Disgusted with politics, and surfeited with life in town, early in 1884 the long man brushed his Stetson, allowed Apolinaria to pluck the lint from his black suit, and met with an Englishman of dubious nobility named Harrison in the office of W. M. Roberts, where he exchanged a bank draft in the amount of five thousand dollars for a thousand acres of range land along Eagle Creek, a tributary of the Rio Hondo in Lincoln County. Hide-through lawyer that he was, Roberts made no mention of his pistol-whipping by Pat two years before as he added his florid signature to the witness blank on the bill of sale. Pat's backers included the Cattlemen's Bank of Lincoln and John Chisum.

From there, the former sheriff went to the Lincoln County Stock Growers Association to register his brand. For years afterward, rustlers who styled themselves after Billy the Kid took a signal delight in spiriting away Eagle Creek cattle with PAT burned in block letters on their hips. Regulators employed by the association dragged one such miscreant from his home and shot him after he displayed a hide with the brand prominent on the wall above his fireplace.

Apolinaria took to the life with fervor. The ranch house, abandoned for months, had become a shelter for every variety of Southwestern wildlife; with a broom she drove out the porcupines and badgers, tied her hair up in a kerchief and climbed into the rafters to poke the little brown bats free of their inverted perches, then swept out the cobwebs and dried dung and scoured the floors and whitewashed the walls. She hung Indian rugs, blacked the stove, and embroidered new sheets for the master bedroom and the guest room where John Chisum stayed when he came to visit on his way back from decorating the cottonwoods in old Mexico with rustlers from north of the border. Señora Garrett was beginning to show with her second child and disguised the evidence behind her prettiest apron when people came to call. As the daughter of a rancher she thought it a fine thing that her children should grow up like desert flowers in the open air, away from the meanness of crowds and the diseases of neighbors packed as closely as blankets in a chest.

Pat envied his wife her complacence. He would not have said it or even thought it, but he was secretly grateful for the thefts from his stock, and for the necessity of ordering his hands into saddle and tracking the path of the rustlers' escape. Routine ranch work vexed him like a boil. He could not comprehend those soft-bellied individuals he met on trains who, in times of upheaval, said they longed for a sameness to their days. The thought that when, exhausted to the soles of his feet from the sheer physical labor of maintaining even such a moderate spread as his ten hundred acres, he retired to his bed knowing that the next day would be identical to the one he had just put behind, filled him with dread. The buffalo were gone, Billy Bonney was gone; sheriff's work had begun to resemble that of a store clerk.

John Poe wore a green eyeshade and sleeve-protectors to the same office where Pat had cleaned and oiled his weapons and interrogated prisoners with his bony, knob-knuckled fists for news of Bonney's movements. If ranch work was all that remained, his life was over. More and more he found himself turning his daily management chores over to his segundo while he went hunting—ostensibly for antelope and boar—but hoping to catch some luckless night-herder in the act of cutting his line fence.

When he did not hunt alone, he was often accompanied by some officers whose acquaintance he'd made at Fort Stanton, where he picked up his mail. One, a straight-backed, stick-up-his-ass lieutenant two years out of West Point, with a puppy moustache, rode like an Apache. Pat considered this a sign of character, and was inclined to overlook a man's less attractive traits if he sat his horse well and took care of the animal. John Pershing had the bad habit of wearing his campaign hat parade-drill fashion, tilted so close to the bridge of his nose that he actually had to tip his head back in order to see game crossing directly in front of him; the long man broke him of it at length, but seeing photographs of him in later years accompanying General Miles on Geronimo's trail was dismayed to learn that he had sunk back into it.

Pershing, a Missourian, was a passing good marksman, but Pat thought his judgment faulty. He based this belief on an incident that took place late one afternoon as the pair were riding not far from the fort. The lieutenant dismounted suddenly, slid his Springfield carbine from its scabbard, and downed a running creature at forty paces with one shot.

"What you fixing to do with that?" asked Pat, when his companion grinned broadly in his direction.

"Make an ammo pouch out of the hide, I suppose. Sell the meat to Mrs. Lisnet at the inn."

"She won't thank you for it."

Pershing produced a skinning knife from his saddle pouch. "And why not?"

"Because that was one of her pigs you just shot." Pat gathered his reins. "Shove back that damn hat."

Later, when the lieutenant was placed in command of black cavalry during the Geronimo campaign, his former hunting companion said, "I knew Nigger Jack Pershing wouldn't amount to a heap of shit when he mistook a tame pig for wild game."

On a steel-cold day in January 1885, weary of shooting jackrabbits along his north fence, Pat crossed into Texas to accept an invitation to dine with the Panhandle Cattlemen's Association in Mobeetie. He was motivated less by the prospect of dinner than by Apolinaria's pregnancy. Mobeetie was near Tascosa, where in times past the Lincoln County sheriff had gone for word of Billy Bonney, and to scrub the crusted dirt from between his toes in a bathtub he shared with one of the city's celebrated whores in Hogtown, south of the tracks. Tascosa's chief exports were mellow cowboys and crabs the size of buffalo. On this occasion the long man separated himself reluctantly from a flat belly, put on his best shirt and the suit he had worn to ask Governor Wallace for his support in the sheriff's election, and feasted on the tenderest beef he had chewed since leaving Louisiana, cooked in champagne sauce and served with a smoky red wine, bottled in the time of Napoleon in a country he had never heard of. He felt out of place among the shirtboards and cutaway coats in the walnut-paneled private dining room on the second floor of Mobeetie's best hotel, and when the brandy came he jerked it down and waited for that old warm rush of confidence he got from tanglefoot.

He was relieved when the company adjourned to the club room, a high-ceilinged chamber with a Brussels carpet whose thickness Pat could feel through the high heels of his boots, scattered with deep leather chairs and sofas arranged in groups for private conversation. There were stacks of local newspapers and *Harper's Weekly*, well read, on tables, and ranks of law books bound in mustard-colored leather, unread, in a massive mahogany case with eagles carved in the corners. An oil painting in a gilt frame the size of a barn door leaned out from one wall, depicting a gaunt cowboy aboard a lathered sorrel chasing a calf down a switchback under a sky crowded with purple clouds. Pat didn't think much of it. The calf was scrawny and probably wouldn't have lived long enough to butcher even if it were captured, and anyway any cowhand with brains enough to move his foot when he was pissing on it would have abandoned a prize bull to run for cover with a storm approaching. He supposed someone had bought the picture to help out some stove-up old hand who could no longer hold anything more worthwhile than a brush, and was shocked when one of his hosts told him the association had commissioned the painting for two thousand dollars from an illustrator who worked for the New York *Herald*. Two thousand would have bought all the available grazing land in New Mexico Territory.

Upon taking his seat in a tall wingback that placed him in the unfamiliar position of feeling dwarfed, Pat was pleased to note the presence of a convenient cuspidor. While the two men who had joined him were snipping the ends off cigars, he used his pocketknife to carve two inches from a plug of Levi Garrett's, popped the length into his mouth, and sat back chewing loose the stubborn shreds of beef that clung between his molars. The moment had arrived for him to be told why he had been invited.

His companions were J. E. McAllister and W. M. D. Lee. McAllister, whom Pat had met before during the spring roundup, managed the sprawling LS Ranch, smack dab in the middle of the Staked Plain. He was a short, wiry Irishman, burned red to within three inches of the crown of his round bald head, with black side-whiskers and a gold tooth in front. From any distance that white cupola of naked scalp, covered by a hat at all times when he was out of doors, looked like some kind of skullcap. Lee, a new acquaintance, was senior partner in the ranch. He was nearly as tall as Pat and terrifyingly thin, the bones of his face standing out like canyon rocks beneath the tight sallow skin. His eyes were sunk in deep hollows and his wing collar, thoroughly buttoned, lay loose around his neck like an open lariat. He seldom spoke, coughing quietly from time to time into a white lawn handkerchief he kept balled up in one bony fist. Pat suspected he was consumptive. His cigar smoked untasted between the first and second fingers of his other hand, moving only to drop ashes into the heavy bronze tray on the table at his elbow.

"How do you find our accommodations?" McAllister opened. "I don't mind telling you they're a far cry from the card room of the saloon where we used to meet. Back then it was buffalo steaks and raw whiskey."

"I like buffalo."

"That's right, you told me you used to hunt them. Not many of the brutes left."

"No, we knocked a hole in the population."

"Not that there was much sport in it. Not like hunting boar."

"Nor men," said Lee.

Pat leaned forward, shot a stream into the cuspidor, and sat back. They were getting to it now.

McAllister said, "I read your book. Splendid blood-and-thunder stuff. I liked it so much I lent it to Bill." He cocked his white-capped head toward Lee, who said nothing.

"That's one reason it didn't make any money. Nobody bought it. Everybody borrowed it from everybody else."

"You knew Billy the Kid."

"I played poker with him."

"I heard he was your friend."

"Bonney didn't have friends. He had men he rode with and men he shot. They wound up just as dead either way."

"You killed your share of the men he rode with," McAllister said.

"I was sheriff then."

"So you were. How do you find the cattle business now you're in it?"

"I like chasing strays over chasing votes."

"I should think it's dull work for a man with your background."

Pat made no answer to that. He wondered where McAllister got his information. The long man confided in no one, including Apolinaria, but he supposed his hands drew the obvious conclusion from his frequent absences. Dinner conversation had been mostly gossip about what the ranchers who weren't present were up to. He had a notion he'd been one of them. He spat again, just to make sure he was among men and hadn't stumbled into a quilting.

A look passed between the ranch manager and the ranch owner, who nodded behind the handkerchief he had pressed to his lips. McAllister settled back into the corner of the sofa and crossed his short bandy legs. "You're aware, no doubt, of our mavericking problem. Chances are you're suffering from some of it yourself."

"Mavericking's no problem. Everybody throws a wide loop one time or another. Herds don't start themselves."

"There's a difference between finding strays and making them. Some of the cowboys looking to start their own outfits have been fencing off unbranded calves belonging to the ranches they work for, separating them from the cows until they're weaned, then slapping their own brands on them. Last month I caught one of the mean bastards burning a calf's feet with a running iron so it couldn't follow its mother."

"What did you do to him?"

"I made him jerk off his boots and marched him sixty miles to the jail in Amarillo; let him feel what the calf felt. He spent the last ten miles begging to be strung up."

"Did you oblige him?"

"Five years ago I would have. I can't abide a man who's cruel to an animal, even one of those flea-bitten sons of bitches. He was just a small thief, though. We've got organized operations stealing whole herds and changing the brands, forged bills of sale, rustlers passing themselves off as officers of the court and confiscating cattle on the grounds they're infested with Texas fever. Last spring the LIT lost a thousand head in one lump. It's gotten out of hand."

"What's the law doing?"

"Oh, they're regular hounds. Whenever they pick up the scent they chase it hell for leather to the New Mexico line. Then they stop."

Pat nodded. "That's a problem."

Again the two Texans exchanged glances. Lee laid down his cigar and drew a long fold of paper from the inside pocket of his dress coat. McAllister took it and thrust it toward Pat.

He read the letter, holding it before his face so the others wouldn't see his lips forming the syllables. It bore an Austin return address and granted W. M. D. Lee permission to organize a *posse comitatus* to apprehend and deliver to justice any and all parties considered a threat to peace and property in the Panhandle region. It was signed by John Ireland, Governor of Texas.

Pat handed it back. "It's a big jurisdiction."

"Effectively, it has no boundaries," McAllister said. "As a private citizen, the leader of this band is at liberty to press pursuit across all state and territorial lines. The job's yours if you want it. You pick the men, you pay and supply them and provide the Panhandle Cattlemen's Association with a record of expenses. It pays five thousand a year. If you accept immediately, I'm authorized to offer you five hundred head of prime breeding stock at a quarter of the market value, to be bought back at full price should you decide to resign."

"Suppose I take it and quit next week?"

"We've agreed to take that chance. I don't think it's much of a gamble. Your honor is well known." The Irishman rotated his cigar. "Have we an arrangement?"

"I need three things."

"State them."

"The first is a free hand. I take the risks, I give the orders. I answer to no one, not you or the association or the governor or Chester-by-God-Arthur."

"I can promise most of that. Bill and I *are* the association, and President Arthur hasn't taken notice of what's been going on out here so far. Ireland may take some talking, but it shouldn't be necessary to remind him who put him in office. What's the second?"

"You can discuss it with the governor when you're getting my free hand. I want a proclamation against carrying six-shooters in this state."

"A handgun prohibition in Texas? You must think he's retiring after this term."

"I won't have my men shot in the belly. I'll take my chances in New Mexico, but I'm a sight less popular here. Bonney didn't raid into Texas."

"We'll convince him it's necessary to attract Eastern investments. Which brings us to the third condition."

"I won't make arrests without warrants. When the dust settles it's always the bounty hunters that wind up on the wrong side of the law. If I didn't learn nothing else from the war in Lincoln County I learned that."

McAllister frowned at his boots. "That's a tall order. You need a judge to issue warrants, and a courthouse for him to sign them in. Tascosa has neither."

"Build one."

Chapter Eight

The Home Rangers

On an unseasonably pleasant morning late in January 1885, the citizens of Tascosa, Texas, awoke to the clatter of a heavy wagon built sturdily of elm delivering a load of rocks smelling of moist earth—the best kind, freshly disinterred and not weakened by exposure to sun and rain and ice—to an empty lot on the respectable side of the tracks. There a crew of stonemasons working under the direction of a great slope-shouldered Greek named Venizelos, who had little English and communicated mainly with sweeping and stabbing motions of his thick arms burned dark as bricks, laid the foundation for the first stone building in the history of the clapboard town. The mayor, beaming as he picked eggs from his teeth at his customary table in the dining room of the railroad hotel, explained to his curious constituents that the philanthropic owners of the great LS Ranch had agreed to loan Oldham County the sum of twenty-five thousand dollars to construct a courthouse and jail.

"Well," said one of his listeners, "that will be the first thing that outfit ever gave us apart from shot-out windows every Saturday night."

The residents of Hogtown, across the tracks, were less easily impressed. Buffalo Lou, a whore of somewhat longer standing in the area than the ranch itself, paused in the midst of soaping the genitals of a customer to wring out her sponge and deliver her own assessment of the situation: "The only good business reason to build your own jail is to be the one to decide who gets put in it."

As it happened, the owner of the genitals, a cowboy named Bob Bassett, worked for the Tabletop Ranch, whose owners, Bill Gatlin and Wade Woods, were identified in the small leatherbound notebook J. E. McAllister carried next to his ribs at all times. In it, written in the Gaelic dialect he preferred to any code, was detailed information on every rustler whose name he intended to appear in the first flurry of warrants issued from the new courthouse. Bassett, who was unaware of the notebook's existence and couldn't read it even if it were to come into his possession and if it were written in English, nevertheless understood the importance of what Buffalo Lou had told him. Upon ejaculating, he went straight to Gatlin with the information. The pair held a brief conference with Wade Woods, whose mouth, paralyzed on one side by a kick from a mule that had knocked out half his bottom teeth, dropped into a lopsided sneer.

"The Home Rangers, they call theirselves. As if Garrett and his pack don't wear the LS burn on both their ass cheeks."

"Burn or no burn, he's the one kilt the Kid." Bassett had read *Billy the Kid and the Preacher's Wife* until the book fell apart in his hands.

The three agreed to transfer their operation to Red River Springs on the great Canadian, where Woods knew of a granite shack that could be defended in case of siege. Gatlin, the only one present with a discernible sense of humor, commented dryly upon the irony of retreating to one stone building to avoid incarceration in another. Woods told him to get his truck together and stop talking Greek. They pulled out under a February sky purple with snow.

"I never heard of an outfit called the Tabletop," Pat said. "It can't be big."

Jim East, Oldham County sheriff and an old acquaintance who had sided Pat in the fight at Stinking Springs, shifted his ubiquitous toothpick from one corner of his mouth to the other. He was a loose-boned former top hand with an uncombed pompadour like a roadrunner's and a sandpapery face that a man might have scratched a match on; but he'd have been stopped by East's ice-blue gaze. "No bigger'n Bill Gatlin's hat," he said. "That's the headquarters. The Tabletop brand's wide and thick enough to cover every other one in the valley except the XIT. I thought at first that's where the rustlers was operating, on account of they had the smallest losses. Then one of Jamie McAllister's boys skinned a winter-killed Tabletop cow on a hunch and came and showed me the inside of the hide. Someone had went and burned the new brand smack on top of one from the LS."

"I do loath and despise a sneaky thief."

"So do I. Bonney just up and shot you when you found him out. He was an honest crook."

Pat, who had dreamt of Bonney again the night before, sealed off that path of conversation. "In or out, Jim? I need ten good men."

"What are you paying?"

"You didn't ask that on the way to Stinking Springs."

"That was different. Times was different. This ain't about rustling, Pat; it's about squeezing out the small fry. The big outfits didn't have anywhere near these losses till the LIT squashed that cowboy strike two years back. All they wanted was fifty a month and the right to do a little mavericking on the side. They got blackballed instead. Couldn't get work shoveling shit anywhere in the Panhandle. That's when the rustling started."

"That why you draw rein at the state line?"

East studied the masticated end of his toothpick and flipped it into the wood box by his office stove. "Talk is you're getting five thousand from the association. How are you splitting it up?"

"Sixty a month and the use of a good horse."

"If they done what the strikers wanted in the first place, they'd have saved ten dollars a man and about five thousand head."

Pat's face grew dark. "If that's how you feel, why don't you unhook that star and haul your freight over to the other side?"

"I didn't say I wouldn't take the job. Who've you got so far?"

"You know them. Barney Mason and Lon Chambers."

"No other takers?"

"I just started looking."

"Come on, Pat. In Lincoln County you had to beat them off with a switch."

"Times was different. You said it yourself." The long man touched his moustaches. "I won't deny there's a deal of bad blood."

"Mason's a son of a bitch, meaner'n a shithouse rat. I don't want him standing over me telling me to take my medicine like he done poor Tom O'Folliard."

"I don't pick them for their character. He's a good shot and he'll grow roots at the backdoor if that's where you post him. You and Chambers get on," he added.

"I'd side Lon to hell and around. What about Poe?"

"John's a civilized man. He likes to scribble in his ledgers and ride around in that buggy of his and get home to his new wife by sundown. Those red wheels won't stand up where we're headed."

"I didn't know you fell out."

"I said he was civilized."

"It ain't a disease, Pat. Though it's spreading."

"In or out, Jim?"

East hesitated an instant; any longer and he'd have been considered a civilized man. Then he nodded. "Assuming we get your ten, where do we look first?"

"My sources claim Red River Springs is a good place to start."

"Yes, I get my best information from Hogtown as well." The sheriff glanced through the window, where a wet snow had begun to fall. The flakes were as large as twenty-dollar gold-pieces and thin as cobwebs. "I don't guess you care to wait for the thaw."

Pat shook his head. "Injuns and outlaws are alike, lazy as niggers. They'd rather sit around a fire than break up drifts and they think everyone else feels the same."

"Everyone else does. Except Pat Garrett."

"Evening, Barney. Shoot any kittens today?"

Barney Mason lifted his thick china mug for Sheriff East to fill from the steaming pot and said nothing. He sported a winter beard that served only to increase his resemblance to a nocturnal rodent of the large-eared, pop-eyed variety.

Most of the Home Rangers were seated around the table in East's big kitchen. Outside, grains of snow like hard dried peas rattled against the siding on the north wall in gusts that searched out the places where putty had fallen from the windowpanes and made the lamp on the table glow fiercely yellow. Coats, hats, and mufflers hung three deep on pegs by the stove, steaming and filling the room with the noxious stench of mothballs and unbathed flesh. The rest of the crew stood and sat about the adjoining small living room. They smoked, conversed in low voices, and stared at their reflections in the night-backed windows. Shotguns and rifles leaned in all the corners.

East returned the pot to the stove, where Pat Garrett stood poking cartridges into the loops on the belt around his waist from a deal box. "Christ, Pat, I've had half these men in my jail more than once."

"They all came recommended."

"Not by me. Those LS men are barroom gladiators. They drink too hard and they don't pick targets. Charlie Reason's as bad as any of the Tabletop outfit."

"I didn't pick them for a choir."

"I won't have nothing to do with them."

Pat looked at him. "Don't wobble on me, Jim. I've got a hundred and fifty-nine warrants and only one man in a position to serve them."

"The jail won't hold ten."

"We'll start with nine."

"Well, I'm riding in back. I'll take my chances with wolves and Comanches."

Lon Chambers, who at Stinking Springs had asked Pat about his friendship with Bonney, got up from the table and came over to refill his cup, using a spoon to hold back the grounds. "We waiting for this storm to let up?" he asked the sheriff.

"Pat's running the show."

"Get your gear." Pat dumped the remaining cartridges into the pocket of his hanging coat and took it off the peg.

"Shit." Chambers gulped down his coffee. "Someday you'll tell me why you got such a hard-on for blizzards."

"Kid Dobbs used to hunt buff in this country. If you lose sight of him, look for Albert Perry. I appointed him first sergeant. He's an old cattle detective."

"He knows the ropes, all right," East said. "He's stole his share."

They rode Indian file across the white plain, shoulders hunched and hats pulled down and secured with their mufflers tied beneath their chins. Snow blew into their faces, drawing them tight as masks. The snowfall gave off its own illumination independent of the skillet-black sky and sculpted the flat landscape into hills and hammocks like dunes. Clouting forward, the horses plunged into hidden hollows with grunts of shock and pain, blowing steam that condensed on the riders' faces and frosted their eyebrows and moustaches, turning them into old men. At Trujillo at two in the morning they fed the horses and kicked at the door of the cafe until the owner came down and built the stove back up and fed them tortillas and chiles and refried beans with scalding coffee and tequila to wash it down. Charlie Reason filled a canteen from the bottle. When Sheriff East protested, Pat drew him aside. "It's medicine for such as him."

The storm blew over at daybreak. Shortly afterward the rangers drew rein on a rise overlooking the Canadian River. All around them for miles were blue-shadowed drifts capped with reflected orange light, unbroken except for the angry puckered path they had made and the black thread of the river chuckling under the ice floes piled like rocks in the bends. "How far's the shack?" Pat asked Dobbs. The words, the first spoken in hours, crackled in the brittle air.

"We'll have a dandy view from the top of the next hill. Trouble is, so will they."

"How far to circle back from upriver?"

"Couple of miles."

"Then put the steel to your horse and lead the way."

Half an hour later, approaching the top of a hill heading upriver, Pat smelled woodsmoke and passed the order along to dismount. They hitched their horses to cottonwoods and spread out, floundering on foot through waist-deep snow to the crest of the rise. There they assumed a semicircular formation with the shack at the base of the hill in the center of their field of fire. The building had been dug into the slope, reinforced with round stones pried from the riverbed and chinked with mud, and roofed with poles. Coming upon it from the side where the snow-covered poles slanted into the hillside, the rangers might have overlooked it but for the crooked stovepipe lisping smoke from the center of the roof.

A figure was moving around thirty yards from the entrance to the dugout, snapping dead branches from a tangle of fallen trees and laying them across the crook of his left arm. "Who's that?" Pat whispered to Jim East.

"Looks like Bob Bassett. He runs with that Tabletop bunch."

Someone said, "Shit!" loudly enough to make echoes. Every head in the vicinity, including Bassett's, swiveled upriver, where Charlie Reason sprawled on his face in the snow, the toe of one boot hooked on a snarled tree-root.

"Charlie and his medicine." East's whisper was savage.

Bassett dropped his armload of wood and sprinted toward the dugout, shouting, "It's the Pat Garrett Rangers!"

Pat sank into a crouch, raised his Winchester, and led the runner with the muzzle. Sheriff East closed his fingers around Pat's wrist.

"They're just cattle thieves," he said.

The long man lowered the carbine.

There followed a shouted dialogue between East and Bill Gatlin, who informed the sheriff that Wade Woods wasn't present. East promised Gatlin and Bassett a fair trial if they gave themselves up without gunplay. Gatlin offered to discuss it if

East would come down in person. East hesitated, then unbuckled his cartridge belt. Pat, still in his crouch, leveled the Winchester at him across his thigh.

East looked at him. "You wouldn't shoot me, would you, Pat?"

"I won't have to if you start down that hill alone."

"I know those boys. They wouldn't shoot a calf with its leg broke."

"The calf wouldn't be fixing to hang them."

After a moment East grinned. "You want to set up another barbecue?"

"We ain't got the provisions, and town's too far." Pat signaled to Albert Perry, who duckwalked over from his position behind a treefall. The former cattle detective had a round soft face with sparse ginger moustaches and the dead eyes of a killer. Pat said, "Send a crew down to strip the poles off that roof."

The delegation mounted the roof from the hillside and got to work.

After three poles had been torn loose and flung to the ground, exposing the interior of the dugout to fire from above, the two men inside announced they were coming out. The rangers surrounded them, tied them up, and took them to Tascosa.

On their first night in jail, a former LIT striker poked a file between the bars.

"I hold Sheriff East responsible." J. E. McAllister dipped the end of his cigar into his glass of whiskey in the association club room. "He used to punch cows with those boys. I wouldn't be surprised if he took a walk while that file was going in."

"Jim's straight as a bull's dick." The long man spat into the cuspidor at his feet.

"Next time you have someone pinned down, go ahead and shoot. We only built that jail to go with the courthouse."

"They're just cattle thieves."

"So was Bonney, but you didn't say that in your book."

Pat said, "Send someone around for your cattle. I quit."

Chapter Nine

Black Cattle

Well, Big Casino."

"Well what, Billy? You're dead."

Bonney showed his big front teeth in a grin, appreciating Pat's joke. He had on his favorite wide sombrero with the Irish green band, a bolero vest over a white linen shirt with the sleeves gathered by garters, tight black trousers split below the knees with tiny silver bells stitched along the vents, and boots with four-inch heels and Mexican spurs. He jingled when he walked and his erection was obvious where the trousers hugged his crotch. The Mexican girls in Fort Sumner and along the Journey of the Dead—the ones who spoke of such things—referred to Billy Bonney's impressive endowment as La Culebra: The Snake. Pat, with customary empirical reasoning, considered that it wasn't that big; it was just that the rest of Billy was that small.

"I hear you stepped out from behind Beaver Smith's bar," Bonney said. "Hooked on a star for Old Elephant Ears and General Wallace."

"For Lincoln County. Chisum don't pay me except in taxes, and Wallace can't vote."

"I never cast no ballot."

"That's because you move around too much. And besides,

you're dead. I blowed you clean through the door of Pete Maxwell's bedroom."

Bonney appeared uncertain for the first time. Then he recovered. He reached inside his vest and Pat's hand went down to his belt, despite the fact he knew he was dreaming. But the weapon Bonney produced was only a deck of cards. He slid off the rubber band and shuffled, the waxed pasteboards hissing between his slim, supple fingers.

"I'm going on the scout," he said. "How about a few hands before I ride out?"

"Go down to old Mexico, Billy. Or up to Texas. Maybe I won't have to kill you this time."

"Straight stud, nothing wild. I'm the only wild card in this here deck."

"Not no more. You're part of the deadwood."

Bonney's hands slipped, an unprecedented event. The cards skidded free and fell to the floor in a slithering cascade. His expression became blank, then frightened. Then a shadow obliterated his features like a cloud sliding over.

"Quien es?" he demanded, from the darkness. "Quien es?"

Pat sat up straight, spilling the sheet from his naked chest. He felt not fear, but a terrible, burning sense of shame, as if he'd been caught masturbating with one of his mother's petticoats. He looked over to see if he'd awakened Apolinaria, but that side of the bed was empty. It wasn't even his bed, nor the room the bedroom they shared at Eagle Creek. The walls were not the familiar whitewashed adobe, but papered plaster, and the sun slanted in greasily through plain muslin curtains instead of the white lace his wife had made by hand. The woman standing by the window smoking a cheroot was thin and slack-breasted in a plain shift through which he could count her ribs. There were hollows beneath her eyes, like depressions in a clay head made by the sculptor's thumbs, and her hair, tinted red, dangled in sweaty strands to her thin shoulders.

"Bad dream, Long Tall?" Her voice was a raspy whisper.

Pat hawked, rolled over, and spat into the china thunder mug on the floor beside the bed. He was in Hogtown: the room smelled of rancid renderings, old semen, and the sweat that soaked the walls to the studs. "What's the damages?" He wiped his lips with the back of his hand.

"Two dollars. I took it out of your poke."

"What else did you take?"

"Go to hell. I could of slit your throat and sold your spurs. You sleep like a old boar."

"You know who I am?"

"Sure. You're P. T. Barnum. I seen your Tom Thumb." She skinned her lips back from a set of nicotine-stained horse teeth.

"You just fucked a famous man."

"They're all famous after I fuck 'em."

"I'm Pat Garrett."

She blew smoke at the curtains. "I knew a Garrity up in Denver."

"Garrett, not Garrity. You never heard of me?"

"You with the railroad?"

"I killed Billy the Kid."

"Who's that?"

"You're full of shit," he said.

She turned away from the window. Face on, she looked a little less emaciated. She was probably still in her twenties. "I hated to see him go."

"You knew him?"

"Never laid eyes on him. I never seen a Comanche, neither, but I miss them just the same. First you clear out the injuns, then you start on the outlaws. When they're all gone, who's left?" She thumped her chest. "That's why I left Denver. Christ knows what's waiting for me after Hogtown."

"You think too much for a whore."

"It's a failing," she agreed.

As was his habit when he was hung over, Pat dressed with particular care, inspecting his collar for smudges, brushing and picking lint from his lapels and trousers, and combing his hair and moustaches with clean water from the basin. When he entered the downstairs parlor on his way out, a man rose from the faded settee, swiftly enough for Pat to touch the pistol scabbard beneath his coat.

"Have I the honor of addressing Sheriff Pat Garrett?"

He took an instant dislike to the stranger. His accent was English, and the long man belonged to a generation that had not forgotten the burning of Washington City. Also his clothing beneath his open bearskin coat, too heavy for the Texas spring, was of a material and tailoring far beyond the budget of one such as Pat, who preferred to be the best-dressed man in any company. The fellow wore his fair hair long, brushed behind his ears, and his vandyke beard received a great deal of attention with scissors and a comb. He was nearly as tall as Pat, and good-looking enough to have had to fight off two or three whores to have the parlor to himself. Pat didn't trust a man who had no weakness for women; it meant he was either a pansy or concerned with some worse vice.

"I'm Garrett. There hasn't been a sheriff in front of my name for a spell."

"Yet there are those of us for whom you will always bear the title to which you have brought so much glory, like Gordon of Khartoum." He smiled. He had good teeth for an Englishman, even and white. "Captain Brandon Kirby." He proferred a slim pale hand.

Pat took it, having first noted that the man's other hand was occupied holding a pair of deerskin gloves; even an ex-Ranger had to look after his skin in Tascosa. "Where's your ship?"

"I was privileged to serve Her Majesty with the Army of Afghanistan." Kirby actually blushed as he said it. His new acquaintance decided that he was an inept liar. "They told me in Lincoln County I'd find you in Mobeetie. I was told there I'd find you here, and so I have." He looked around, at the parched furniture and dust that showed in the shafts of sunlight. "Are the women clean, by the way?"

"I wouldn't eat off them. What's your business, Captain? I quit the Association three days ago."

"So I was informed, and all the better for my mission. My employer is James Cree. Do you know the name?"

"Creek?"

"Cree. The name is Scottish, as indeed is the man himself. He's outgrown the Highlands and wishes to increase his considerable fortune by raising cattle in New Mexico Territory. I'm representing him in his quest for land."

"Tell him to invest in a whorehouse. Easy women are quicker to come by than cattle when your stock gets run off."

Kirby exposed some more of his teeth to show he was a man of the world. Pat was fascinated by the growing depth of his distaste. "Unfortunately, Mr. Cree is respectable. In any case, he's concocted a scheme that promises to make the practice of cattle rustling in the West as obsolete as piracy on the high seas."

The long man, intrigued despite himself, said he'd pay to hear it.

"You won't have to; rather the other way around. I would admire to discuss it with you, if it's not too early to drink."

"In England, maybe."

They walked to the first saloon on the Tascosa side of the

tracks, where the bartender drew a beer for Pat, added bitters to a glass of gin for Kirby, and banged the drinks down on the bar. "I say," the Englishman complained, brushing drops of gin from his waistcoat. But the man had turned his back on him to wipe down the beer pulls.

Pat said, "Forget it. He punched cows for the LIT until the strike. A lot of these town boys are on the blacklist."

"I had nothing to do with that."

"You have now. You've been seen with me. From now on you want to watch to see your glass don't get pissed in." Pat carried his glass to a gaming table unoccupied at that hour of the morning and sat down. Kirby joined him.

"Mr. Cree began his search in Montana Territory, but found the climate too much like Scotland's for his taste. The Southwest is not so good for grazing, but the land is cheap. He hopes to control a million acres in New Mexico and the Panhandle."

"Nobody can afford to keep up a spread that size."

"But a very rich man can easily afford to acquire all the parcels in the region which contain water, granting him virtual ownership of an area as large as all of western Europe."

"He'd need ten million men to protect it."

"Hence the scheme." Kirby drew a flat wallet from inside his suitcoat and unfolded a rectangular scrap of newsprint containing a steelpoint engraving in profile of a heavy-shouldered bull. It was an advertisement for a stock auction cut from an Aberdeen newspaper.

Pat read the legend. "What's Black Angus?"

"A breed of cattle, far superior in meat production to any in this country. I attended this auction last month and bought one hundred and fifty bulls for breeding. They're not as hearty as the local red cattle, but by crossing the strains, Cree expects to create a supreme hybrid that will outproduce all the others in the world."

"Where are the bulls now?"

"They're currently in quarantine in Canada. I hope to arrange for their release in time for an autumn drive. By then we should have all the land we require."

"You better leave them where they are. The thieves in this country will steal everything but the hoofprints before they get ten miles."

Kirby drained his glass, bringing an orange flush to his face. Pat had never met an Englishman who could carry his liquor. "I understand you're a rancher, Mr. Garrett. How do you protect your stock from theft?"

"Burn them like everyone else. But any rustler with a running-iron can change a brand."

"Cree's idea will make branding a thing of the past." He thumped the clipping on the table with a forefinger. "These bulls are *black*. They sire black calves. Any man not connected with the Cree organization found running black cattle will be apprehended on the spot. I promise you that after the first round of trials and convictions, the remaining rustlers will seek else-where for their livelihoods."

"It makes too much sense," Pat said. "I'm suspicious of some-thing nobody thought of before."

"It's in your nature to suspect. Surely everyone out here knows that. Which brings me to why I have come all this way to seek you out."

"I'm through regulating for Big Cattle, black calves or no. There's no satisfaction in it."

"You don't understand. It isn't Pat Garrett's gun I wish to hire. It's his regard."

"I wouldn't try living on it here in the Panhandle," Pat said.

"It's a different story in Lincoln County, where we intend to concentrate our efforts. The name Cree inspires either indifference or avarice there. When the landholders agree to discuss a transaction at all, they dictate terms more suitable to a Stuart king than a simple speculator in cattle. I hold the conviction that a union with the man who slew Billy the Kid would enable us to negotiate something far more to our advantage."

The long man swallowed the last of his beer. "Still thirsty, Captain?"

A glimmer of greed appeared in Kirby's eye, which he sought to dissemble by unpocketing a watch the size and thickness of a silver dollar. "I suppose I have time for another."

This time, when the bartender banged the glasses, Pat asked him in his quiet drawl if he wouldn't care to pick them up again and set them down gentle-like. The man tried to return his gaze, wavered. "Pardon." He reached for the glasses. Pat slapped down the exact change and whisked them away, leaving the bartender's hands cupping empty air.

"Supposing I agree to front for your Mr. Cree," Pat said, reclaiming his seat. "What's my end?"

The effort of not looking at the glass of gin still in the long man's grasp stiffened the muscles in Kirby's face. "I think I could persuade him to agree to a finder's fee of ten percent, with a substantial bonus should you succeed in delivering the deeds under the amount budgeted."

"How much is that?"

"I've been instructed not to go over three hundred thousand dollars."

"Done." Pat withdrew his hand. "We'll start the ball with my spread on Eagle Creek."

Camping out that night on the road back to Lincoln County, Pat drank the very last of the nostrum he had acquired from my hut in old Mexico. He awoke with the sun full in his face and no dreams in his memory.

Chapter Ten

White Wind

They can't *walk*?" Pat was amused.

Kirby, perspiring freely in his tweeds on the verandah of the Angus Ranch headquarters (the role of English country gentleman had caught his fancy in the jaws of a gila monster and he would no sooner surrender it than he would his North Country accent), shook his head in no particular response to Pat's question. "It seems the worst quality the indigenous red longhorn possesses is also its greatest strength. That tough stringiness diners complain of when they try to chew the meat is the very thing that allows the steers to cover so many miles in a day without dropping dead from exhaustion. I selected the black bulls for the succulence of their hams, never dreaming that they were simply too fat to waddle more than a hundred yards at a stretch. The cost of shipping them here by wagon from Canada will annihilate this year's profits."

Pat laughed. He felt he could afford to. He had sold James Cree his own ranch at a substantial profit, along with four hundred head of stock, and delivered a hundred thousand acres besides. The porch they were standing on was brand new, constructed along with the rest of the house on the site of John Poe's old house and barn, whose sale Pat had negotiated on the strength of their past association. Privately, he thought it was to

Poe's pure profit, since the current Lincoln County sheriff had grown too fat sitting behind his desk going over his highly regarded ledgers even to ride comfortably in his fancy buggy, let alone hoist himself into a saddle for the long trip to Lincoln from his ranch. In any case he enjoyed laughing at anything that caused Captain Kirby displeasure.

"I had hoped to fold the expense into the profits from last spring's calf crop, but the numbers are far below what I estimated." The Englishman steadfastly ignored his companion's mirth. "The local brigands appear to have wasted no time. Perhaps they hope to offset their losses when the cows begin throwing black calves."

"I wouldn't count too much on that." Pat wiped the tears from his eyes and lit a cheroot, striking the match on a freshly painted post and leaving a scar.

"Why not? What are they going to do, paint them?"

"All I'm saying is you're laying down a mighty lot on them bulls being around long enough to rut."

Kirby didn't appear to pay much attention to the answer. He was looking out across the scraped plain, where a wind had sprung up, pushing cottonwood leaves ahead of it and combing the short grass between the bulbs of mesquite, which had begun to turn color. "And now it's cold. A moment ago it was sweltering. I was told the winters were mild in this country."

"Depends on the winter. I hear the buff up north are putting on their woolies early. That's a sign, or maybe not. One thing you can count on about the weather here is you can't count on the weather."

"How very picturesque." Kirby went inside.

Pat remained on the verandah, smoking and watching the wind from the north grow horns.

* * *

Most of Lincoln turned out to see the first wagonload of Black Angus rattle down the same street Billy Bonney had taken out of town after gunning down deputies Bell and Olinger. Extensions had been built up on the sideboards, but the spaces between were wide, and everyone got a good look at the future of the American cattle industry. The bulls appeared not to belong to the same species as the red longhorn, wild-eyed, gaunt in the hips, their bones standing out like angle irons in a gunnysack: More fist-shaped than rangy, the Angus were rounded all over and stood low to the ground on legs as big around as telegraph poles and were shaggy all over like buffalo. Their coats were dead black, more charcoal than India ink, and the light of intelligence did not shine in their eyes. Their lowing had not the arrogant edge of the longhorn's bellow; one onlooker likened it to a fat woman's fart. Nobody was much impressed except the representatives Captain Kirby had invited from the meat-packing plants in Chicago, who informed him that if his first generation of cattle looked as good as their sires they would take them all off his hands. The owner of Lincoln's butcher shop confided to his customers that those loose-bellied Easterners wouldn't know a steak from a tin of sardines. "What's the point of eating meat you don't have to pound the hell out of to get it to lay down on your plate?"

When the first bull was found castrated, Captain Kirby's gentlemanly repose went up the chimney. He told Pat he wanted the culprit tracked down and hanged.

"Not without a warrant," Pat said. "Anyway, the tracks'd just lead to the bunkhouse."

"We're employing a traitor?" Aroused from bed, the Englishman had pulled on a soiled shirt without a collar. He was unshaven and his hair stood up on one side.

•

"Likely more'n one. There's a deal of bad blood around since the strike. The way you treat the hands don't help the situation. This ain't Scotland, and they ain't tenant farmers."

"If they think I've been harsh before this, they have a surprise coming."

"Let it go, Captain. One bull's just a reminder. He could've went ahead and sliced the balls off the bunch."

"Only at the peril of his own. I'll not have these animals mutilated. My God! Do you know what it cost to bring them here?"

"A cowboy has to be plenty hot to choose such work. You got them out stringing wire now. Give them Saturday off if they string five miles by Friday. It's heaps better to offer them sugar than a singletree across the ass."

Kirby filled a tumbler with brandy from a cut-glass decanter bearing the Cree family crest. "Well, who the hell are they?"

"New Mexicans. They fought Maximilian and Geronimo and the whole Comanche nation. The rest of the time they fought each other. I wouldn't go so far as to say they look down on anybody, but they sure as hell don't look *up* to anybody this side of God Almighty."

"Tell them that until the man who castrated that bull comes forward they work Sundays."

"You tell them. I don't cherish getting shot out from under my hat."

"That's another thing. From now on the carrying of pistols on company property is prohibited. Violators will be dismissed immediately without pay."

"You'd best throw in their knives and rifles. Boots, too. They'll stomp you to death otherwise."

"I'll take that chance. Anyone who would take his revenge in this cowardly way will surely hesitate to face a man who can defend himself."

Pat, accompanied by a group of Cree employees who had been with the outfit since Montana, enforced the antifirearms regulation with dispatch. They surrounded lone hands along the fence line, disarmed them, and sent them on their way. When the hands caught on and began carrying their weapons inside their trousers and in shoulder rigs under their vests and coats, Pat moved in close and slammed the barrel of his big Colt's across their skulls, apologizing curtly on those occasions when a subsequent search failed to turn up contraband. Whenever a running-iron came to light, proving the man a rustler, Pat took him into custody and delivered him to John Poe for prosecution. A second bull was found castrated, then a third. Kirby fired twenty men suspected of complicity in the mutilations. Still they continued: a dozen in a single night, sixty by the end of the first month.

The country through which the long man rode on his patrols became increasingly white and bare from drought. The water holes controlled by the Cree company were fenced in with barbed wire, and armed riders were stationed to prevent men employed by the surrounding ranches from cutting it. Where no riders were to be seen, there was a hole that had dried up. As the rainless weeks crawled past like thirsty vagabonds on their hands and knees, the abandoned stations multiplied. Dry rot consumed the fence posts. The wires drooped like neglected debutantes. Even the vultures deserted the holes for better pickings nearer the ranch buildings. The deep roots of the indestructible feathergrass drew up, the tufts fell over and blew away with the dust. The topsoil and then the subsoil dried out and was peeled aside, seeking shelter between jambs and sills and hammocking in the corners of interior cabinets. The land turned brown, fading like old cloth.

Then came the winter of 1886.

The last morning of 1885 was cloudless and balmy. In the forenoon the wind shifted toward the south, drawing a dirty gray veil across the sky from Canada. The air smelled of iron. The first long icy drops of an afternoon-long drizzle struck the pulverized earth, darkening it momentarily, then disappearing beneath it like burrowing insects. They froze on the blades of grass that remained, turning them into glass filaments. The wind steepened. By nightfall the rain had given way to a fine, powdery snow that clung to the cottonwoods, piled up on roofs, and snaked along the wind-scraped ground until it stacked up against the walls of barns and curled back on itself in the hollows of hills like a barber's last flourish with brush and pomade. The wind turned white. It shrieked around cornices, shook shutters in its teeth, and stung the eyes of beast and man, burning exposed flesh like sheets of flame. From northern Dakota to the belly of Texas, from Topeka to the Great Salt Lake, the storm bellowed. It continued without letup for three days and three nights. Eighteen inches of snow dropped like a great smothering mattress, obliterating roads and fences. The temperature plummeted to twenty below zero. Trains were held up in Kansas and Colorado. The mail stopped. Telegraph lines, embrittled with ice and whipped about like scourges, snapped, and where they did not part, the poles that held them leaned over and were buried beneath the drifts. By the end of the blow, the High Plains had been catapulted back forty years, to the time before the Transcontinental Railroad and Western Union. One-half of the United States was cut off from the rest.

Three hundred people lost their lives in the blizzard. They were found frozen in the snow near the remains of their blasted houses, huddled together stiff as cordwood in covered wagons whose teams stood frozen in their traces, curled into fetal positions in the dubious shelter of sheds and lean-tos forty yards from their own hearths. When the snow began to recede, seas of cattle dead from cold and starvation appeared in wallows and ar-royos, driven there before the wind like debris. Bloated, stick-legged carcasses bobbed in the spring runoff. Faced with losses of eighty-five to a hundred percent of their stock, the buildings, fences, gates, and ledger books that encompassed the great beat-ing heart of the great cattle ranches showed themselves to be mere shells. Correspondence from the eastern banks whose funds fueled the traffic in beef ceased to be cordial, then ceased altogether, replaced by the letterheads of collection agencies based in Chicago and St. Louis. When another drought came in the summer of 1886, killing the new grass and scraping away the bottomsoil, the smaller ranches dried up and blew away with it.

Prairie fires gorged themselves on the dead blades, naked branches, and empty line shacks, carving black swaths across the land. Range hands, Pat among them, pulled bandannas up over their faces, slapped out what flames they could with blan-kets doused with water, felled trees, and dragged burning bunches of mesquite across the brown hills to create firebreaks. The mountain ridges glowed red in the evenings. The sun came up behind a haze of smoke and floating ash. As the drought and fires spread eastward, destroying the wheat and corn crops of the Middle West, shipments of feed slowed to a trickle. Cat-tle grew hollow in the flanks and starved to death in the middle of the very grasslands that had fed the buffalo for ten thousand years.

Then came the winter of 1886–87.

Snow began to fall in October. By Christmas the mercury in the thermometers had dropped to forty below, and stayed there through February. In early January the sky turned black as a skillet and dumped sixteen inches of snow over most of North America in sixteen hours. From New York to Washington State, the continent was as a thing dead beneath a shroud of blinding white. The last of Cree's Black Angus bulls perished of thirst while standing up to its chin in snow, unaware that the stuff could be eaten. Pat and others donned two suits of underwear and as many flannel shirts as would allow them to move their arms in their fleece-lined coats, smeared lampblack beneath their eyes to forestall blindness, and waded through waist-deep drifts to extricate foundered cows and deliver fodder to herds stranded in ravines. The hearts of two of the older hands burst from the strain; their bodies were carried back and stored in a barn to await the thaw, when the ground would be soft enough to dig graves without breaking a spade. Two weeks later a chinook wind blew warm air across the plains, but before the snow finished melting, an icy blast issued from Alberta, freezing it into a crust as hard as iron. The cattle who had survived the blizzards could not break through it to forage for the grass beneath. Maddened, half-blind bulls, cows, and steers, their ribs standing out like umbrella staves, staggered into town, pushed down fences, and ate the tar paper off the sides of shacks. They heeled over in backyards and school playgrounds and putrefied when the thaw came. Teams and wagons were employed to drag the carcasses to a mass grave, where lime was shoveled over them to prevent plague.

Captain Brandon Kirby, looking nearly as gaunt as any of the remaining Cree cattle, counted banknotes out of the strongbox on his desk and pushed them across the blotter toward Pat. "You'll find it's all there, and you may count yourself fortunate for that. There won't be enough if all the hands ask for their time."

"I never did trust to luck." Pat counted the notes for himself and put them in his inside pocket. "I been waiting outside since before sunup."

Kirby was looking out the window of the ground-floor study he used as his office. "The Stock Growers Association has ordered a thousand rolls of barbed wire. They're going to fence in the open range, trim the herds. It's the only way to keep count and feed them in the event of drought and blizzards. I never thought I'd see the day."

"I seen my share. You get so you take what comes. What's next?"

"Mr. Cree sets sail for Scotland on the twelfth. I'm to sell off the rest and take my commission. After that, I don't know. California, perhaps."

"All the gold's dug out there."

"There's gold and gold. What about yourself? Back to sheriffing?"

"No, irrigation."

"You're starting a water company?"

"Yeah. Well, not exactly. I'm getting together an investment partnership to dam the Rio Hondo and flume it out across the desert. The territory's seen what drought can do. I figure to make something off the water rights."

"You'll lose your shirt. God doesn't want this country to have water. Snow, yes. Water, no. You'll be broke in a year."

"I'm broke now. Anyway it beats going to California without a plan."

"I didn't say I didn't have a plan." Kirby uncorked his pocket flask, swigged from it, and looked at the flask. "Maybe I'll try the liquor business. Make wine."

"Lose your shirt."

The Englishman found a glass in a drawer of the desk, blew

dust out of it, and poured from the flask. He pushed the glass across the blotter and lifted the flask once again. "Here's to your water," he said.

Pat picked up the glass. "Here's to your wine." He drank.

SILVER

Chapter Eleven

The Cyclone and the Peccary

In the autumn of my one hundred fifth year, the rain fell for three days in the desert in a month with a blue moon.

Three days of rain in the desert is a rarity during the monsoon season of spring; that it should happen in the time of the harvest was a thing unknown in my lifetime, nor could I find any reference to such an incident in the journals of my father and grandfather. That it should take place between two full moons appearing in the same month assigned it to a unique category, shared by the Immaculate Conception and the Detonation of the Godhead, and thus the creation of the universe. It was a time—if ever there was a time—to forage for the Black Maria.

La Maria Negrita is a desert mushroom, whose span is measured in hours. It grows in heavy moisture and dense shade—two things not to be found in that burning land except under the scarcest of circumstances—and sheer chance governs its discovery by one knowledgable enough to recognize it and to harvest it immediately. It cannot be domesticated. I had never seen the Black Maria in nature, although I had searched for it when I thought the conditions friendly. My experience of it was confined to a single paragraph in my great-grandfather's journal and three dessicated specimens in the bottom of an apothecary jar labeled in his hand. It was said to cure the Plague, leprosy, and male-pattern baldness, to restore fecundity to the barren womb, and, when pulverized and mixed with the menstrual blood of a virgin, to rejuvenate the soil in a field exhausted by poor agricultural planning.

I had no interest in curatives and placed no faith in the last property, which smacked of quackery and even if true served only to sanction the farmer's incompetence. My keenness to secure a fresh specimen of La Maria Negrita was based entirely upon the results of experiments recorded by my great-grandfather, who claimed to have managed the transmutation of silver to quicksilver with the introduction of eighteen grains of new Maria to a forty percent solution of molten silver in purified water. His conviction that an additional eighteen grains would complete the transmutation from quicksilver to gold, was obstructed by the fugitive nature of the fungus, whose properties fled when it was exposed to the dry air. If his belief was correct, the spore of the Black Maria contained the secret of the Philosopher's Stone.

The blue moon doubles the force of lunar gravity. It steepens the tides, stimulates crop growth, and elevates all things created of nature to the second power. It increases the ability of the male sperm to impregnate the female egg, and of the egg to reproduce. Infants born between the pull of the two moons are wiser, healthier, and more fertile than others of their generation. That property of the cinchona bark that cures fever is pronounced when it is harvested and applied during that period, and the yarrow plant that blossoms then will cauterize and heal at an accelerated rate. It follows that the power of the Black Maria to alter the molecular structure of base metal will be heightened and its span of effectiveness will be extended.

This, at least, was the theory; and since a theory had driven all the males in my line to the last ounce of their life force before the earth was known to circumnavigate the sun, I prepared for my first journey in a decade from my rock to the desert floor with all the solemnity of a Christian priest assuming his vestments.

First, I filled a goatskin bag with water from the barrel the boy kept filled for me. Should my energy flag, I placed in a pouch seven pemmican cakes made from chokecherries and coca leaves, with animal lard as an adhesive. I removed my sandals, pulled on thick woolen stockings, and stamped my feet into a stout pair of infantry boots given to me by a Mexican Army deserter in return for a compass to find his way to the sea while avoiding contact with patrols. These were chosen not so much to protect the pickled and hardened soles of my feet as to shield my lower legs from snakebite. Over the tops I dropped the hem of my heaviest sackcloth, for my skin had grown too thin with age to withstand the scorching rays of the sun. Last I put on a broad-brimmed hat woven of soft straw, the gift of an itinerant missionary who had last been seen riding a burro south on his way to convert the pagan Indians residing below the ruins of Popocatepétl. (Nothing more was heard of him for six years. Then a Yaqui who stopped in the village to visit his sister and stayed to tell of his experiences as a slave to the people of Popocatepétl reported upon the missionary's fate. Remembering from the tales handed down by their ancestors that Spanish-speaking warriors valued gold above all else, a delegation of Indians had sought to please a company of federales who camped near their village by presenting them with the gift of seven gold teeth. They explained that the teeth had been torn from the head of the living missionary before he was split down the middle and roasted upon an altar for the pleasure of their omnipotent god. The outraged captain had the delegation seized and hanged and the village put to the torch, enabling the Yaqui to escape and relate his sad tale.) After forty years the hat the missionary had made was still supple, and resiliant enough to roll into a cylinder and pass through a copper bracelet, resuming its original shape without a crease or a crumple. The shade of the brim was as cool as the patch beneath a plane tree, and the hat itself was as light as air.

I slung the water bag behind my back after the fashion of a quiver, appended an oilcloth pouch to my belt for the collection of specimens, took up my ironwood staff, and went out. The herb garden, moist in the early light, slumbered through my passage. I threw the staff to the desert floor to free my hands for the descent. Even at that tender hour I felt the sun heavy across my shoulders, the warmth of the weathered rungs as my hands gripped them. My exhilaration was complete. I felt as if I were ninety again.

The village was not yet awake. I had told no one of my plans, and as I walked down the deserted street behind my elongated shadow, the thump of my staff echoing off the adobe walls dozing on both sides, I felt a tug of apprehension. If the boy who brought my water should visit during my absence, he would surely raise the alarm. I had been a part of the village since before its oldest resident was born—indeed, since before the first course was laid to the first house—and even those whom I had not met held a proprietary interest in me. If I were to be returned under escort by a search party, would they understand the importance of my mission and that it must be solitary, or would they assume that my mind had begun to wander, and seek to confine me to my rock for my protection? If the excursion was successful I cared not to venture forth again, and yet that was not the same as being informed that I could not. Not at all the same. I was not, I am not a sorcerer, I cannot combat the determination of a whole village, not even a well-meaning one. Upon reflection, however, I was serene in my chosen course. It is always easier to ask forgiveness than permission.

Rain makes of the desert a new place, too beautiful and good for this wicked earth. The sand retained enough moisture to adhere to my fingers when I stooped to study it, and as the sun on the horizon went from cherry red to oxblood, pushing away the shadows, the great barren scape became a bright Oriental carpet: yellow primrose, scarlet Indian paintbrush, magenta fireweed, blue lupine, and the crimson pulp of saguaro blossoms, limned in white. Against the ocher and umber and pewter of the caves, canyons, and formations of granite and shale and sandstone and slate, the flaming colors of the hidden life came to glory—for me alone, it seemed, as nary a sandfly nor a lizard stirred on the rugged surface nor vulture nor eagle glided in the invisible currents of the sky, the stomach-tightening blue sky. Although before dressing for my journey I had purified my body with scalding water and borax, had fasted the day before and sterilized my system with purgatives, I felt unclean in Eden, a despicable piece of foul refuse washed up on the shore of Arcadia.

And then the sensation was gone. With the ascent of the sun, the flowers closed their petals and the features of the terrain lost their vivid and virile individuality. Everything withdrew behind a brown and swirling curtain. A breath of fetid wind blew up from the belly of old Mexico, raising billows of dust that eddied in the hollows, clumps of dead earth and decapitated cactus whirling about like exasperated rats snapping at their own tails. Diablos de polvo, these phenomenae were called locally— dust devils—and truly they gamboled about like damned imps, profaning the land with their self-centered play. As I watched, several of them banded together, forming a vortex the size of a city plaza; into the spinning void vanished shards of stone shaved thin by wind and flying sand, pebbles, clumps of feath-

ergrass, to reappear inside the brown funnel, bobbing and colliding and darkening the outer ring. The funnel grew, skipping
and skidding and whipping its tail, gorging itself upon larger and
larger flotsam: Rocks now, the size of fists, bunches of mescal
torn from their roots. Larger still, then narrowing at the base as
it expanded in height, a plume the color of sand, transparent no
longer, snarling like a panther in fierce combat, gouging a path
in the surface of the desert; a cyclone now, twenty feet high and
growing, now charging forward in a straight line like a locomotive, now turning back along its own trail, now knifing off ninety
degrees, quick as thought. Its slipstream blew stinging bits of
sand in my face and lifted the brim of my straw hat, pasting it
back against the crown. I held onto it with both hands and sank
into a crouch in a shallow wash, frightened out of my native fa-
talism by a force containing more energy than my entire male
line combined. Channel it, and in less than a heartbeat the Great
Secret would be known. But to channel it required a force
greater yet.

Thirty feet, now forty. A titan rising straight out of the desert,
swallowing everything in its path and turning it into raw de-
structive power. I had seen its kind before, but always at a distance, a thing remote. Set loose amid a great population like
that of Mexico City, any one of them would have accounted for
hundreds, thousands dead, and damages to empty the treasury
of the Republic. Here they were a daily occurrence and whirled
out their brief voracious lives unnoticed.

I saw a thing dart from behind a rock, and thought at first it
was a mesquite bush torn loose by the great cushion of air at the
base of the cyclone. Then it changed directions and I saw it in
silhouette, recognized the rounded tubular body with its quill-
like coat, balanced upon four thin legs, the head as big around
at the base as the rest of the body, tapering to a flat snout with

tusks clamping tight its upper jaw like thick white sutures: a peccary and a large one, at least sixty pounds, running fast. It seemed at first to sense the cyclone's shifts and take evasive action a split second ahead of them.

Then it misjudged, wheeling left when it should have wheeled right. The tail of the twister snapped, caught the peccary, and sucked it inside before it could even squeal its distress.

I thought the pathetic creature lost. Presently, however, the funnel struck the edge of a pile of broken shale, ricocheted, and skipped to the top of a narrow butte, jettisoning debris when it landed. It continued to the edge of the butte, then leapt to the desert floor. Now my attention was diverted from it for the first time; for something moved among the pile of debris it had left behind. It was the peccary, which rose upon unsteady legs and shook its great thick-based head, appearing none the worse for its experience. This I judged a miracle. Then, perhaps in a fit of delayed panic, the creature broke into a run. I expected it to stop before it reached the edge of the butte, but it did not even slow down. It may have been blinded while inside the vortex. It ran straight off the edge and plunged, shrieking pitiably, twenty feet to the hard surface of the desert.

It took me several minutes to make my way to the spot where the peccary had landed. The cyclone had by this time vanished over a ridge. The beast lay on its side, with its head doubled under its right foreleg at an unnatural angle. Plainly its neck was broken, but it was breathing; I saw the rise and fall of its chest beneath its coarse coat. Tentatively—for the peccary is a wily, vengeful animal, capable of feigning injury to finesse its enemies within range, then lunging to rip and grind with its terrible jaws—I put out a hand and laid it upon the creature's side. I felt the double-thump of its beating heart through thick hide and wiry hair, the heat of its blood coursing through its veins. I felt the heart slowing, I felt it stop. I heard the beast's last breath rattling as it left its lungs. I knew silence.

For a long time after the peccary died I remained in a crouch with my hand on its ribcage. The cyclone was gone—left or blown out—but the beauty and tranquility that had preceded it did not return. I sensed the festering wrath of the pagan gods of the world, the beast-headed, two-faced, jealous and duplicitous immortals driven from both hemispheres by the spread of Christianity to their last refuge in the desert, where mercy and good were punished as severely as pride and evil. Here they still reigned, weakened for want of believers but powerful in their exiled union, and woe to the wanderer who depended upon his piety to see him through.

An omen, this; but I knew not its meaning. Salvation, then destruction. Why?

I did not find the Black Maria, although I carried a detailed sketch drawn by my great-grandfather in colored inks that would not allow me to mistake it. My concentration was shattered by the vision I had seen. I cut off the peccary's ropelike tail, and as I record these observations I can see it suspended over my bench from a nail in the shelf above the athanor, but I am no closer to the meaning it represents than I was upon the day I acquired it.

Salvation, then destruction.

It vexes. It maddens.

Chapter Twelve

Water and Whiskey

The senior partner in the Pecos Valley Irrigation and Investment Company stretched his long body in his stirrups and watched a twenty-mule team gouge the earth outside Roswell. Dragging a ditcher shaped like a giant spade weighted with lead, the teams followed a path outlined by a plow, to in turn be followed by a six-hitch rig pulling a scraper to smooth the ragged edges. In time, when the company finished diverting the Pecos River to fill the ditch, it would live up to the grandiose name the partners had given it: The Great Northern Canal. Just now it was an unsightly raw gash, and the stench of freshly turned earth reminded Pat Garrett of his father's plantation, with all its bad associations.

A horse drew alongside his, and Pat looked into the face of his partner. Charles B. Eddy, thick-built and sandpapery, with a short-stemmed brier pipe screwed perpetually between his molars, wrapped his reins around the horn of his saddle and glowered at the open wound. "Pure-dee ugly, ain't it?" he said. "As a cattleman I always set myself up above the damn sodbusters, but I don't see much difference now."

"You'll change your mind once it's flooded."

"Though when that'll be I don't know. I got a last notice from Chicago. They're threatening to seize the equipment."

"How much do they say we owe?"

"Twice what we got."

"What about Charlie Greene?" Pat's former publisher had joined the venture.

"Bottomed out, same as us. I'm going to Colorado Springs tomorrow. I've got an appointment with Tansill."

"The cigar man?"

Eddy nodded. "He has money to invest and he's warm on the idea. If he likes our plans, he might bring in J. J. Hagerman. Railroad man, money to burn."

"I don't like it. You can only slice up a pie so many ways."

"There's no help for it, Pat. We're in over our heads."

"Just so I don't wind up the one holding the empty pan." Pat turned his horse around and headed back toward town.

Eddy cleaned out the account and chartered a private train to bring Robert Weems Tansill, the manufacturer of Punch Cigars, and James John Hagerman, retired, to Toyah, Texas, a three-day buggy ride from Roswell and the site of the nearest station. Pat put on his good suit and a new Stetson and extended his hand when Hagerman stepped onto the platform. The railroad man, stout and rumpled from the ride, with gray in his noose-shaped beard, ignored the hand, brushing cinders from his coat. He squinted toward the sun-baked plain west of town. "This country doesn't spell water to me."

"That there's the idea," said Pat.

"Is there a hotel here without scorpions?" Hagerman looked at Eddy.

Pat said, "I lined you up with the presidential suite. Harrison stayed there last year."

The railroad man met his gaze for the first time. "I supported Cleveland."

Hagerman never addressed Pat after that. Eddy conducted

the prospective stockholders on a tour of the forty-mile canal and the pipelines in varying stages of completion that would eventually connect it to the Pecos River. Back in his hotel suite, Hagerman and Tansill conferred, then sent out for champagne and cigars—General Gordons, not Tansill's five-cent Punches—to celebrate the new partnership. Hagerman produced a checkbook bound in calfskin, dipped a pen with a flourish, and made out a check to the Pecos Valley Irrigation and Improvement Company for forty thousand dollars.

Pat, watching, said, "That's Irrigation and *Investment*. You need to draw up another check."

Hagerman blotted it. "That's just the first change."

Pat now had eighteen hundred acres three miles east of Roswell, with a two-story adobe house standing calm as a monastery in a shady grove of oak and pecan trees. Apolinaria had planted roses near the porch, and Pat himself had dug up a quarter-acre of bluegrass sod and laid it in front, making a lawn as tidy as any in town. He fed his cattle from alfalfa he grew himself, selling the rest to neighboring ranches, and had spent much of his first year's profits planting and pruning the eight hundred apple and peach trees in his orchard. Returning from Toyah, he fed and watered his big sorrel, rubbed it down with burlap, and went into the house, exhausted to the soles of his feet.

Apolinaria met him at the door. She was carrying Annie, their youngest. Dudley Poe, four, peeped out from behind his mother's skirts until he recognized his father, then came around to greet him solemnly; the boy, who knew Pat's rages, was slightly afraid of him, although the long man had never raised a hand to any of his children. Pat had spotted the oldest, Ida, beating a rug in the backyard. Five-year-old Elizabeth sat on the sofa, embroidering in a hoop and pausing from time to time to run her hand over the stitches, her blue eyes vacant. A bout with scarlet fever when she was three had left her totally blind.

"The man from the bank was here," Apolinaria said by way of greeting. "He can't give us any more extensions. He said he was sorry, but it isn't his decision."

Pat said, "I'm out."

"Out?"

"Hagerman bought up all the shares with one check. He liked my idea so much he stole it."

"Are you going to sue him?"

He laughed. Dudley Poe scampered back behind his mother's skirts. "I sold him my shares."

"Where is the money?"

"At the bottom of a ditch in the Pecos Valley. The shares were worth less than I owed."

She looked away, bouncing the baby in her arms. Her face was as pretty as when they were married, but folds of flesh had begun to appear at the corners of her mouth. Her waist had thickened and there were filaments of silver in her thick black hair. Pat had gone all silver at the temples, the tips of his moustaches were darker than the roots. He had found himself shaving his father's face.

He went into the bedroom. The bed and the chest of drawers had followed him from house to house: wedding gifts from his father-in-law, so that the house he had also given them would not be empty. His wedding picture, Pat seated with Apolinaria standing beside his chair, her hand resting on the back, shared the top of the chest with his wife's silver brush and mirror, a bottle of whiskey and a glass, and a cabinet photograph Pat had had taken with his earnings from shooting buffalo. He looked young and fierce in a new suit with his hat resting on his forearm. It had been a life without debts, a life of nights slept through without a single bad dream.

He filled the glass from the bottle and drank it down. Filled it again and opened the top drawer, groping under the stacks of shirts Apolinaria had washed and ironed and folded, until he found the long-barreled Colt's he had used to kill Billy Bonney. To protect the children he kept the shells on the top shelf of the walnut wardrobe. He unlocked the wardrobe with the key on his watch chain, took down the box, and thumbed a cartridge into each of the Colt's six chambers. John Poe and some others he had known made it a practice to keep an empty chamber under the hammer, but Pat didn't hold with that, more lawmen having died for want of a bullet than from shooting themselves by accident. Someone knocked on the front door, but it might have been someone else's house for all he paid heed to it. He heard Apolinaria's voice and a deep rumbling response. He was plugging the last chamber when Ash Upson walked into the bedroom without knocking.

Pat glared at the old journalist's reflection in the mirror in front of him. He had on a soiled collar and the same old suit, looking as if it would fall apart if it ever came into contact with a brush or an iron. His goatee was pure white now except for the yellow stain around his mouth, and his hair stood up on one side. His pouchy face was yellow beneath its customary gray pallor. With scarcely a glance toward Pat, he headed straight for the glass of whiskey.

He drank, then tipped his head in the direction of the big revolver. "Who's that for? Not yourself. You aren't marksman enough to hit a target as small as your brain."

"Even if I was to try it, your liver'd go first." Pat spun the cylinder.

"Your brain and my liver. I'd sooner vote for U. S. Grant." He took another drink, then picked up the bottle. "You going to shoot the son of a bitch, or just buffalo him like that lawyer Roberts?"

"Who, Grant?"

He refilled the glass and drank, swallowing hard. "Hagerman, squirrelhead. Apolinaria told me he skinned you pretty."

"You fixing to stop me?"

"No. Hell, no. The only thing worse than making your own mistakes is trying to stop another man from making his. In any case there hasn't been a good shooting in this territory since you put down the Kid. Also when they hang you it might just liven up the market for that piece of shit of a book you and I perpetrated."

"I never should of shot Billy."

Upson paused with the glass halfway to his lips. "Well, now's the time to think of *that*."

"I'm serious, Ash. Carpetbaggers like Hagerman stayed clear of this country while Bonney was about."

"Professional courtesy, I suspect. The territorial imperative." He drank.

But Pat wasn't listening. He was looking at the picture of the young buffalo hunter. "Tote up all the cattle and horses Billy stole, put it in dollars and cents, it don't come up to the interest on what Hagerman stole with just a scratch pen and a checkbook."

"The twenty-one men the Kid killed might make up part of the balance."

"That was your figure. I put it nearer four. But you see what I'm saying."

"It's a wicked old world, my friend. Why do you suppose it is I drink?"

"It wouldn't be because you got no other choice."

"Choices are for children. Bonney didn't have one. He was what he was. So are you. The difference is he knew it." Filling the glass once again, he waggled his elbow at the Colt's. "Put that back or use it the way God and Governor Wallace taught you."

Pat hefted it. His expression in the mirror was sheepish. Then he bared his teeth. "You'll always be there to pull me back, won't you, Ash?"

"Don't bet the ranch on it." Upson drank.

In 1890, the eastern half of Lincoln County, containing the town of Roswell and a substantial portion of the Pecos River, broke off and renamed itself Chaves. The majority of its residents, mountain-dwelling Mexican sheepherders, had voted to honor Colonel J. Francisco Chávez, a frequent president of the New Mexico Territorial Council and the latest in a long and distinguished line to bear the name of a pioneering Spanish family with ties to Coronado, but the Anglo lowlanders who farmed and grazed their cattle in the valley persuaded the council to scrap the Hispanic z in favor of a Gallic s. The new district, in itself larger than some eastern seaboard states, needed a sheriff.

"You will hunt bad men?" Apolinaria, rocking in the parlor and nursing Annie, looked tired.

"That part of the job's changed," Pat said. "I'll probably get fat by the office stove while the deputies do the hunting, like John Poe."

"You will never grow fat."

Pat kissed her, smoothed the wiry black hair on Annie's head, and went to the barn for his bedroll. Much of Chaves was rugged country, with long empty stretches between houses, and those mostly mud shacks; hunting for votes there would be as rigorous as the search for Billy Bonney.

His first stop was the Poe ranch, where his successor in the Lincoln County sheriff's office had retired. He found a green spread with freshly strung barbed wire, a rambling house with a red tile roof and new paint on the siding. Pat's former deputy had invested his profits from the Cree sale, arranged by Pat, in a bigger and better operation than the one he had let go.

"Sheriffing isn't the same as when you left it, Pat." Poe sat on a splat-bottomed chair on his front porch, scratching the head of a big woolly dog with its chin resting on his knee. He wore white Mexican pajamas and straw slippers in the middle of the afternoon and looked like Buddha.

"That's what I told Apolinaria." Pat perched on the edge of a glider with his knees on a level with his chest and circled the brim of his hat through his fingers. In the yard a Negro stable-hand washed down the spokes of Poe's buggy with a sponge and a bucket of oil soap, whistling softly. Sophie Poe was clattering china inside the house. Pat had engineered the couple's introduction, had practically pushed his old friend into the union to cinch his election in Lincoln. They had been together eight years.

"It's an administrative post. You run the county, collect taxes. There is bookkeeping involved. The irrigation project promises to bring in a lot of business from the East in the coming years. It's a big job. Complicated."

"Get to the getting, John."

Poe exhaled. "I'm supporting young Campbell. He's a successful rancher, has a good head on his shoulders, and doesn't lose it. He was just a boy when the war broke out in Lincoln. He's the first candidate we've had in years who isn't still fighting it."

Pat stood and put on his hat. Poe's eyes followed him. "It isn't personal, Pat."

"Nothing ever is with you."

"You have your ranch and your investments and your reputation. You shouldn't jeopardize them by playing around with politics."

"I should sit around in long-handles getting all suet-gutted."

Poe said nothing.

Pat turned to leave. At the top of the steps he looked back. "I'm running as a maverick. See if your boy Campbell can keep up with me."

"That would be a mistake."

"We all of us make them, John. Like when you and Tip McKinney sat playing with your peckers on Pete Maxwell's front porch while Bonney walked right past you."

The long man campaigned as an independent write-in candidate opposite the Democratic favorite. The Mexican-American majority, who harbored fond memories of Billy the Kid, including those who had never seen him, elected the young ranchman over Bonney's slayer. In April 1891, Pat disposed of his holdings in New Mexico, packed his family into a buckboard and spring wagon, and quit the territory for Texas.

Chapter Thirteen

The White Sands Murders

They'd gone and brushed and pressed Ash Upson's suit, trimmed and combed his whiskers and run a brush through his hair. Pat didn't know him at first. His skin looked healthy and they'd stuffed his cheeks with something that filled out the hollows. His nails were rounded and pink and he had a rosary wound around both hands.

"I'm not certain he was Roman Catholic," said the mortuary director, a small, china-faced man with elaborate waves of creamy hair, so florid in the face that Pat suspected him of dipping into the rouge reserved for customers. "The rosary helped explain the bend in his fingers, which could not be corrected without extreme measures."

"He usually had them around a glass," Pat said. "How much for the box and burial and what you done so far?"

"Twenty-five dollars is the basic rate. For thirty I can offer six pallbearers, and two mourners for another dollar."

Pat counted two tens, a five, and five silver dollars into the director's palm. "I'll take the pallbearers. Ash didn't have that many friends to hold him up when he was alive. You can keep the mourners."

"I'll just write up a receipt."

Alone with the remains, Pat looked into the painted face.

"Well, Ash," he said, "who's going to throw me down and hog-tie me next time?"

The director returned, blowing on a slip of paper to dry the ink. Pat touched one of the corpse's hands and turned to take the receipt. "Shut the box and nail it."

"Before the vigil?"

"The time to watch over him's past."

Ash Upson was buried in Uvalde, Texas. He had come there to bet on Pat's mare, which Pat had entered in the mile race at the fairgrounds outside town. After the horse had won, the old journalist had stood everyone to a drink in a local saloon, and continued drinking there after everyone else had left. Early the next morning, summoned by the agitated bartender, Pat had carried the unconscious Upson out to his buckboard and taken him to a doctor, who listened to the man's heart, pried open each of his eyelids, and told Pat he had better make arrangements.

"Well, Ash," Pat had said, smoothing back his comatose friend's unruly hair, "you quit winners."

After the graveside service—attended by Pat, Apolinaria, their four children, the professional pallbearers, and a local minister, who referred to Upson by his formal Christian name "Marshall"—Pat went to El Paso to take in the heavyweight championship fight between Bob Fitzsimmons and Peter Maher. He was getting set to leave his hotel room for the arena when a bellhop informed him that the governor of Texas had dispatched eleven Rangers to stop the fight.

"I heard they'll fight in Juarez if not in Texas," Pat said.

"So did the president of Mexico, sir. He's sending troops to stop it there."

"Where's that leave?"

"Well, Judge Bean has issued them an invitation to fight in

Langtry. There's an island in the Rio Grande close by that can't rightly be claimed by the U.S. or Mexico. But there'll be a delay."

"If Wallace had sent half that many men to stop the war in Lincoln, there wouldn't of been a war."

"Where's that, Cuba?"

Pat tipped the boy a dollar for the information. "Who's in the bar?"

"A man named Raymond was there a little while ago, asking for you. He's from New Mexico."

"I don't know any Raymond. What's he look like?"

"He's a curly-headed greaser with a pointy beard. He looks clean and he talks good American, so the bartender didn't boot him out."

"He's lucky he didn't try. Numa Reymond's running for sheriff in Doña Ana County. Not Raymond." Pat gave him another dollar and went down to the bar. Reymond spotted him and waved him over to his table. The sheriff's candidate was a sleepy-eyed Mexican-American with pomade glittering in his tight curls and an obsession for clean collars. Pat had heard he changed them five times a day.

"How's the race?" Pat asked when they were seated with a fresh bottle on the table between them.

"Crooked as a dog's hind leg. There's a little matter of eighty-eight forged ballots standing between me and the sheriff's office. I'm suing to have them set aside."

"I can't help with that."

"That's not why I wanted to talk to you, Pat. The governor's here."

"Culberson?"

"No, Thornton from New Mexico. He's staying in the hotel. He wants to see you."

"What's Poker Bill want with me?"

"It's the Fountain murders."

"Ah."

Reymond drank whiskey and ran a finger along his moustaches, flicking away the drops. "Don't act ignorant with me, Pat. You know what's being said about you in the papers."

"I heard a thing or two."

"The disappearance of Colonel Fountain and his son is all caught up in territorial politics, but at bottom it's just another range feud. Everyone thinks you're the one to get to the heart of it."

"Everyone except Oliver Lee."

"Lee as much as anyone; that's why he fixed the election to put his man Guadalupe Ascarate in charge of the investigation. Ascarate's sheriff pending the outcome of my suit; his is the name on those eighty-eight ballots. *I* know Oliver Lee had the Fountains killed on the Mesilla Road to keep the colonel from indicting him for stock theft; *you* know it, and so does the governor. But everyone in Doña Ana's either beholden to Lee or too much his enemy to make a real investigation of it. You've been away from New Mexico five years now."

"Nearer six."

"So much the better. No one's got any hobbles on you. Also you're the man who killed Billy the Kid. That counts for plenty."

"Not in Chaves it didn't."

"That was a long time ago. They've had time to think things over, and six years of pettifogging politicians strutting around pinned to badges. Gun law doesn't look so terrible next to that."

"If they think that, they must all of them have been born since Lincoln County," Pat said.

"Hear me out. Thornton's going to press Ascarate to appoint you chief deputy and place you in charge of the Fountain case. I'm prepared to drop my suit if Ascarate complies."

"Why should you do that?"

"Ascarate can't last, especially if the trail leads back to his boss. You'll succeed him as sheriff. Then you can appoint me chief deputy."

"What if Ascarate won't bite?"

"Then I'll press my suit. I'm bound to lose at the local level, but I'll appeal it right up to the territorial council. Poker Bill holds the majority there. I'll win, and when I'm sheriff I'll make you chief deputy. All I need is one term to put me in the running for the council. Then I'll resign in your favor."

"It's got more thorns on it than a prickly pear."

"I've never known you to steer clear of thorns," Reymond said. "What's your answer?"

"Let's go talk to Poker Bill."

In the presidential suite they found Governor Thornton, mournful-looking as an undertaker with his white handlebars and deepset eyes, dressed all in black to his collar, in heated conference with two men, one of whom was known to Pat. In fact, Thornton was a jovial man of healthy appetites, the joy of his family and close friends, who had nicknamed him Poker Bill for his ability to dissemble his true nature among company and settings crucial to the conduct of his territory. Even so, when he was exhausted or distracted, his wit would sometimes expose itself, to be gathered in quickly like a loose shirttail before it was noticed or remarked upon.

Pat shook John Nance Garner's hand before the governor could complete their introduction. The dapper young Texan, who held Washington aspirations, had been after Pat for so long to sell him his property in Uvalde, and so charmingly, that Pat had named his favorite mare after him. Nancy's winning performance at the fairgrounds had only added to the long man's affection.

He looked at the other man, square-built and bitter-featured, with no expression when Thornton identified him as Guadalupe Ascarate, sheriff-elect in Doña Ana County. Ascarate, in his turn, flicked ashes from the end of his cigar to the carpet and made no move to rise from the leather armchair in which he sat. His boots were exquisitely tooled and blacked to a high shine. Pat had never known a certain kind of Mexican to make a loan to a family member in need if the money could just as well be spent on a new pair of boots.

"I assume you're familiar with this Fountain business," said the governor when they had all found places. Pat, sitting legs crossed on the end of a horsehair sofa, had accepted a cigar when Poker Bill offered it from a cedar box, but declined the favor of a light. The air was blue with smoke as it was.

"Just what's been in the papers," Pat said.

"Oliver Lee's been mixed up in one way or another with every skirmish that's taken place in the Tularosa Valley since the winter of '87. In '93 he stood trial for murdering two rustlers and was acquitted on a plea of self-defense. The following year he was implicated in the ambush murder of a rancher named Frenchy Rochas, who controlled the clear-water rights in Dog Canyon. No charges were brought against Lee, but the fact is he's been piping water down to the valley from the canyon ever since. About that same time, Albert Fountain was named the lawyer for the Southeastern New Mexico Livestock Association, and announced his plans to prosecute Lee for rustling and murder.

"Last month, a range detective in Fountain's employ bought a steer from Lee's top hand, Bill McNew. When it was killed and skinned and the underside of the hide examined, the fact that the brand had been changed was indisputable. Fountain took the hide to the courthouse in Lincoln. I believe you know the place."

"I know it." Pat chewed on the end of his unlit cigar. The graves of deputies Olinger and Bell were still visible from the building.

"When the hide was added to the rest of the evidence in its possession, the grand jury in Lincoln handed down thirty-two indictments against Lee and McNew. Colonel Fountain was handed something else, no one knows by whom: a note informing him that if he didn't withdraw the charges, he wouldn't reach home alive."

"Lee says he never wrote it," Ascarate put in. "Nobody knows who did."

Numa Reymond said, "Nobody knows what happened to Fountain, either. He and his son went missing somewhere in the White Sands on their way back to Mesilla."

Poker Bill laid his cigar stub atop the pile in a crystal ashtray, where it was allowed to smolder out. "The colonel knew his chances. Little Henry's another matter. The people of the Territory of New Mexico don't lose much sleep over what befalls a middle-aged lawyer, but when a nine-year-old boy's blood is spilled, they will have justice."

"That's guesswork." Ascarate relit his cigar. "Mariana Fountain's a jealous woman, everyone knows that. Maybe the colonel got fed up and jumped the fence."

"Along with his son." Reymond's tone was dry.

Ascarate shrugged.

"The posse found a deal of old blood on the ground where a buggy had swerved off the road near Chalk Hill," continued the governor. "Twelve miles farther on they found the buggy, abandoned, with the horses gone. Henry's hat was there, also the threatening note and Fountain's cartridge belt, with twelve shells missing. His wooden dispatch case with all his court documents was nowhere to be found."

Ascarate said, "If I was Fountain and wanted to kick over the traces and didn't want anyone coming after to drag me back, I'd write just such a note. I'd unhitch the horses, put Henry on one and climb on the other, and take off for old Mexico."

"What about the blood?" Garner looked amused. His delight in the human carnival had cut him out for a career in politics.

"It was old. It could have been cow blood. Could have been paint."

Garner smiled. "What do *you* say, Pat?"

"I didn't see it."

"Quite apart from the tragedy involved, this incident couldn't have taken place at a worse time for the territory. We're petitioning for statehood. So fresh an unsolved crime can only weaken our case in Washington." Thornton looked at Reymond. "This contretemps over the sheriff's election in Doña Ana County serves notice to the nation that we are incapable of sorting out our affairs at the local level. Will you withdraw your suit until such time as we have a suspect in custody?"

"I can't promise that, Your Honor, for the very reason that without pressure from outside the sheriff's office, Mr. Ascarate will never lift a finger to deliver a suspect to justice."

"That's a damn lie," Ascarate said calmly.

Poker Bill turned his attention his way. "May I ask what action the sheriff's office *has* taken?"

"I've had men all over that ground. That white sand won't hold a track. The county commissioners have added five hundred dollars to Santa Fe's offer of two thousand and amnesty to the man who turns state's evidence. The Masons have pledged another ten thousand. If there's anything to the talk of murder, that should shake something loose. When that happens, my deputies and I will be on hand to catch it."

"I was wrong," Reymond said. "You have lifted a finger."

"You're a damn liar."

Reymond stabbed a finger at Ascarate. "Ask *him* how those eighty-eight forged ballots got counted. Ask him who waltzed into the commissioners' court with a six-shooter on his hip and a deputy U.S. marshal's badge tacked to his shirt. It was his boss, Oliver Lee."

Ascarate started up out of his chair. The flare of Poker Bill's match distracted him. "Sit down, Lupe," said the governor out the side of his mouth, puffing life into a fresh cigar. "You back off too, Numa. Just because Fitzsimmons and Maher can't fight doesn't mean you two have to fill in. That's better." He shook out the match and tossed it onto the heap in the ashtray. "I invited Mr. Garrett so he could be present when I asked you, Sheriff Ascarate, if you would consent to assign him to a post as chief deputy with jurisdiction in the Fountain case. I suggest you pay him five hundred dollars per month, with half that sum to be provided from the territorial treasury."

"Keep your money, Governor. I run the sheriff's office. I pick my own deputies."

Reymond said, "Everyone knows who runs the sheriff's office." He looked at Thornton. "I'll drop my suit here and now if Ascarate agrees to resign. Then you can appoint Mr. Garrett sheriff."

Ascarate smiled at his cigar. "Reymond keeps forgetting he lost the election."

John Nance Garner scratched an ear. "This meeting stinks clear to Canada. I don't think it has anything more to do with who killed Albert Fountain than the moon."

Thornton sat back. He looked like an old widower. "Gentlemen, if you will all step out and let Mr. Garrett and me speak in private, I believe we can bring an end to all this wrangling without bloodshed."

Ascarate stopped smiling. "I won't be back-doored out of the office I won fair and square."

Reymond laughed. Ascarate shot to his feet, his fists balled at his sides. Reymond rose to face him. Pat stood, towering over both of them. All eyes went to him.

"I'm going down to the bar."

Garner got his hat off the peg and followed him.

Ten minutes later, Poker Bill Thornton joined them in the card room. No greetings were exchanged and he took a seat while Pat and Garner played out their hand. Pat won. Garner left to drink at the bar.

Pat shuffled. "Take a hand, Governor?"

"Draw's my game. I never saw the percentage in turning anything face up."

Pat dealt. Thornton studied his cards without rearranging them, discarded two. "What do you want, Pat?"

Pat skinned two his way. "Money."

"I heard you were well off."

"I'm broke as Job. Apolinaria's expecting again. I can't feed the four I have."

"Discussing your money problems isn't the best way to begin a negotiation." Thornton opened for a dollar.

Pat took one card for himself, saw Thornton's bet, and raised him a dollar. He said nothing.

The governor deliberated. "How much would it take to decide you to accept a post as independent investigator in the Fountain murders?"

"Who's offering, you or Ascarate?"

"Ascarate can't put on his pants without asking Oliver Lee which leg goes first. Lee will never agree to it." Thornton saw the raise and bumped him another dollar.

"That two-fifty a month from the territory still stand?"

"I'll make it up out of my own pocket if the council won't bite. It will, though. Statehood is everything."

"Throw in a hundred and a half for expenses and a bonus of ten thousand on conviction and you got yourself a detective."

"I can only manage five thousand. Money's tight in Santa Fe."

"Ten's the figure."

"Fifty-five hundred then."

"Ten."

"Six. I'm gambling with my political future here."

"Ten."

Poker Bill drummed his cards on the table. "Eight thousand, damn it. I'm calling your hand."

Pat spread out his cards. He had an ace high straight. Thornton had a full house, sixes over treys. As Pat scooped up the pot he said, "Stud's my game. I'm your man."

Chapter Fourteen

Wildy Well

N ow I know why they call this the Journey of the Dead."

Kent Kearney, slender and mild-eyed, uncorked his canteen and looked out across the dunes of naked gypsum for which the White Sands was named. The frozen waves put him in mind of a chart of the surface of the moon he had displayed on the corkboard in his old classroom.

"The Dead's on the other side of the San Andres," said Pat. "I prefer it to this."

Privately, the long man, who loved New Mexico in all its many moods, loathed this stretch, eighteen miles long and three miles wide, between the foothills of the San Andres and the Sacramento range. By day the sun hammered the white hills, bringing to a boil even the cold blood of the rattlesnakes that burrowed deep into them to escape the heat. By night grains of gypsum blew across the naked dunes in fine clouds like ground glass, changing the shape of the terrain like an ocean. He was unmoved by the crippling heat and the heart-emptying bleakness of the frozen waves of inescapable white; he simply had no use for country he couldn't track a man through.

The five men, mounted well and heavily armed, had drawn rein to drink from their canteens and look out across the bloodless plain. They included Pat, Kearney, a former schoolteacher who had joined the posse out of a commitment to his community, Jose Espalin, a Mexican who had shopped his gun on both sides of the border, and Clint Llewellyn and Ben Williams, Doña Ana deputies who had proven themselves enemies of county politics.

Kearney, who revered Pat Garrett's reputation, had expressed reservations about Espalin. The Mexican, tall and darkly handsome until his lips parted to show his missing front teeth, had blue eyes with all the depth of cheap silver plate. No one seemed to know what went on behind them: Not Pat, who appeared sometimes to place a man's abilities ahead of his motives, and not Oliver Lee, for whom Espalin had ridden in the past and was rumored to have taken part in the bushwhacking murder of Frenchy Rochas in Dog Canyon. When Kearney had asked Pat why he'd brought the Mexican along, the long man had shrugged and said, "He puts me in mind of Billy Bonney."

"But you killed Bonney."

"I never didn't like him."

From Chalk Hill the posse retraced the path Colonel Albert Fountain's buggy had taken on his way home to Mesilla, shortly before he and nine-year-old Henry had dropped off the face of the earth. It had not rained nor snowed heavily since that day, and the ruts their wheels had cut were still visible. They found the place where the buggy had swerved off the road, five miles short of San Augustine Pass. The sun had faded the discolored circle of earth and grass nearby, but the horses caught the scent of old blood and balked, tossing their heads and shaking their manes in protest.

"There's Ascarate's paint," Llewellyn said.

Pat studied the terrain, then pointed at a clump of mesquite atop a stationary dune. "That's the high point."

They rode to the spot, where Llewellyn and Williams dismounted and walked around, spreading the feathergrass with the toes of their boots. Former cowhands who had wintered as wolfers, they were expert trackers who knew the country well. Williams grunted, stooped to retrieve something from the ground, and went up to Pat, jingling a pair of spent brass cartridges in the palm of his hand.

"Winchester," said Pat after a glance.

"Here's a knee print." Llewellyn was crouching where Williams had found the shells.

Pat said, "I wonder how long he waited."

"Is this where it happened?" Kearney asked. "They were killed here?"

"Not here." Espalin, face invisible in the shade of his flat-brimmed sombrero, rolled a cigarette. "This was just to turn them off the road. The rifleman probably shot the boy so Fountain could operate the buggy. Too much chance someone coming along the road might see them."

Later, Kearney confided to Pat his suspicion that Espalin had spoken more as a participant than as a speculator. Pat made no response.

Williams pointed south. "Albert Junior's posse found the buggy twelve miles that way. The Colonel made a chase of it."

Pat kneed his sorrel back down to the road and started west. Kearney caught up. "Aren't we going to search for the bodies?"

"There's a hundred thousand square miles of New Mexico," Pat said. "I don't propose to dig up all of it looking for buzzard pickings."

"What *do* you propose to do?"

"Have a talk with Oliver Lee."

"I heard he went into hiding after you arrested Bill McNew."

"Lee's brother-in-law, Dub Cox, owns a spread on the other side of the San Augustine. He might know something about where he went."

"What makes you think he'll tell you?"

"Oh, he'd never tell me."

They made camp on the western slope of the Organs. Kearney started off to look for wood, but Pat called him back. "Cold camp," he said. "No fire."

Everyone unsaddled his mount except Espalin, who unloaded his short-barreled Colt's and brace of Walker horse pistols, cleaned them, and reloaded them with fresh cartridges from his belt. His fingers moved so fast Kearney could hardly follow them.

"Leave the carbine," Pat said. "That way they might let you in close."

The Mexican unstrapped and laid the scabbard containing his Henry on the ground. He swung aboard the piebald and started down the slope at a walk.

"How long do we wait?" Llewellyn asked.

Pat cut himself a plug. "Till morning, if we don't hear gunshots first."

In the chill of dawn, Kearney, on lookout, challenged a figure picking his way up the slope leading a horse.

"Stand down," came Espalin's voice from the shadows. "Is me." He walked past the schoolteacher without stopping.

Pat was sitting up in his bedroll, scratching his head. His long-barreled Colt's rested in his lap. When he recognized the Mexican in the starlight he asked him if there were any holes in him.

"Just my gut. Dub's wife cannot cook for shit." Espalin sat

down on a rock and tugged off his boots. "Lee's there. He's got Jimmy Gililland with him."

"Gililland's a bad hat," Pat said. "He ain't got sense enough to want to see thirty. You're lucky he didn't shoot you in the back."

"I'd of done the same, but he didn't give me the opportunity any more than I gave it to him. Anyway they think I'm their man in your camp."

"Which you ain't." This from Clint Llewellyn. He and Ben Williams were both sitting up now.

Espalin grinned, showing the gap in his teeth. Then he shrugged. "Lee's finished. He knows there's paper out on him and he has no faith McNew won't give him up. He means to make a fight of it. I don't like his odds."

"Did he say where he's headed?" asked Pat.

"He and Gililland lit out at first light, same as me. He said he's fixing to hole up with Jim and Mary Madison at Wildy Well. They look after Lee's cattle at Dog Canyon and sell water to the El Paso and Northeastern. Their shack's just off the spur."

Kearney started breaking camp. When the others protested: "They have a head start. We should get mounted."

Pat threw aside his blanket and stood, stretched his long back. Bones crackled in rapid succession, like twigs igniting. "Why? We know where they're headed."

"Shouldn't we catch them in the open?"

"They've got fresh mounts. They'd just run away from us and then we'd have to start looking for them all over again." He strode outside the circle of light.

It was Williams' turn to grin. "Getting lazy in your old age, ain't you, Pat?"

"The only way to shoot a badger is to catch him when he comes up out of his hole." Water trickled in the darkness.

* * *

They rode thirty-eight miles across the desert, stopping every few miles to water the horses from their cupped hands and lead them. Their clothes were black with sweat. Leading his gray near the end of the line, Kearney asked Llewellyn how old he figured Pat was. He got the words out between pants.

"I don't know. Right around forty-six or seven, I reckon."

"What do you reckon he eats?"

Llewellyn contemplated the long straight figure loping ahead at the front. "Bull's balls boiled in rattlesnake piss."

"I'd admire to know if he brought any extra."

"Llewellyn!" barked Pat.

He straightened. "Yo!"

"You've been to Wildy Well. What's there?"

"There's a house with a wagon shed attached. There's a barn and a pumphouse and a big old water tank on a platform."

"What's the house built of?"

"Adobe."

"Well, there's no shooting through adobe. We'll have to go in."

Sometime past dark they smelled woodsmoke. Llewellyn took note of the mountains and said he thought they were within a mile of Wildy Well. They tethered their animals and walked the rest of the way carrying their rifles and carbines. As the ranch buildings separated themselves from the general darkness, Jose Espalin took off his boots and led the way in his stockings. The house was a rectangular box, blue-white in the moonlight. The outbuildings Llewellyn had described threw square flat shadows on the ground. The galvanized water tank stood four feet above the ground on a wooden scaffold with loose earth piled around the base to discourage nocturnal creatures from nesting beneath it. Dark rust marbled with streaks of white lime bled down the tank's corrugated sides and clung to the bottom in calcified drips like stalactites. The windows in the house were dark.

The others hung back while Espalin crept up to the front door. There he swept off his sombrero and stood bent over for a full minute, listening. When he straightened, raising his hat, Pat drew his revolver and signaled with it to Williams and Llewellyn to station themselves at the ends of the house. He motioned to Kearney to follow him. Espalin stood aside as Pat leaned his shoulder against the front door, testing it in its frame. He handed his Winchester to the Mexican, fisted the Colt's, spread his feet, and threw all his weight against the door.

It sprang open with a splintering sound, swung all the way around on its hinges, and struck the wall with a boom that shook the house and brought a shower of dirt and old clay down from the protruding roof poles onto Kearney's hat. Pat lunged across the threshold. Locating the bed under one of the end windows, he pivoted that way and thrust his Colt's into the mounded blankets. "Throw up your hands!"

A pale-haired woman jackknifed into a sitting position, the counterpane slipping down and exposing a naked breast. She screamed.

Pat showed her the revolver. The screaming stopped as if a door had been shut.

The man lying next to her had roused himself more slowly. His face was stubbled and his hair was in his eyes. His face was puffy with sleep. He stared at the Colt's as if he were trying to identify its purpose.

"Who are you?" Pat demanded.

"Jim and Mary Madison." Espalin, standing in the doorway, aimed his gap-toothed grin at the woman's breast. She glanced down, gasped, and drew up the counterpane.

Kearney came in from another room, wide-eyed and breathing in shallow gusts. He had the muzzle of his Springfield tilted up behind the head of a man walking in front of him with his hands in the air. The man was barefoot and wearing a nightshirt. "I found this one trying to let himself out through the wagon shed," Kearney said.

"What's your name?" Pat asked.

"Lon McVey. I don't know these people. I just stopped for a meal and a bed on my way to Roswell."

"Where are Lee and Gililland?"

McVey shook his head. Pat looked at the Madisons, who said nothing.

"I'll take the woman," Espalin said. "Women just generally open up to me."

Pat ignored him. "Get dressed, all of you. Watch them," he told the Mexican.

"What do I do?" Kearney asked.

"Watch Espalin." He went out.

Pat assigned the pumphouse to Llewellyn, the barn to Williams, and searched the wagon shed himself. Finding nothing there but a water wagon, he circled behind the house. A white ash ladder leaned against the wall. Pat walked past it without looking at it directly, spotted Williams coming out of the barn, and waved him over. As Williams drew near, Pat saw his gaze light on the ladder, then move on.

"Wait here," Pat said.

Williams nodded.

The long man returned to the house. Mary Madison, wearing a skirt and blouse with her hair tied behind her head, was scooping coffee from an Arbuckle's sack into a pot on the stove. Her husband and McVey sat on a pair of straight chairs, their hands clamped on their knees. Pat looked at Espalin, who shook his head and spat into a bucket.

"Anything outside?" Kearney asked.

"I found a ladder."

McVey glanced toward the ceiling.

Chapter Fifteen

Two Minutes

Clint Llewellyn came in from outside. Pat looked from him to Madison. "You've got a root cellar?"

The ranch manager nodded. "Back of the kitchen."

"Take your wife and get in it. There may be shooting." To Llewellyn: "See they stay there."

McVey said, "What about me?"

"You come with us."

Jose Espalin twisted his hand inside McVey's shirt collar and followed Pat and Kent Kearney outside. They found Ben Williams still guarding the ladder. Pat pointed his Colt's at McVey.

"If you're so concerned about your friends, why don't you climb up and tell them we're here?"

McVey shook his head.

Pat raised the revolver and brought the barrel down on the man's skull. McVey's knees buckled. Kearney caught him beneath the arms.

"Put him in the root cellar and come back," Pat said.

Kearney handed Espalin his Springfield and scuttled backwards, McVey's heels dragging ruts in the earth. When he returned, the ladder had been moved to the wagon shed, whose lean-to roof slanted down from the flat roof of the house. A two-foot wall shielded the house roof on two sides. Moonlight shone through chinks in the adobe.

"They can shoot down on us through those holes." Pat's voice was a murmur. To Williams: "Shoot anything that moves on top of the house. Use the water tank for cover."

When Williams was in position, Pat started up the ladder and signaled for Espalin and Kearney to follow.

The roof was covered with the same galvanized iron that had been used to make the water tank. Pat and Kearney pulled the ladder up behind them and leaned it against the roof of the house, bending up the sheet of iron along the bottom edge to keep the legs from slipping. Kearney got on the ladder and inched his way to the top, carrying his Springfield. Pat and Espalin stationed themselves at the corners.

Pat cupped his free hand around his mouth. "Give it up, boys! There's no place to go from up there but straight to hell!"

The muzzle of a rifle slithered over the top of the low wall. Kearney shouldered his rifle and fired. The big ball knocked a scallop out of the adobe.

Pat fired behind Kearney and ducked. The muzzle on the wall flashed. The slug split the air above Pat's head with a crack. There was another report from the roof. Kearney shouted and rolled off the ladder. He skidded to the edge of the shed roof, where he hung on for a moment to the bent metal. Then his grip lost its strength and he fell the rest of the way to the ground.

Williams opened fire from behind the water tank. Bullets from the roof whanged into the tank. Thin streams of water sprang out. Williams, stretched out on his stomach behind his Winchester, hunched his shoulders while the cold water splattered over him.

Pat crawled on his belly to the edge of the shed roof and lowered himself to the ground. Kearney lay moaning nearby.

"Where you hit, Kent?"

"Jesus, Pat." His voice was a thin whine.

Groping in the darkness, Pat felt the moist pulp of the man's shoulder. "It's bad, Kent. The bone's shattered."

"It's worse than that, Pat."

"Hang on."

Espalin leapt down to the ground, cursing shrilly in Spanish when spines from a clump of mescal pierced the soles of his stockinged feet. A volley of shots clattered from the roof, pinning him against the wall.

The shooting ceased. Echoes of the reports growled away toward the mountains and died hissing. Two minutes had elapsed since the fighting began.

"Garrett, you hit?"

"That you, Lee?" Pat pried the spent shell out of his cylinder and replaced it with a cartridge from his belt. He was seated on the ground near Kearney with his back against the wall of the wagon shed.

"You are a hell of a lot of bastards to order a man to throw up his hands and shoot him at the same time."

"Kearney fired without orders. Are you ready to surrender?"

"I don't think I will. I've heard that you intend to kill me."

"That's just newspaper talk. All I'm fixing to do is take you and Gililland in for trial."

"Just like you done with the Kid?"

"I brought Bonney in alive once. He killed two of my deputies escaping and that's all I have to say about Bonney. You're safe in my hands. Now, will you surrender?"

Lee's laughter was louder than it needed to be. "Who do you think has the best of it? You've got yourself into a hell of a close place."

Kearney had begun talking to himself. The ground felt damper than it should. Pat pushed himself up into a crouch. From that position he could make out Williams stretched out on his stomach beneath the geyser that was the water tank. Llewellyn was still inside with the Madisons and he had lost track of Jose Espalin.

"I know it," he said then. "The question is, how are we going to get out of here?"

There was a pause on the rooftop. Then Lee said, "If you pull off, we won't shoot you."

"Just like you done Frenchy Rochas?"

"I wasn't in on that."

Pat wiped his hand on his shirt. The dampness definitely wasn't dew. "What about Kearney? He's bad hit."

"Jimmy and Mary Madison will see to him."

"I'm depending on you to hold your fire," Pat said.

Kearney stirred when Pat's clothing rustled. "Don't leave me, Pat!"

"You're in good hands, Kent. Lee has nothing to gain by not keeping his word."

"You're four to their two. You going to just tuck in your tail and slanch off?"

"I'll be seeing you," Pat said.

"In hell."

Kent Kearney died in Tularosa, where a railroad section crew Pat sent back from Turquoise Siding took him after Mrs. Madison had used a butcher knife to remove a second slug from his groin.

In Las Cruces, the newspapers were already trumpeting Pat Garrett's humiliation when the posse dragged into town. A journalist who reminded Pat a little of Ash Upson found him pouring himself a drink behind the sheriff's desk. The long man made no objection when the newcomer pulled up a chair and sat down.

"Oliver Lee says you and your posse ambushed him and Gililland in their sleep." He put on a pair of gold-rimmed spectacles and thumbed through the pages of a tattered and grubby notebook. A gnawed stub of yellow pencil rested between the fingers of one hand like a cigar.

"What they were doing sleeping on the roof is anyone's guess, I reckon," Pat said.

"I've slept on a roof of a hot night."

"Well, if I were Lee and had any pride in myself as a frontiersman, I'd come up with a better account of what I was doing. Men who could sleep through the ruckus we put up downstairs aren't the caliber that brought civilization to the wilderness."

"Did you intend to kill Lee and Gililland?"

"No. Had I intended that, I never would have gone to the trouble to obtain warrants for their arrest."

"Lee's attorney says Lee and Gililland are refusing to turn themselves in until some kind of ironclad arrangement is made to protect them from assassination."

"Everyone knows Albert Fall represents the El Paso and Northeastern Railroad, which depends on Lee's Dog Canyon station for water. It's all part of the railroad's scheme to lop another county out of Doña Ana so it can buy a whole new set of politicians. That would remove the White Sands from this county's jurisdiction. Gililland has been boasting about his part in the Fountain killings. Fall's afraid he'll confess when he's behind bars. If anything, Fall's statements are an endorsement of my ability to apprehend his clients."

"That's a fairly complex observation for our readers to grasp."

"They were all brought up on dime novels, where there's no room for politics. They all think it comes down to a fair fight between me and Lee. It's never that simple. I'd never have killed Billy Bonney if Lew Wallace didn't want to be president."

"Some people are saying that the Wildy Well fight has sullied your reputation as a lawman."

"I know who's saying it." Pat drained his glass.

"Others are saying it's typical of how you work, that you set out to assassinate Bonney and his closest friends and carried out your intentions in cold blood."

"Them that say that weren't freezing their asses off in the snow with me at Stinking Springs or sitting in the dark with Pete Maxwell waiting for Bonney to show himself."

The journalist transcribed Pat's response into his notebook, automatically editing out the phrase *their asses off*. He had more questions, but Pat got to his feet, explaining he had appointments to keep. The man looked a lot less like Ash Upson than he had when he'd come in.

"Well, Big Casino."

"What you doing, Billy?"

It was obvious to the long man what Bonney was doing. Riding across country to meet with John Chisum, Pat had altered his course when he saw a figure crouching along Chisum's north fence and recognized the green band on his hat. Billy, dressed in his working clothes and a pair of leather gauntlets that covered his arms to the elbows, was using wire-cutters to snip through the taut strands. Recognizing Pat with a broad grin, he had sat back on his heels, tugged off the gloves, and drawn a blue flannel sleeve across his glistening forehead.

"Just giving Old Jug Ears a hand with his problem," he said.

"What problem's that?"

"Cattle-poor. Poor old son's got more'n he can afford to feed. Me and the boys took pity on him and decided to help him out."

"How many are you fixing to help him out of?"

Billy was truly ugly except when he smiled; it went all over his face and provided justification for his big front teeth. Pat thought it was the young man's good fortune that he found so many things to smile about. There were women throughout the territory, devout women who would swear on a Bible that Edwin Booth in his prime had never had anything on Billy Bonney, simply because they had never seen him in a somber study.

"Now, Pat, don't you stretch me no blankets about how you didn't cut out no calves for your own self when you was working somebody else's spread."

"No one told me you were getting up your own outfit, Little Casino. Where's your acres?"

"That's the hard part. Charlie Bowdre and I are looking to buy some land with what we realize from Chisum's beeves."

"You're not long on loyal. Seems to me you and Chisum was fighting on the same side not so long ago."

"I'm mighty glad you remember it. Old Jug Ears seems to have forgot. If I was to claim what he owed me for the Murphy men I seen to, he wouldn't have nothing to raise on this here range but a big old ruckus."

"I don't intend to sit here arguing with you, Billy. You're dead."

Bonney took off his sombrero and ran his fingers through his hair, already thinning, as if his superabundance of energy were aging his body ahead of its season. He tugged the hat back on. "I'm dead for a fact," he said, drawing up the string beneath his long wobbly jaw. "I keep on, though. They know about me in Germany, I reckon, and maybe even Rooshia. Right now the king of China might be soaking his yellow ass in his jade bath-tub and reading about my exploits and derring-do. Meantime you're alive, getting all squeaky in the joints and watching your phizzle shrink up and just generally disappointing everybody that sees you, on account of you ain't as young and good-looking and full of piss as they been reading about. I ain't walking around with no wife and no litter of kids that I got to think about before I ride in with guns blazing. I don't need to lay down my arms and run away from no two outlaws on a shed roof. There's dead and dead."

"I didn't lay down my arms."

Billy got up and tucked his gauntlets inside his belt. Then he swung a leg over the bony buckskin he had ridden away from Lincoln and the bodies of Olinger and Bell. "I got to fly, Big Casino. I'm supposed to meet you in Fort Sumner tonight and get myself kilt. It says so in your book."

Pat drew his Colt's. "Hold on there, Billy. I'm arresting you."

"Sorry, Pat. I got a rule about never surrendering to a man without his britches on."

He looked down and saw that he was naked from the waist down, his long hairy legs laughably pale against the coat of the big bay he had ridden in Lincoln County. His face grew hot. "Stay put or I'll shoot you in the back!"

Bonney appeared not to hear. He gathered his reins and turned the buckskin east.

Pat jerked his trigger finger. Nothing happened. Again he looked down. He was holding not his pistol but his own limp phallus. He sat there and watched as Billy Bonney rode away at a walk, whistling "Silver Threads Among the Gold."

* * *

The long man jerked awake, feeling a hot flush of shame throughout his body. He looked down and was comforted to note that he was fully dressed, in the worn leather-reinforced corduroys and old canvas coat he preferred for traveling. He did not know immediately where he was, and the rumbling beneath his feet and the swaying of the coach, lighted only by the buttery glow of oil lamps suspended from the ceiling at the front and back, did not help. Then he remembered. He was on board the Santa Fe–Las Cruces train, headed home from Hilsboro and the trial of Oliver Lee and James Gililland for the Fountain murders. The pair had turned themselves in to Miguel Otero, the new governor of New Mexico Territory, upon the promise of safe conduct through the legal process. Pat groped in his breast pocket for a cigar, retrieving as he did so stray scraps of his cross-examination by Albert Fall:

"What did you say would be your course if given any warrants for the arrest of Lee? Did you not say that you would go after him by yourself?"

"Yes sir."

"Upon what were these warrants based?"

"Upon affidavits."

"What did you do when these warrants were sworn out?"

"Sent out a posse to serve them."

"Isn't it a fact that this posse was composed of militia—and that they pressed food from citizens?"

"Not to my knowledge."

"What was your object in sending this mob after Lee and Gililland?"

"It was not a mob, it was a posse."

* * *

Delicately, with soft-spoken phrases, the resplendent Fall, twirling with his fingers the platinum watch chain slung across his silk printed vest, embroidered a violent tapestry in which Pat headed up a ruthless gang of handpicked killers galloping roughshod across the territory, terrorizing settlers in their determination to execute Lee and Gililland without trial. Pat thought of Kent Kearney, the country schoolteacher, dead of his wounds; but by then the attorney was coming at him from another direction and he was forced to abandon Kearney—again—to defend himself. At no time did Fall's voice rise above the tone of polite conversation, nor did he address the famous former sheriff of Lincoln County in terms other than those of oily respect, and in this way he assassinated Pat's character for good and all. When the long man stepped down, he was conscious of the fact that he had been made to seem a monster, a hoary horned throwback to the dark time before the triumph of civilization and the closing of the frontier. It was 1899; the new century held no safe billet for the killer of Billy the Kid. After eighteen days of testimony the jury deliberated for eight minutes, then voted in favor of acquittal. Lee and Gililland swept out of the courtroom on a swell of backslapping, handshaking, and celebratory cigars.

Pat didn't light his when he found it, but chewed on the end, thinking about this latest dream. He had not before dreamt of encountering Bonney on the range, and in fact had never so encountered him in life; his memories of their times together were illuminated by smoky lamps suspended from pressed-tin ceilings and accompanied by the thud of broken piano keys outside card rooms packed with unwashed men. He did not wonder what the dream signified—the thoroughness of his disbelief in God and fate was such that he accepted all things as random and without design—but he was curious about where it had come from. Probably he was just getting old, pushing fifty with all his weight, and thinking too much about what he would do next.

In any case, there was nothing to be done about the former, and he was damned if he would even try to do anything about the other. In his valise in the brass rack over his head rode a letter signed by John Nance Garner, introducing Patrick Garrett to President William McKinley.

Chapter Sixteen

The Pledge

The interior of El Paso's Acme Saloon was a long varnished wooden box that gleamed in as many ways as a room could gleam. Ceiling lights installed by one of the city's two electric plants reflected off the polished maroon top of the mahogany bar, the rows of bottles and white china beer pulls, and long mirror in its gilded frame behind the three bartenders in their white shirts and aprons, the oar-shaped, oiled-oak blades of the big fans swooping ten feet overhead, and the diamond stud in the green satin necktie of the faro dealer standing flaccid-cheeked and granite-eyed at parade rest behind his table awaiting his first customer of the morning. A large oil portrait of McKinley, the recently martyred president, hung wreathed in black velvet above the backbar. Pat, who had had an audience with the chief executive in this city shortly after the trial of Lee and Gililland, could scarcely connect the statesmanlike face in the painting with the blank broad countenance of the man who had told him blandly that he would consider seriously Pat's request for a federal appointment. No such action had resulted, and for two years Pat's political hopes had been as dead as McKinley.

At that hour, before the first drink was spilled and the first cigar fired up, the place smelled cleanly of moustache wax and pomade, vanilla oil and fresh-brewed coffee, bootblack and peppermint and the warm soapy water into which the glasses were plunged between patrons. The barmen, newly bathed and starched, with talcum on their pink palms, paused during setup to snatch glimpses of their reflections in the mirror, like infantrymen inspecting their uniforms before parade. Pat, the former bartender, loved that brief moment in the daily life of a saloon. In a little while the place would start to fill up with sweaty gamblers and shaky drunks. The first splatter of tobacco juice would defile the first polished brass cuspidor, and as if a starting gun had been fired the first loud braggart of the day would come strutting in on the arm of some hungry-eyed whore in her rustling skirts, layers of paint and powder, and cheap scent. Before Pat finished his inaugural beer the scrub-faced maiden of the morning would be well on her way to becoming the foulmouthed, spraddle-legged slut of the vomity night.

The man who drew his beer, a contemporary of Pat's with handlebars artificially blacked and hair combed carefully across his naked scalp, asked him if he was new to El Paso.

"New to no place," Pat said. "But this is my first visit this century. I generally do all my drinking at the Metropole, but it's all torn up now."

"They're wiring the place for electricity. We had us a mess here when our turn came, and I don't know that it was worth it. I miss gas. These damn bulbs light up places that don't need to be lit. We're always sweeping cobwebs out of the corners."

"One ducked the broom, looks like. Right up there."

He didn't look. "I don't miss coal oil, though. When I came here I was the tallest bartender in the place, and I got the job of climbing the ladder and scrubbing the soot off the ceiling. In those days the new man was expected to do everything, even empty and clean the spitoons. Now we get some drunk."

"You've worked here a spell."

"I'm the only man left who was here when John Wesley Hardin got shot. He was standing right about where you are, shaking dice with Harry Brown. Old John Selman stood in the door and shot him clean in the back of the head." The bartender stopped mopping the bartop to fix Pat with his eyes, big as brown marbles. "Now, nobody else saw this nor believes me when I tell it, but I'll swear to it on a stack of Bibles as high as your chin. Old Wes Hardin, he gave that dice cup two shakes *after* he was shot. Just stood there with his brains on his face, still trying to make the point. That's how keen he was on winning."

"Did he win?"

The bartender blinked. Then he dropped his head and resumed mopping. "I don't rightly remember whether he did or he didn't. I don't guess it means much either way."

"Seems to me it does. Seems to me anything a man does after he's dead signifies something."

"All the same, this city's a mighty dull place for his passing. There hasn't been a killing worth talking about in years, and I can't remember the last time one of the banks was robbed."

"What's doing in the Tenderloin?" Pat had been thinking of going around and looking up a whore whose services he'd enjoyed in the past.

"Oh, somebody bottoms up dead every week or so in the opium dens, but it's usually some greaser gone to spend the pesos they get from politicians to wade across the river and vote. You don't count Mexicans. There's just too much law here. It's bad for business."

"I reckon Hardin's brains on his face was good for a few rounds."

"For a month we couldn't keep the glasses filled. We could've used ten bartenders if they could move around back here without falling over each other. Everybody wanted to stand where old Wes stood and hear the tale."

"It don't matter how a man lived if he died right."

"That's the truth, mister. Old Wes just stood there and gave that cup two shakes. Stack of Bibles." He wrung out his rag over the slop bucket. "You hear Teddy's coming to town?"

"Roosevelt? I heard."

"That's how homey we've gotten here in El Paso. Old U.S. Grant wouldn't have come within a hundred miles when Hardin was around. The army wouldn't have let him. You know they started up the Rangers again just to get Hardin. The first time it took the whole Comanche Nation. Where you from, mister?"

"New Mexico."

"Billy the Kid country. Well, you know what I'm talking about then. They say Teddy's thinking of putting in New Mexico for statehood. That wouldn't have happened if the Kid was still around. He wouldn't have let it."

"Bonney couldn't even help himself."

"I guess you don't know his kind, his and old Wes Hardin's. You can kill them, but you can't civilize them. They won't stand still for it."

"They stood still when it counted." Pat paid for his beer and left. The saloon had begun to fill up.

He went back to his hotel and stretched out fully clothed on the bed to stare at the ceiling and wait for noon. That's when Roosevelt's train was expected.

Arriving at the platform, Pat found the press of rubberneckers, reporters, policemen in helmets, and angry anarchists impenetrable. The locomotive, flags flying in front of the boiler, had just sneezed to a halt, steam boiled around its wheels and drifted across the cinderbed. The long man had on a new suit with the stiffness still in the seams and his Stetson had been cleaned and blocked recently; he had no desire to risk mussing himself. He cut himself a plug and, chewing, leaned inside the doorway to the telegrapher's while the city police sorted out the crowd. The train consisted of three cars festooned with red-white-and-blue bunting. The caboose and the coach just behind the tender would be for soldiers and the Secret Service, which had been re-cruiting furiously since the McKinley killing. An army sharp-shooter in a sergeant's uniform stood atop the president's Pull-man with feet spread, holding a Krag repeater and scanning the crowd from beneath the flat brim of his dimpled campaign hat for likely targets. Plainclothesmen in straw boaters and tight coats, virtually the only ones so attired in the blistering heat of west Texas in late summer, worked their way through the throngs, studying faces and bumping against people in search of hidden weapons. Pat, who had seen three presidents assassi-nated in his lifetime, thought it was all show; if Billy Bonney, wanted throughout the territory for the murders of Buck Mor-ton and Frank Baker, could gun down Sheriff Brady on Lincoln's main street in broad daylight and ride away bold as brass spurs, then anyone could kill anyone else—anywhere, anytime he chose to do it. He'd heard the Germans were working on a gun, fed directly from a cartridge belt, that could fire several dozen rounds a minute, and the French were debating the possibility of dropping dynamite onto the heads of enemy troops from hot-air balloons. Such reports disturbed him in ways he couldn't de-fine, although he thought it might have something to do with the fact that he had six children.

At length, the police succeeded in herding the crowd beyond the sawhorses erected at opposite ends of the platform. A group of shaggy-headed socialists laid down their signs to help away one of their number, bleeding from a scalp wound inflicted by an officer with a stick. Pat waited for them to pass, then approached one of the plainclothesmen standing inside the nearest barricade. The man, lean and Yankee-looking beneath the brim of his boater, drew himself up a little. He was better than six feet tall and plainly unaccustomed to having to look up at anyone in order to address him.

"I've got an appointment," Pat said.

"You and everyone else both sides of the Potomac." The man had a New England accent, metallic and bitter. "Got a pass?"

He drew from his breast pocket a paragraph typed under the new White House letterhead; those he had received from McKinley had referred to the place as the executive mansion. The plainclothesman snatched it from him and read it without moving his eyes. Then he looked up. "You're Garrett?"

"I am."

"Wait here."

In a little while he came back from the train, carrying the folded letter before him like a saber. "Surrender your weapons."

Pat unbuttoned his coat and opened it to show he was unarmed.

"Thought you were *that* Garrett."

"I didn't figure Billy the Kid to be riding this train." He felt strange saying it. He had never referred to Bonney by that name.

The plainclothesman pulled a long face of contempt. He jerked his chin at the policeman nearest him, who stepped forward and pulled one of the sawhorses out of line so Pat could pass. Wiry fingers closed around Pat's upper arm. "Spit out that plug."

Pat missed the polished toe of the plainclothesman's right boot, but only because he jerked it back at the last instant.

· On the platform of the private Pullman another Straw Hat, rounder in the face and kind in the eyes if one didn't look past the surface, found Pat's name in a leather-bound notebook and opened the door for him, using his left hand. Pat saw the bulge of the pistol rig beneath his left arm.

The interior of the car reminded Pat of the Acme Saloon, only no smell of peppermint or pomade and no sign of alcohol or any promise of it. The walls were paneled in red oak, and a deep fern-print carpet covered the floor from end to end. Curtains of burgundy velvet hung over the windows, tied back with ropes of gold, a row of Chesterfield lamps with copper shades swung from the ceiling between ranks of oils in gilt frames leaning out from the walls; Pat, who had little patience with *Harper's Weekly* but sometimes paused to study the lithographs while waiting his turn in the barber's chair, thought they were original Remingtons. There was a small portable bookcase, much scarred from travel, packed with volumes, a pair of deep armchairs upholstered in green plush, and a half-size rolltop desk against one wall with letters and rolled-up documents in every pigeonhole. A captured Spanish battle flag decorated the back wall next to the door and a grizzly rug, slightly moth-eaten and greatly at odds with the car's civilized appointments, sprawled at the foot of the larger of the two armchairs with yet another scrolled paper clamped in its jaws.

In the smaller chair, legs crossed to show an immaculate expanse of dove-gray gaiter, sat a trim man of sixty or so, with beautiful white whiskers and gold-rimmed half-glasses, scribbling on a sheet of foolscap on a lap desk. This was not the president. That individual, whose square stern face with its drop-wing moustaches and beribboned pince-nez hung in post offices, barbershops, and private parlors from Long Island to

Long Beach, was seated at the rolltop desk in his vest and shirt-sleeves with his cuffs rolled to his elbows. Pat assumed at first he was writing—the new president and most of the members of his cabinet were perhaps the most literary in the nation's history, and had been responsible collectively for more than thirty-five books now decomposing decorously in matched sets behind glass in doctors' waiting rooms in Maine and lawyers' offices in Dakota—but as he stepped farther into the car, removing his hat, he saw that Roosevelt was busy dismantling a coiled steel contraption with screwdriver in hand and his famous spectacles dangling from their gold clip.

When after a full minute neither man had acknowledged the newcomer's presence, Pat cleared his throat. He felt like a damned fool doing it. One of the advantages of having killed Billy the Kid was he had grown accustomed to all activity coming to a stop whenever he entered a room.

The man in the armchair went on writing. "Matters of state must take patience, Mr. Garrett. Theodore is in the midst of inventing a better mousetrap."

"*Rat* trap, Hay. You needn't bother pretending you don't know the difference. You saw your share when you took Lincoln's dictation." Roosevelt dropped his screwdriver, sprang to his feet, and closed the distance between himself and Pat in a bound, right hand outstretched. "Please accept my apologies for the behavior of my secretary of state. He's quite absorbed in yet another dreary volume about his years as Honest Abe's personal secretary."

"*Assistant* secretary." John Hay dipped his pen. "In any case, twenty thousand readers have not found them dreary so far. How many copies did you say you sold of *The Naval War of 1812*?"

"It went into a second printing, blast you." The president's grip was firmer than it had to be, but Pat had been warned by John Nance Garner, and gave as good as he got. Roosevelt's gray eyes sparked approval. "What about you, Garrett? *The Authentic Life of Billy the Kid* got me through three weeks of white weather holed up in my ranch house in the Badlands in '84. I made Hay read it on the way here from Washington."

"Well, that's two."

Roosevelt laughed, a high honking bray, and straddled his nose with his spectacles. They were very thick and made his eyes seem to swim. "What do you know about mechanisms? I bought that blasted trap in Denver and haven't been able to figure out how it works. There's a rat abroad in the White House, big gray jasper whose snout puts me in mind of Henry Cabot Lodge. The staff has nicknamed him General Linares, after my esteemed opponent at San Juan Hill. Can't have that. I mean to have him stuffed and sent to the Smithsonian, but I must catch him first. I don't trust a weapon I can't understand."

"The only reliable way to kill a varmint is to wait for it outside its hole and shoot it when it shows."

"Delightful! Perfect! You hear that, Hay? Perhaps if I'd had Garrett with me in New York I'd have been spared Boss Platt. Sit down, sir. Take off your coat. It's much too hot in here for a man with blood in his veins." He glanced theatrically at the coated Hay. As Pat complied, hanging his coat on the back of the vacant armchair, Roosevelt tugged at a bellpull. When a black orderly in a white coat presented himself: "Bring us some lemonade, Atticus. Mr. Garrett is thirsty."

Pat, who had not been consulted, would have preferred a tall whiskey; but he'd heard the president kept temperance and so sat down without comment while the servant went to fetch the refreshment.

When the lemonade was poured—John Hay, Pat noticed, let

his glass stand untouched on a table, the ice melting, while he went on writing—Roosevelt gulped down half of his, set down the rest, and tramped up and down the length of the car, flapping his arms. On his way back he paused by an open window to breathe in the hot dry air. "I love the smell of this country," said he. "If you have any sort of imagination you can detect the stench of dry Aztec bones and conquistadors' armor baking in the sun. I cannot believe dear old Bill contented himself during his visit with a buggy tour and Methodist services. Had he known how little time was left him, I daresay he'd have dipped his beak deeper."

"At the risk of parroting our friends in the Secret Service, I might point out that if a certain chief executive insists upon standing before open windows in Wild West train stations, he hasn't much time left himself." Hay spoke without looking up from his foolscap.

"I've old hens enough fluttering about without another in the flock." But Roosevelt came away and sat down. Perched on the edge of his wooden swivel, facing Pat with his hands on his knees, he looked as if he were set to take off and fly upon no notice. "I'll get to the point, Garrett. I've chosen not to reappoint H. M. Dillon as collector of customs in El Paso. I'm considering you to replace him."

Pat, who had been lobbying for the position since his visit with Roosevelt's predecessor, expressed no surprise. He kept a tight rein on his elation. He had been around politicians long enough to sense an approaching *but.*

"There are no secrets on Capitol Hill." Turning slightly, the president riffled a sheaf of papers held down by the rat trap. "Since my preference became known, I've been awash in telegrams and letters urging me to reconsider. I won't name names. I'm sure you know who your enemies are."

"There's some around I haven't killed."

John Hay made a hoarse sound in his throat. Roosevelt looked as stern as his photographs, and Pat questioned the timing of his experiment in levity.

"Enemies are an inevitable byproduct of effective public service," Roosevelt said then. "I haven't much use for saints in my bureaucracy. In any case the naysayers have been counterbalanced by an equal number of endorsements from prominent local citizens and a former governor of New Mexico Territory."

Pat said nothing.

"A man of sterling qualities is needed to oversee the border between the United States and Mexico. Mind you, I'm a former frontiersman myself, and know how slight is the value of what we are pleased to call the higher principles in certain venues. I do require, however, an abstemious man in a rigorous office." The president reached into a pigeonhole. Pat, watching, could scarcely believe that all this talk of sterling qualities and effective public service had come down to a question of drink. He felt a nearly uncontrollable desire to laugh.

"Would you read this aloud, Garrett?"

Pat took the sheet of stiff paper and pronounced the words typewritten there:

"I, the undersigned Patrick F. Garrett, hearby give my word of honor that if I am appointed collector of customs at El Paso, Texas, I will totally abstain from the use of intoxicating liquors during my term of office."

"Well?"

The single syllable, dropped into the silence that followed the recitation, startled Pat out of his mounting mirth. He smiled slowly.

"Mr. Roosevelt, it suits me exactly." He held out a hand.

The president dipped a pen in the inkwell on the rolltop and passed it over, along with a ledger. Pat rested the book on his knee, placed the document on top of it, and signed with all the flourish he had.

Roosevelt beamed. "Bully."

Chapter Seventeen

On the Border

Horseshit. He said it? Horseshit."

Pat, blowing a hole through the foam in his beer, nodded solemnly. " 'Bully.' That's what he said."

"Say it the way he said it."

"Can't. Not enough teeth."

"Shit. I thought that was just something them Eastie journalists made up." Tom Powers' broad Irish smile reached clear to his good eye. The other, a glass replica with the iris painted on, remained motionless in its socket. He topped off his glass from the bottle on the desk and offered to pour one for Pat, who shook his head and lifted his glass of beer in a sort of toast. They were seated in the back room of Powers' Coney Island Saloon in El Paso, which Pat had made his headquarters while the Metropole was being electrified. The Acme was too toney for him; he preferred the cigar burns on the Coney bar and the balding moose head mounted above the coatrack, collateral from an Idaho hunter who couldn't settle his tab. The back room had yet to be wired. Pat, feeling the first cricks and catches of a cantankerous old age, considered himself more at home in the soft orange glow of the oil lamp on the desk than in the glare of a tin-shaded bulb. He found the exposed cables that ran up the walls of downtown El Paso from grubby Bakelite turning-switches no improvement over gas pipe. Moreover he liked his host, who couldn't care less who shot Billy Bonney, or if he was shot at all. Scratch Home Rule for Ireland and Powers had no interest in anything that didn't directly affect his inventory.

"You serious about that pledge you signed?" Powers heeled the cork back into the bottle.

"I signed it."

"But beer's an intoxicating liquor."

"Not the way you serve it."

"That's a damn lie." The saloonkeeper grinned. "So you're a tax collector now?"

"Customs," Pat said. "I see the duty gets paid."

"Take a cut?"

Pat shook his head.

"That's good." Powers drank. "That's proper. Teddy's an honest one. I'd shake his hand."

"Not much chance of that, unless you want to get out of the saloon business."

Powers turned his glass eye Pat's way but said nothing.

The long man's office was reached by a flight of outside stairs, from the top of which a window looked out on the broad flat bend of the Rio Grande and the bridge connecting the U.S. and old Mexico; when the wind blew strong from the north, he could snap his cigar stub out the window and watch it land in one of the busy streets of Ciudad Juárez. When it turned up from the south, it brought with it the stench of the cattle pens in quarantine, the sharp-metal stink from the smelting stacks along the river, and the occasional bray of an automobile horn as one of the vehicles, shaped like a bathtub mounted on four wire-spoked bicycle wheels, chugged up Mesa Street, backfiring and startling horses. The window in the adjacent wall faced east toward Washington and the residential streets, where Queen Anne spires towered over territorial adobe and boys in cloth caps and corduroy knickers chased hoops with sticks, a practice whose point escaped the collector of customs.

The building was new and smelled pungently of fresh-sawn pine and lead paint. Pat had installed neither shades nor curtains, preferring to let the sun pour in; by afternoon the heat was so overpowering that no work could be done, at which point he adjourned to the Coney Island. There, at a corner table out of the direct line of sight from the bat-wing doors, meetings were conducted over an ostentatious pitcher of lemonade, or when the winter winds defeated the Gulf Stream, a steaming pot of coffee. Aside from that he drank beer exclusively, and then only in the privacy of Tom Powers' back room. Visitors who came to see him in the office were met by an astonishingly tall man with salt-and-pepper moustaches in a vested suit with an elk's tooth on a fob, who rose from behind his cluttered desk to grasp their hands in a dry firm grip and offer them, if they were male, a cigar from a wooden box on the desk, or if they were female, a paper cone filled with mossy water from an earthenware crock installed in the corner between the windows. Frontier history buffs looking to meet Billy the Kid's slayer were disappointed to learn that he did not use a big Colt's pistol for a paperweight, that no mementos of his peacekeeping past decorated the room, whose only ornaments were an American flag on a staff, the president's portrait in a walnut frame, and large-scale parchment maps of Texas and Chihuahua hanging side by side on the only wall not interrupted by a door or a window. His soft Alabama drawl confused them, and when he drew a pair of wire-rimmed glasses from the tortoiseshell case in his breast pocket to read a document or a letter of introduction, some of them decided that this must be a different Pat Garrett.

If, however, that visitor were to say or do something to test the temper of the collector of customs, the point was settled with a speed uncommon to the sedentary life of the conventional bureaucrat.

In the spring of 1903, Pat's office door opened to an undersize man in an outsize collar, crosshatched with dirt, and cinders still on his suit from a long ride by rail. He had a narrow forehead, hollow in the temples, ears that stuck out worse than old John Chisum's, rimless eyeglasses, and a moustache like a caterpillar, from one end of which drooped a smoldering cigarette. He was carrying a broad-brimmed Panama hat that he could not have worn aboard the train; it was the only truly clean thing about him, white as milk against fingers stained black with nicotine. He held it nearly at arm's length to prevent the ashes of his cigarette from falling on it and placed it on the only clear corner of Pat's desk.

"Garrett? I'm Joseph Evans. I'm a special Treasury agent. Secretary Shaw sent me."

Pat stood and shook his hand. The man seemed to have no bones in his fingers. The collector indicated the straight chair facing the desk, but Evans missed the gesture. He strolled the room with his hands thrust deep in his pockets, looking at the maps, the portrait, the view from the windows. "Mr. Shaw is in receipt of a petition signed by sixty-three prominent El Paso businessmen calling for your removal. He asked me to look into it."

"I've seen the petition," Pat said. "I know who sent it. I. A. Barnes represents an American importing firm that does business here. He's after my job."

"Sixty-three men appear to think he's qualified."

"I'm not surprised, seeing as how they're most of them connected with the Corralitas Ranch down in Casas Grandes."

"Mr. Shaw is well aware of the Corralitas controversy. The New York Board of Appraisers did not agree with your estimate of the Corralitas cattle's age. They reckoned between ten and thirty percent of them to be one year old or older. Your figure was slightly over half. The difference is between three dollars and seventy-five cents per head and two dollars. A substantial error."

"I've had to do with cattle for better than thirty years. I know a good deal more about their age than anyone in New York."

"Nevertheless, the decision went against you. It made the administration look bad in the papers."

"The papers here sided with me. The *Herald* knows Barnes's petition for a sham."

"Of course I was referring to the *eastern* newspapers. El Paso is the end of the world as far as most of the voters in this country are concerned."

"I'm sorry you wasted the fare," Pat said.

Evans stood with his back to the flag. The sunlight pouring through the east window made blank cutouts of his spectacles. "The party has a long-time loyal supporter here in George M. Gaither. I want you to consider appointing him cattle inspector. It will remove some of the pressure from you and recognize him for his efforts on our behalf."

"Gaither's a hack."

"This request comes directly from Secretary Shaw."

"Gaither's had his snout in the public trough for years. When the wind shifts he turns with it. He's absolutely unfit for any position under the government."

"I urge you to reconsider."

Pat played with a yellow pencil on the desk. It bore the impressions of his teeth, as did all the others in the mason jar. "I'll appoint him for thirty days. That should give him time enough to prove even to Washington he's a horse's ass."

"I felt certain you'd see reason." Evans turned to leave, then went back and retrieved his hat. Pat wondered if he'd bought it brand new in El Paso.

Tom Powers accompanied Pat aboard the Santa Fe Railroad for the trip to the long man's neglected ranch in Doña Ana County. Pat had not invited him, and Powers had offered no reason for his decision to go. In truth, neither man had given the situation much thought. It had taken Pat the better part of ten years to find a companion with whom he felt as comfortable, and as little as if he were on display, as he had with Ash Upson. He had presented Powers with the long-barreled Colt's with which he had killed Billy Bonney, and now it hung among the arsenal that decorated the wall behind the Coney Island bar.

The saloonkeeper, still attired in his town suit and fedora, perched himself on an intact section of weathered rail fence, sipping whiskey from a flat bottle while Pat wandered the yard in front of the house, kicking up clumps of drought-killed grass and testing the gate, which collapsed with a shove. The house's tile roof had fallen in and there were holes in the adobe through which a child could crawl. A family of armadillos had moved into the front parlor, building a nest inside the kiva fireplace. The nearsighted, armor-plated mammals had been migrating ever northward for three seasons, as if the end of the old century had been some sort of signal releasing them from their ancestral insect-hunting grounds. Pat, dressed as of old in a sweat-penetrated Stetson, canvas coat, denims faded white, and scarred boots, looked grim.

"What can I get for the place, Tom?"

"It depends. Any furniture in the house?"

"It's worth more than that. What do you know about land?"

"I know better than to ask someone like me what I can get for it."

"Maybe I shouldn't sell. This government job can't last. Roosevelt won't be president forever."

"Seems like he already has. But then I'm a Democrat."

"I thought you favored him."

"That's before I found out this teetotaling business was permanent. I thought he put it on to get votes. All this dry talk in Washington makes me nervous." He drank.

"Prohibition's in Kansas, I hear. Even Dodge City."

"Country's gone to hell since McKinley bought the farm."

"I ought to fix the place up, rent out what I can't ranch myself. Real estate's bound to jump now the frontier's closed."

"I wonder how you go about closing a frontier."

"I don't know. All I know is they closed it."

Powers changed the subject. "How's Gaither working out?"

"I let him go last week. He had his thirty days."

"That pettifogging Evans won't like it. They've got tight."

"Evans don't concern me. Leslie Shaw's another story. He's marked me to fall. He's in the pocket of Barnes and that Corralitas crowd. But if I can't run the El Paso office my way I'd just as soon pick Texas ticks off New Mexico cows."

The Irishman stuck his short legs out in front of him, balancing himself on his tailbone. He drank as heavily as Upson without ever showing any adverse results. Pat sometimes said he had a glass leg to go with his eye. "I'd still shake Teddy's hand," he said.

"The hand of a teetotaler?" Pat was amused.

"A popular one. If I had my picture taken with him I'd hang

it behind the bar. Business would improve. I could afford to electrify the card room."

"Roosevelt's as down on gambling as he is on liquor. You'd sooner have the chance to get your picture taken with Pancho Villa."

"I don't know anybody who knows Pancho Villa."

A bench had been installed on the front porch of the Nation's Meat and Supply Company on San Antonio Street for passengers waiting to board the traction car that ran past it to put up their feet and cool the back of their necks in the shade. On his way to his office, Pat paused to take stock of the tableau presented by Special Agent Joseph Evans and George M. Gaither sharing the slatted seat. Evans sat with his head down, knees spread, and the Panama hat dangling from his fingers between them; the front of the brim and the pinch of the crown now bore the stains of handling. Gaither, all soft fat and black muttonchop whiskers in loose seersucker, small red bow tie, and a straw boater with a red silk band, worn as square across his forehead as if he'd put it on with a mitre, sat back with his elbows on the back of the bench and the soles of his saddle shoes showing, picking his teeth with a cedar splinter.

"Good morning to you, Collector Garrett," Gaither said.

Evans raised his head then. The eternal cigarette smoldered short, threatening to ignite his caterpillar moustache.

"I'd wish you the same," Pat said, "if I meant it."

"That's no way to carry on," said Evans.

Pat stood in front of Gaither. "You've been talking about me around town."

"I guess I can talk."

"You've been telling all your friends you'll have my job."

Gaither picked his teeth and said nothing.

"Did you tell anybody I said your position was permanent?" Evans put his hat on. "Garrett, have you been drinking?"

"Answer the question."

Gaither removed the toothpick from his mouth and studied the frayed end. "I did not. I said you promised, with the assistance of Mr. Evans, to make it permanent if possible."

"You're a goddamn liar."

"Now, hold on." Evans gathered his feet to push himself off the bench.

"You're a goddamn liar too."

Gaither moved swiftly for a heavy man. He threw away the toothpick, sprang up, and hurled a fist that glanced off the customs collector's jaw. Pat swung one of his long arms in a loop that caught Gaither on the ear. After that, the fight lost its outward shape, the two men grabbing at each other's coats and wrestling rather than exchanging blows. Evans kept his distance—afraid, perhaps, of further soiling his panama. In a little while the street corner was a mob of interested citizens, some of them prominent, who seized the combatants and separated them. Police Chief Peyton Edwards elbowed his way through the throng and placed Pat and Gaither under arrest for disturbing the public peace.

"What'd they soak you?" Powers asked.

"Five bucks apiece." Pat puffed furiously at his cigar as if it were a cigarette. The Coney Island's back room was blue with smoke.

"Could've been worse."

"Only if they put us in the same cell. We had to stay overnight. I never was in jail before."

"There's not a whole hell of a lot of politicians can claim that."

"I had a wire from Washington sitting on my desk when I got out. That pettifogging Evans don't let the grass grow."

"What'd it say?"

"Shaw's appointing a special investigator to find out what Gaither and I already told Chief Edwards. He's appointing that petition-slinging son of a bitch I. A. Barnes."

"I don't know why you take it."

Pat puffed. "I never was in jail before."

Powers poured himself a whiskey. "He's going to be in San Antonio next year."

"Who, Barnes?"

"Who cares buffalo shit where Barnes goes? I mean Teddy. They're getting up a Rough Riders reunion. They're all coming, the Colonel included."

"He's up for reelection. I don't guess he can refuse."

"You going?"

"Next year's a ways off."

"That'd be the time to get my picture taken with Roosevelt, if ever there was one."

"Not if you're still in the saloon business."

"I don't have to be in the saloon business where Teddy's concerned. Tell him I'm a cattleman."

"What do you know about cattle?"

"I know enough to stay out of the business. That's more than Teddy knew."

"All right," Pat said.

"You mean it?"

"If I didn't I wouldn't be saying it."

"Thanks, Pat. I owe you."

"Just pour me one and we'll call it square."

"Beer?"

"Whiskey. What the hell."

GOLD

Chapter Eighteen

The Return of the Long Man

Salvation, then destruction.

Salvatio convenire destructio.

Salvación, despues destrucción.

I could not in any language, ancient nor modern, fathom the meaning of the vision of the cyclone and the peccary.

Years had elapsed since the day it was revealed to me in the desert. In the time between I had during the course of my experiments expended enough pewter to place a foaming stein in the hand of every customer in every Rathskeller in Munich, smelted nickel sufficient to plate the pivoting doors of New York and Chicago, sent enough bauxite up my chimney to build an aluminum road shining from Madrid to the Straits of Gibraltar. I had invented and prepared a solution consisting of three parts cinchona bark to one part cave mold dissolved in alcohol that had defeated an epidemic of malaria in the village, treated a score of cases of syphilis among transients, lain near death from scarlet fever for a fortnight, and been nursed back to health by the grandson of the boy who had first brought water to my rock, losing most of what remained of my hearing in the recovery. Yet I was no closer to the Philosopher's Stone and could not even guess at the answer to the riddle I had been asked.

The ancient gods that paced the barren reaches, despised and forgotten by the peoples who had paid them homage through the million dark years before the Revelation, were low and devious. Arrogant at their height, cruel in their largesse, in their bleak exile they fed their resentment on needles and venom and amused themselves preying upon the minds and hearts of those scattered few who still heeded them. Their catechisms were meaningless, their visions conducted no light. They spent their scaly-headed, pendulous-breasted, Grendl-bodied immortality scheming new ways to bedevil those who were wise enough to mark that they did not vanish with the smashing of their temples, did not quit this world when the first unlettered Christian hoisted his cassock and shit on their altars and walked away to spread the tale. The lesson was not a lesson. The promised wisdom was muzzle.

And yet.

I kept no faith. Gentle Christianity was as dead to me as the remains of my great-grandfather's family, torn and twisted on the Grand Inquisitor's rack and flung into a pit reserved for the disposal of Unbelievers. Of the pagan creeds of the native tribes, none was as vivid as my father's narrative of my grandfather's last moments, hurled broken, blinded, and burned from the summit of a cliff by the Pueblos whose malaises he had treated, and for whose labors on his behalf he had paid them in gold and silk. I had read and been unmoved by the Book of Mormon. I found no succor in Mohammed or Buddha and thought Devil-worship a waste of expensive candle wax. The pursuit of pure Science had left me no time for pilgrimages or obsequies, even had I cared to partake in them.

But to lack faith is not to disbelieve. Whether the gods invented man or man invented the gods is immaterial; the sheer collective weight of the unthinking masses that turned out offering fealty to avoid or transcend destruction, whose solitary devotions kept lights burning in a billion bedchambers from Ice Age to Industrial Revolution, must perforce by weight of will heap flesh on graven idols and quicken it. They were unseen, these Once Exalted, but then so was the cyclone, and like the cyclone it was by their visible effect upon material earth that their strength and stature was measured.

I knew not the mechanics of augury, but thought it probable the portent I had witnessed had taxed the strength of deities already eroded by their diminishing congregation. They had not the stores to mount a practical joke. No, there was meaning to the peccary's rescue and immediate death; but I, who now had lived in three centuries, had not the wisdom to read it. Was I then a fool, a contemptible puffer like my great-great-grandfather, whose longevity was his sole virtue? Was *that* the jest engineered by the vengeful deposed gods of antiquity? I groaned and hung my head in my hands above the litter of filings and instruments that profaned my worn bench.

"Well, you ain't no ghost, and that's a fact. You told me once there's no end to a ghost's patience."

I started; for although I had not heard his footsteps on the polished stone floor, age and command had brought an edge to his tone that pierced the callosities on my eardrums. I turned around on the stool and looked upon the long man for the first time in a quarter-century.

Gaunt he was now rather than lean, like an ancient wolf in harsh winter when prey was scarce. The bones of his face stuck out like architecture, his eyes glittering like blue glass shards in the caves of Chihuahua. The long countenance was as brown and cracked as a dry lake bed. His hair and moustaches were white, and the years of stooping to hear and to be heard had rounded his back permanently. His suit of clothes was smarter than the one he had worn on his first visit, exquisitely cut from better material, and now that the railroads had come it had no need of brushing after the long journey. He no longer smelled like a French king, but entirely like harnesses that had been left out in the sun and rain. Where the nickel-plated star had been, there now depended a platinum chain with an ivory fob. The hat in his hand was a fedora, dove-gray, with a four-inch brim and a wide black silk band. The sorrow he wore was the same.

"The nostrum has run out," said I.

"Years and years ago. It never did stop even one dream."

"Did you follow the instructions I gave you?"

"A quarter of a jigger a night for two years. After it run out I switched to whiskey. That didn't stop them neither, though it did sunny up my disposition. We had us some fine talks, Billy and me."

"I have thought of you often."

He did not address that. "I didn't know the place at first. Last time I was here it was just adobe huts and the only bath in four hundred miles. Dogs taking a dump in the street. I didn't expect it would change. Funny. Where I come from just about everything has."

"A company from El Paso is testing for oil in the sand hills. If they are successful, refineries will follow. At night, they say, the flames from the chimneys reflect blue off the bellies of the clouds. They say it looks like an ocean."

"Looks like hell."

"I would not know."

"I would." He cast his splintery gaze about the room. "Nothing's changed here. I don't reckon you ever found that trick for making gold."

"If I had, it would make no difference to the way I live. My goal is perfection, not wealth." I moved my shoulders. "I am still searching. And you?"

"Well, I ain't perfect by a long shot."

It was taking longer this time for the long man to come to the reason for his visit. He had grown older, but with age had not come contentment. He was more guarded, less trustful. The years of meeting gunshot with gunshot were far behind him. In the arena in which he'd been competing, the opponent was more difficult to identify, and the weapons to fear were not those he could see. The fatal blow was as likely to come from the man at his side as from the one he faced. Words were nets, thoughts were tridents. To share intelligence was to stand naked before the enemy.

I sought to put him at his ease. "I am ancient. I have no ambitions and only one illusion. Here of all places you may speak your heart."

He nodded, and appeared to go on nodding after he'd forgotten the reason. Then he spoke.

After a time—so Pat Garrett told it—the half-naked Bonney of Pete Maxwell's bedroom in Fort Sumner came less often to his somnolent mind. Mostly it was Billy in his Spanish costume and green-banded sombrero, although sometimes he appeared in the same black hat caved in on one side and heavy ribbed sweater he had worn in the photograph that still circulated on cigarette cards throughout the southwestern United States and had even found its way to the papered wall of the cantina that had been built upon the site of Juan Flores' barbershop. He spoke to Pat of old times with Big Ear John Chisum and John Henry Tunstall the Englishman, whose death in the range war in Lincoln County had set in motion the events that cast in steel the remainder of Bonney's life and Pat's. He spoke of dealing monte in Beaver Smith's saloon. On occasion he brought cards, and the pair played until dawn, or until Pat awoke. Sometimes Pat was receptive, and asked Billy what had become of Tom O'Folliard and Charlie Bowdre, and why they didn't come to visit. Bonney would explain that Tom and Charlie were still sore about getting killed, particularly during cold weather so that they could never warm up, and envied the long man his warm blood. "Them boys always did miss the whole point," Billy said. "They was in for the cash."

"What about you?" asked Pat.

"With me it's like cards. If you're just playing for money, you can't help but lose."

"But you lost."

"There's losing and losing."

"Billy never did make a lick of sense," Pat said. "Being dead hasn't changed him none."

Often the visits were quite ordinary, with nothing of note passing between them. Pat might as well have dreamt of branding calves on his ranch or stamping duty records at the border. The thing he dreaded—and because he could not predict when it would happen, even the ordinary visits were torturous—was the times when Bonney's amiable, slack-jawed expression would change abruptly in the middle of some folksy anecdote or while he was drawing from the deck; when his skin would grow ashen and a black band of shadow would fall across the top half of his visage, and he would shout:

"Quien es?"

Then there would be an explosion, very loud, well beyond the volume entrusted to a mere dream, and Pat would wake up, bathed in icy sweat, his nostrils burning with the stench of sulphur and cordite.

It required the half of a bottle of whiskey to help him back to sleep; whereupon another dream would come, or it would not. When it came there was no determining whether it would play itself out peacefully or end in the same disturbing way. Sometimes he put off returning to bed, and was useless all the next day for exhaustion. He feared nothing in life as much as he feared the phantasms of the night.

He did not always dream. When he did not, and when the dreams were uneventful, his life the next day would go one way or the other, as do all our days. In time, however, he came to see that the death-dream, in which he killed his friend, invariably preceded a black day in his passage.

He had slain Billy Bonney the night before he pistol-whipped W. M. Roberts on Lincoln's main street over the insulting letter to the *Rio Grande Republican*, and subsequently lost the New Mexico Territorial Council election. He was defeated for sheriff in Chaves County on a day following a night during which he had slain Billy Bonney. Bonney's death had awakened him in camp on the way to the disastrous gun battle at Wildy Well, and on the morning he traded blows with George M. Gaither he was tired and irritable from lack of sleep after a death-dream the previous night. He had not dreamt at all before the meeting with Theodore Roosevelt at the El Paso railroad station, where he was appointed collector of customs. During Roosevelt's second term, Pat one night relived in all their ghastly detail the circumstances of the night of July 14, 1881; the next day he orchestrated the infamous photograph of the president at the Rough Riders reunion with Tom Powers, notorious throughout Texas and northern Mexico for his Coney Island Saloon. Treasury Secretary Leslie Shaw made haste to bring the truth to the attention of Roosevelt, who chose not to renew Pat's appointment.

There were other such episodes, but the above serves to establish the pattern.

"Is it your belief that Bonney is responsible for all your misfortunes?" I asked.

"Not all. The sun don't shine on the same dog's ass all day, and no man's lucky all the time. But the ones I brung up suit Billy's damn sense of humor down to the ground. Take that time he kilt Olinger and Bell and jumped jail in Lincoln. He done it to vex me as much as to keep from getting hung."

"Ghosts enjoy a joke as well as the next man."

"It never did seem to matter to him that he was the only one laughing."

"Have you considered that the dreams may be intended as a warning?"

"Billy wasn't one to look out after other men's hides. It's what kept him alive long after he should've been cold and planted. Anyway, a warning's not much good if it don't tell you what to look out for."

I turned up a palm.

"What is it you ask of me?"

"I come down here thinking you'd have some nostrum that works where the other didn't. It's been better'n twenty-five years. I reckon that makes you somewhere around a hunnert and a quarter." Teeth showed behind his white moustaches.

"I cannot help you."

"I can't believe that. They can cure yellow fever and consumption. There's a doc in Europe claims he can make a crazy man sane. I rode from the station in a gas-powered buggy and I read where two brothers back East built a machine that flies, without a balloon or nothing."

"Time does not move so rapidly on this rock. There have been no developments."

Again he nodded.

"That tears it, then. I'm fixing up the ranch, bringing in some of them Scottish cattle Cree and Kirby went bust on. The range is fenced in, so I shouldn't have to worry about feeding them come a bad winter. I learnt a thing or two about irrigation when I was getting took by Eddy and Hagerman. What I don't ranch I'll hire out. It's still a risky living. I wanted to try and make sure I didn't dream about killing Billy before I got in so deep I couldn't get out."

"I am sorry."

He straightened his shoulders with a shrug and pulled on his fedora with the same gesture he had used a quarter century before. Perhaps it was this similarity that brought to his mind our words of parting on that occasion. The same gradual grin deepened the cracks in his face.

"I clean forgot to bring any of that wisdom you asked for," he said. "I told you I'm slow settling debts."

"I am confident you pay the ones that matter."

Pat Garrett turned and strode out, ducking below the lintel. I followed as far as the door and watched as he descended the ladder. The crown of his hat vanished below the edge of the rock. A moment later I heard a backfire from the desert floor, as sharp as a rifle report, and the rataplan of pistons. Gears meshed with a groan and then the noise faded away. I never saw the long man again.

Chapter Nineteen

The Deacon

Jim Miller was not as tall nor as prosperous as he appeared. Standing at a little over medium height in two-inch heels, a sober black broadcloth frock coat (dubbed the "Prince Albert" by a canny eastern tailor who had never been closer to Victoria's late consort than his likeness on a can of tobacco) sheathing and concealing his short trunk, emphasizing the length of his legs in well-cut gray flannel trousers, he managed to maintain the illusion of height even when shaking hands with six-foot-five Pat Garrett before the bar in Tom Powers' Coney Island Saloon in El Paso. He wore a soft black hat with its wide flat brim straight as a ruler across his brows, barber-trimmed handlebars, and a brief Imperial beard in the hollow of his chin. His fair skin was burned red from the sun glaring off the snow north of Fort Worth, where he had received Pat's wire, and against it the startling blue of his eyes shone like ice shards under a threatening sky. He wore his Colt's in a special holster inside the waistband of his trousers in deference to the city ordinance against carrying firearms, but Pat spotted the yellow-ivory handle against his vest when his coattail slipped open.

"Do I call you Mr. Miller or Deacon?" Pat asked.

"Miller will answer, or Jim if you're the friendly type. Every day but Sunday." His soft accent was Texan. He had left his native Arkansas while still in his infancy and no trace of it remained.

"Tom says we can use his card room."

"I don't play."

As many people claimed Miller was a duly appointed deacon in the Southern Baptist Church as claimed he had simply donned that title along with his black coat; but in speech and general behavior he conducted himself as if it were legitimate. On the rare occasion that he drank to excess, he acknowledged that he had broken but one commandment in his forty-three years, and that one fifty times. Those who had overheard him called him Killin' Jim Miller.

The photograph of Tom Powers standing among Theodore Roosevelt, Pat, and the Rough Riders, blown up and hung in a silver frame, had improved business at the Coney Island to the desired extent: the gaming room was now wired for electricity. Bright bulbs with hammered funnel shades swung low over the card stations and billiard table, their light reflecting green off the baize and illuminating the pictures of prize-fighters on the walls and the scaled-down replica of the bar in the main room. At that hour of the morning the room was deserted. Pat and Miller strode to the table farthest from the door and sat down without taking their hats off. Thus by tacit agreement they declared it a brief conference.

Pat noted with grim amusement the adjustments his companion made to avoid prodding himself with his concealed pistol. "I heard you favored a scattergun."

"I didn't figure I needed it to get a table in a saloon. They tell me El Paso's simmered down since Wes Hardin got it."

"You knew Hardin."

"Only after he got out of jail. I retained him to prosecute Bud Frazer for trying to kill me."

"I heard you killed Frazer."

"I found two barrels did the job where two juries wouldn't."

Pat, remembering the verdict in the Lee–Gililland trial, nodded. "Civilization's a deal slower in coming than electric light."

"I'm thinking it can take its time." Miller turned his concentration toward rolling a cigarette. His pink-nailed fingers were meticulous.

Pat got to it. "You know Brazel?"

"We've not met. I heard there's black blood between the two of you. Something about goats."

"Wayne Brazel's a sprout. It's the men behind him I can't stomach, chiefly W. W. Cox."

"Cox holds the paper on your ranch by Las Cruces."

"The son of a bitch is holding my cattle in Mexico till I pay it off. Only I can't pay it off without cattle. Now he's partnered up with Brazel to run goats on my property out by Bear Canyon. I can't abide a goat. More than that, I can't abide the way Cox and Brazel went around me through my boy Dudley Poe to lease the property. The deal was Brazel would deliver ten heifer calves to Dudley each July for five years. Only you don't get heifer calves from goats. All you get from goats is goats. They crop the grass down to bare ground and ruin it for cattle. Also they stink worse'n sheep. Beyond that I got personal reasons for hating goats."

Miller lit his cigarette and said nothing.

"I got Brazel arrested for herding livestock near a residence," Pat said, "but he's out on bail and court won't convene till spring; meanwhile them goats are eating my grass. If this thing is allowed to run its course I'll lose the ranch no matter which way the jury jumps. I want that goat man off my land."

"Permanent?"

The long man shifted his weight in his chair. "I'm not hiring your gun, just what goes with it. I want you to sit in on a meeting between Brazel and me. I think he'll see reason with you in attendance."

"It's not my area."

"I'll make it worth your time." When Miller made no response, Pat went on. "I've had my life's portion of ranching. If you ain't cut out for it, it breaks your heart and your back and leaves you with nothing but dirt. If Brazel moves his goats I'll sell you the place for three thousand and pay off the mortgage out of that. Now, that's a bargain."

"You figure I'm cut out for it?"

"You can turn around and sell it if you like. Cox knows what it's worth. He'll make you a fair price, and that's damn more than you're paying. He's a mean old cob but he won't cross you the way he done my boy Dudley Poe. He's smarter than that."

"I'm not tempted."

"It's fifteen hundred acres. They aren't making any more of it. There's a spring, a house, and outbuildings. Then there's the stock."

"Cox has the stock."

"He'll free it up once the mortgage is paid. I'll run it up for you personal. Dollar a head." Pat kept his tone matter-of-fact. He had three hundred dollars in the bank in Las Cruces and owed almost a thousand in taxes.

"I've made as much as two thousand just for uncasing my shotgun. I didn't have to wait for no deeds to clear." The man in the black coat flicked his ashes into the glass tray recessed in the table for that purpose. "Where can I find Brazel?"

"To talk to him about setting up a meeting."

Miller smiled for the first time behind his moustaches. It did nothing to take the chill from his eyes. "Of course. I get paid in advance for the other."

"Let me know when you have an answer. I'm staying at Mrs. Brown's here in town."

"I know."

Pat lifted his brows. "I only moved in last week."

"Pat Garrett can't unbutton his fly without the whole Southwest knowing about it." Miller got up and left.

Alone in the large room, Pat went to the bar and leaned over it to retrieve the measured bottle from the shelf beneath. He blew into a glass, filled it, and was drinking with a heel hooked over the brass rail when Tom Powers came in. The saloonkeeper turned his good eye Pat's way. "I saw the Deacon going out."

Pat drank and said nothing.

"You know he's an assassin."

"If you barred your place to assassins, you'd be out of business in a month."

"If I was to take that notion, I'd start with him. They say he killed his own grandparents when he was eight."

"They said something like it about Billy. The true facts are never enough for some people."

"Miller blew Sheriff Frazer's head out from under his hat in Texas and stood trial for killing an Indian policeman named Collins in the Nations. That ought to be facts enough for anyone."

"I'm not a lawman anymore, Tom."

"Neither are Frazer and Collins."

"My business with Miller's legitimate. Anyway, it ain't your concern."

"It is if it goes on under my roof. I didn't electrify this place to have dark plots bandied about in it."

"You wouldn't have electrified it at all if it wasn't for me,

Tom." Pat measured himself another glassful. "It cost me my job."

"I'm guessing they'll put that on my headstone."

"You owe me."

"If I didn't I wouldn't be here." Powers stepped behind the bar and held the bottle up to the light. "You're hitting this stuff square on the head these days, Pat."

"I reckon that makes me your second best customer."

"It don't matter that I'm a drunk. You've got a standing to maintain."

Pat looked at him for the first time. He had a headache. He could feel his pulse pounding in the veins in his eyeballs: Quien es? Quien es? "You ever try standing on shit, Tom? You just keep sinking. Pretty soon you're lower than the shit. I've never stood so tall as the night I shot Billy. Wish to hell I could say the same for him."

"That's whiskey talk."

"Whiskey don't lie. I believe if you was to put Billy Bonney up for governor of New Mexico State he'd win it running away."

"You ought to get out of El Paso. The town's unlucky for you. Just the way it was for Wes Hardin."

"Old Wes Hardin. They came from all over both sides of the border just to look on his corpse. More folks saw Hardin dead than Lincoln alive. You reckon they'd turn out like that to look on my corpse?"

Powers laughed and poured himself a drink. "I'll let you know in twenty or thirty years. You're a young man yet, Pat. I've got ten years on you."

"John Selman shot Hardin in the back of the head. He was standing at the bar, just like I am now. He couldn't have done it better if he'd had his pick."

"You told me you had a job waiting for you in Santa Fe. Governor Curry's set to appoint you superintendent of the territorial prison."

"That was three months back. I'm still awaiting a wire."

"Maybe it's waiting for you in Las Cruces."

"The only thing waiting for me in Las Cruces is a cattle ranch without cattle. A situation like that sure cuts down on the chores."

"You're forgetting your wife and parcel of kids. What you want to take up with that Brown woman for? She's a grass widow and not near as handsome as Apolinaria."

"She's my landlady."

"She's a whore."

"I didn't ask her profession."

"Boarders don't take their landladies on buggy rides all over town and along the river road. Not married boarders whose faces are known."

"The church ain't your true calling, Tom. I'd give it a pass."

Powers slammed the cork into the bottle. "That's a hell of a thing for you to say to me."

"I reckon it is." Pat was contrite. "Don't take it personal. I didn't sleep much last night. I had a dream."

"You'd sleep heaps better in your own bed with your own wife. If I had a wife like Apolinaria and a parcel of kids I'd sell the saloon and never leave home."

"You don't know what you're talking about."

"You don't know the company you're keeping. Whores and murderers."

Pat fished a silver dollar out of his pocket and bounced it on the bar. "I'm going back to bed."

"Wait for your change." Powers rummaged among the coins in the cigar box on the shelf under the bar.

"Put it toward a pulpit." Pat walked out with the exaggerated dignity of the true drunk.

Mrs. Brown was out when he got home. He let himself in with his own key and sank into the feather mattress on the old brass bed without taking off his boots. He fell asleep quickly, snoring to rattle the blinds on the windows, and dreamed of Billy. It was the death-dream.

Chapter Twenty

Mrs. Brown

It's wildly impractical," Mrs. Brown said.

Pat nodded agreement and sipped coffee from his thin china cup, thick and strong and black as molasses, the way he preferred it and the way only Mexicans knew how to brew it; his own attempts always wound up bitter beyond words. He wasn't really listening. They were sitting on the terrace of the El Capitan Restaurant overlooking the Mexican Quarter, and he was watching some kind of pageant going on a few blocks away. Practically every day of the year belonged to some saint or other, and the occasion was rare when one of them wasn't being celebrated. This one made use of a tall adolescent—chosen, no doubt, for his height—got up in a death's-head mask of papier-mâché, with a white linen sheet for a shroud, aboard a pale horse being led by a bent-over crone dressed all in black. A cassocked padre and a little girl in a Communion gown briskly smacking a tambourine headed the procession, looking like scraps of white paper skipping ahead of a groundwind, and the usual three-piece mariachi band—guitar, trumpet, and drum—brought up the rear playing something drunken and tinny. Pat wondered if all musicians in old Mexico were chosen for their inability to carry a tune in a bucket.

Whatever it was about, everyone was having a good time.

Children ran shouting after the performers and the watchers on the boardwalk beat their hands and cheered and sang along with the music: "La muerta, la muerta, viva la muerta." The more macabre the trappings, Pat reflected, the more greasers seemed to like it. It was no wonder they had so many revolutions.

"It's burgundy velvet, with a robin's-egg blue linen yoke and a full skirt that wraps around," Mrs. Brown was saying. "The hem is trimmed with chantilly." She pronounced the word with a hard *ch*. Pat had never heard it before, but assumed it was French and that she was making a mess of it. He'd been to New Orleans, and Mrs. Brown had spent her whole life in Texas, and not more than a day or two of that on the polite side of town. "I saw it in Birnbaum's window."

"How much?" Pat asked.

"Forty dollars. Mrs. Birnbaum said they're selling the same dress in St. Louis for sixty," she added quickly.

"Tell her to sell it in St. Louis."

She looked down at her plate of ham. It had grown cold and she had not so much as dented it with her fork. "You haven't bought me anything in a long time."

"I bought the dress you've got on, and the hat." He'd thought it was a damn silly hat at the time, the black straw brim bent up on one side and pinned to the crown, dyed ostrich plumes on the other, and time hadn't increased his affection. "I'm buying that supper you didn't eat." He resolved to smoke a cigar and put it out in the center of the ham slice when he left, just to keep the management from serving it to another customer and collecting twice. He had lost a young fortune at cards and horse races in his lifetime and didn't mind wasting his money so much as paying to look the fool.

"If you loved me you wouldn't keep track."

He got out his wallet to pay the bill and leave, with or without her. Then he took out a twenty-dollar bank note and two tens and laid them on her side of the table. "Tell Mrs. Blumberg I ain't paying no tax."

"Birnbaum." She made a purring noise and placed the notes in the bottom of her reticule. She had fine eyes, large and dark like his wife's, but heavy-lidded, as if she hadn't got enough sleep; which in his experience was a true thing. Her nose was thin and too long and she had bad skin, but she made up for these faults with an abundance of tawny hair that he didn't think was dyed. She wore it swept up; when the pins were removed, it spilled like rich grain to her shoulders. Although soft and doughy around the middle when she undid her corset, in bed she grappled ferociously, all teeth and sharp nails and sinewy coils that kept him from breathing, making the release when it came as explosive as a Howitzer. Apolinaria by contrast lay submissive and unmoving, neither resenting his needs nor enjoying them, accepting them with the passive gratitude of a penitent. He loved Apolinaria; not as passionately as he had loved her sister, dead these thirty years, but with the fullness of affection due the mother of his children and the companion of his age. He needed Mrs. Brown. Her conversation bored him, and it had occurred to him that if she were to drop out of his life—fall into the Rio Grande and drown on her way across the bridge to purchase her medicinal opium, or leave him for the Mexican policeman he knew she stayed with while in Juarez—he would miss her for a while the way he'd miss masturbating if his wrist were sprained, but that would be all. Her absence would cause him more irritation than grief.

He was still a little cloudy on how they had come to keep company. Tom Powers, whose taste in whiskey Pat also considered inferior, had been working on her romantically, and had introduced her to him along with her girlfriend, a younger and far more interesting woman with an infectious wit, to whom Powers had presented Pat as the famous Sheriff Garrett of Lincoln County. The long man, pleasantly drunk and in a mood to charm, had barely noticed Mrs. Brown in favor of her friend, but as the evening wore on and the Coney Island grew crowded and smoky he found himself standing with his arm around her waist while the other woman receded into the predominately male assemblage. One-eyed Tom, diplomatic to a fault, withdrew as well. The next day Pat awoke in Mrs. Brown's bed, and by the end of the week he had moved his belongings from his rented rooms on Texas Avenue to her house on Eighth Street, from the bedroom of which could be heard the cries of merchants selling avocados and melons in the farmers' market in Juarez. He was contented enough with her favors, whose variety convinced him, if indeed her general manner did not, that she had at one time or another made ends meet with their assistance, and was seldom bothered by the empty-headed prattle that in her passed for conversation, but in his darker moments he could not avoid the conviction that somehow in the course of that alcoholic evening she had bewitched him against his will. He did not trust her.

She had a first name, something classical that he couldn't pronounce (*Apolinaria* had thrown him for a year, and even after all this time he could not say it the way a Mexican did), and so when he made reference to her and thought of her it was as Mrs. Brown. He never addressed her by name or private endearment. In truth, every conversation they had had, she had initiated. His relationship with her was entirely responsive except in bed, and even there she commenced matters as often as he. The first time this happened he was surprised, and perhaps shocked; for he was accustomed to a degree of passivity even in those partners for whose time he paid. Certainly this was always the case in the marital chambers. To find the positions reversed disconcerted and excited him in equal measures. Mrs. Brown appeared to enjoy herself whether she was giving pleasure or taking it. She had never once refused him. He made that allowance for her, and when he bothered to contemplate the affair he decided that was the one thing that sustained it. When it came to the physical act of love she was a giving creature, generous and sweet. He came as close to loving her then as he ever would.

She claimed to have lost her husband in the siege of Santiago, but the circumstances of his death as they were explained in a wire she insisted she had received from the War Department kept changing. Pat had heard from various sources that "Mr. Brown" was alive and operating a house of loose ethics in Fort Worth, that he had expired of a belly wound inflicted by a mulatto named Pullman Beal during a fight over Mrs. Brown in an Amarillo saloon, and that she was married simultaneously to a Brown in Del Rio and the Mexican policeman in Juarez. Pat believed none of the stories. He believed all of them. He didn't lose any sleep wondering whether any of them was true and would not have cared if the most sordid turned out to be fact. In his fifty-eighth year, he was a man without illusions.

He knew what was said about him when he was seen piloting a buggy through city traffic with Mrs. Brown beside him on the seat, hatted and shaded beneath a spread parasol, or strolling down San Antonio with her on his arm, pausing at every store window to admire the merchandise on the other side of the glass. They said—these cattlemen's wives in silk drawing rooms only once removed from the parlors of whorehouses where they had met their husbands, these oilmen in their silk hats and morning coats who nipped into the Mexican quarter at dusk to explore the pleasures of working women—that Pat Garrett had "gone to the bad" in the company of his hired whore, that her wicked wiles had besotted him and turned him off the true path. She was responsible for every wrong decision he had made since he came to El Paso. But for her, they said, he would have restrained himself from fighting George Gaither on a public street in broad daylight like a common tough. Her influence had caused him to throw reason to the winds and smuggle Tom Powers, that one-eyed whiskey-slinger, into a photograph next to President Roosevelt, soiling the dignity of that high office. Time and the actual order of things had no effect upon such talk. Such talk made no room for a man's ability to make his own mistakes. They had to be charged to liquor or, preferably, a woman of slim virtue. It made for more entertaining discourse.

For all their whispers they cared nothing for respectability or appearances. They were the sons and daughters of embezzlers and consumptives, driven west to escape their pasts or to prolong their lives; civilization had come with them like lint caught in the cuffs of their trousers and on the hems of their skirts. Their heirs pretended to guard that fragile culture against the actions of that same breed that had brought it. In fact they would find life intolerable without the diversion of an occasional fall from grace. Pat compared himself to the *Police Gazette* and the herky-jerky images of frantic firefighters and disrobing women projected twice a month onto the stage of the opera house for the enjoyment of patrons, and had commented to Mrs. Brown that they ought to charge admission every time they went out in public. He was the same man he had always been, he had not changed. The generation that had grown up since Billy Bonney's death expected his slayer to behave like the abstemious, poetry-spouting heroes in *Beadle's Dime Library*, and when he had not, they drowned their disappointment in lascivious gossip. He despised himself whenever he thought about how much of his life he had squandered currying the favor of such as they. Everything he had done since he left Pete Maxwell's bedroom in Fort Sumner he had done for their approval.

Not killing Billy, though; no matter what they said about that, that he had done for himself alone. He had not killed the badger to protect his mother's chickens. He had killed the badger because he had wanted to kill the badger.

"Patrick, are you listening?"

"No."

"Silly man." Mrs. Brown was pulling on her elbow-length gloves, elaborately attending to the details. She smoothed the gauntlets along her forearms and worked a fingertip between all the fingers, seating the material firmly. At her insistence, Pat had bought them for her from a shop that catered to gringos on the Mexican side of the river. He had been in a good humor at the time, and had even foreborn to point out that it seldom got cold enough on the Gulf Stream to make them anything more than a nuisance. She was forever forgetting them and sending him back for them; as if anyone would bother to steal them unless he was on his way to Montana. "I said a new dress isn't much good if I haven't a place to show it off."

"Put it on and take a walk down San Antonio. You'll see everyone you know and some you don't."

"I was thinking of the opera."

"No."

She thrust out her lower lip. It made her look like a rat terrier Pat had had when he was eight. "You haven't taken me anywhere in a long time."

He started to sweep a long arm around the El Capitan's terrace, to force her to give evidence that it didn't qualify as somewhere. His gaze fell upon Jim Miller, making his way toward Pat's table from the interior of the restaurant. He resembled a

Mormon in his long black coat and flat-brimmed hat. When he spotted Pat he stopped and jerked his head. Pat placed his crumpled napkin on his plate and rose.

"You're not leaving me alone to talk to that horrible man." Mrs. Brown's face was pale, a danger sign.

"Pretend I'm in the crapper."

He joined Miller on the other side of the arched passage, where they crowded next to the wall to avoid collisions with steaming tamales and cooked pheasants. They didn't shake hands.

"You're not hard to find," Miller said in greeting.

"I wasn't hiding."

"I meant you cut a wide swath in town. Everyone seems to know what you're about."

"Tell it."

"Brazel's willing to sell out if his price is met."

"I ain't buying any goats."

"You don't have to. I can find a buyer who'll make me a better price than what Brazel's asking. He's got twelve hundred goats he'll let go for three-fifty a head, then he'll cancel his lease. He's having a contract drawn up."

"For a man who says ranching ain't his area, you're sure starting to sound like one," Pat said. "I didn't figure you for a goat man."

"I don't intend to keep them long enough to be one. Your offer still stand?"

"I don't make any I'm not prepared to back up."

"All right, then."

When Miller left, Pat returned to his table and sat down. Mrs. Brown's face was dead white. "I loathe being stared at in restaurants."

"You get used to it."

"Now you're having fun at my expense. I don't see what there is to grin about."

"Calm down, old girl," Pat said. "What opera you thinking of going to see?"

Chapter Twenty-one

Old Haunts

No city, as Pat saw it, managed to look more like itself than Santa Fe, while having changed so much in everything that counted.

The Palace of the Governors looked the same. Strings of dried chiles still decorated the verandah, and Indians still sold their pots and beadwork in its shade, never once looking up into the faces of customers as they haggled. But Lew Wallace no longer spread terror inside its six-foot-thick walls, calling for more and better maps of the territory like the general he was while Jorge, his old manservant, hastened back and forth emptying and replacing his brimming spitoons. In the governor's chair, clean-shaven, quiet-spoken George Curry now sat placidly signing ordinances against the operation of automobiles during peak hours and drafting addresses to the Women's Christian Temperence Union. Outside the plaza, the gubernatorial term of Miguel Otero had furred the lines between the Mexican quarter and the city proper, but to Pat's mind, emancipation had only served to make the Spanish-speaking population as edgy as the Anglos. Free now to compete commercially with their fair-skinned neighbors, the Mexicans were less cheerful, more guarded, and tended to contaminate the bills of fare in their cantinas with veal in champagne sauce, strawberry shortcake, and Kentucky rye. In the largest Hispanic enclave north of Chihuahua, it was sometimes impossible to order a decent tortilla with green chiles or a bottle of mescal that didn't taste like horse liniment.

Pat's first stop, after pausing to cut the cinders in a saloon run by a young Spaniard who entertained his clientele with Caruso playing on a Parlograph behind the bar, was at Señora Leones' whorehouse, respite in years past from Wallace's harangues, only to find that an ice cream parlor had moved in. From there he went to a three-chair barbershop and paid nearly a dollar to have his neck trimmed, his chin scraped, his nails pared, and his boots shined to a finish like black oil. He spent his last quarter on a Hidalgo Perfecto and had to bum a light off the apprentice barber, a sullen-faced half-caste in his teens with vaseline in his hair and pimples on his forehead. The train ticket had cost twice as much as anticipated. Pat was broke.

After waiting some little time in the narrow wainscoted reception area where a secretary in a shirtwaist and long skirt with her hair tied up with ribbon chattered at a big black Remington typewriter, Pat was allowed into Governor Curry's sun-splashed office. The window overlooking the plaza left so baldly open gave him pause. In the past he had been accustomed to meeting Lew Wallace there in the dim golden light of a globe on the desk, blinds drawn and shutters latched against Billy Bonney's threats to kill the governor for breaking his promise of pardon; that the chief of the territory should go about his business naked to the world struck the long man as unseemly and somehow indecent. He was scarcely mollified by the pudgy Curry's obsequious greeting and flabby handshake. Wallace, ever the general and conscious of the gulf that separated the commander from his subordinates, had never offered his hand nor risen from behind the great leather-topped desk with great brass tacks all around.

"I believe this is your first visit to the capital in some years," said Curry when the pair were seated, Pat in a straight-backed chair of Mexican design with his fedora in his lap. "What do you think of the place?"

"It's grown a mite. More brick buildings, less adobe."

"We're encouraging that. Mud walls don't hold up to the vibration of heavy machinery. There's talk of an automobile plant and a print factory. Bit of a shock for you old-timers, I imagine."

"I was the same age as you when you ran the Brock Ranch. I reckon we're both older by the same thirty years."

"So we are. Those days seem a long time gone. Dead as old John Chisum. Now when you bring up the war, most folks think you're talking about the one with Spain. I suppose that's as it should be. Living in the past has been the ruin of Dodge City and Tombstone. Wyatt Earp's a fight referee. Bill Tilghman's gone into national politics. The new breed of marshals and sheriffs make their rounds in flivvers with court orders in their pockets. I don't believe half of them bother to carry weapons." His liquid brown gaze went toward the bulge of the bulldog revolver in Pat's side pocket.

Pat saw where this was going. He leaned forward and helped himself to a cigar from the humidor on the desk, carved from native piñon. Curry had not offered. "Once every couple of years, some young cowboy gets a pimple on his ass and takes a shot at me. They all want to be Bonney, you see. I ain't as popular as Tilghman, and Earp always was a sack of horseshit. That business in Arizona should never have happened. I got brothers too, but we don't travel in a herd. What about that appointment, George?" He bit the end off the cigar and, unable to locate a cuspidor, took the piece out of his mouth and put it in his pocket.

Curry shifted his weight in his swivel. He had taken a bad

spill off a mustang during the trouble in Lincoln County, and Pat suspected his back still bothered him. "I've decided to keep Olaf Burnsum in the prison superintendent's position for the time being. He's doing an adequate job. There hasn't been a disturbance among the convicts in years."

"That's because they go over the walls like water."

"That's not at all true. This is a difficult time to make changes, Pat. I have no guarantee that my own appointment will survive the next administration. Roosevelt has indicated he won't seek a third term. He wants to run his secretary of state. If Taft loses to the Democrats—" He spread his hands, then let them drop to the arms of his chair. "Let's just say, this isn't the time. After the elections in November, assuming we carry the day, if you care to resubmit your application—"

"Damn it, George, I was counting on this job. My ass is poking through my drawers. I got eight kids and they all have to eat till November."

"Perhaps if you stayed at home more, and worked the ranch." Curry's jowls folded over the corners of his disapproving mouth.

"My ranch is overrun with goats," said Pat darkly, "and I reckon I ought to have thanked you more for carrying the sheriff's election for me in '80 with a jug of whiskey and the wetback vote."

The governor's broad brow clouded. "That was the frontier. If you can't see the difference, maybe it's time you retired from public life." He softened his expression. "Do you need money?"

Pat clenched and unclenched both fists. He reached up and took the unlit cigar out of his mouth. "George, I'm in a hell of a tight. I've been trying to sell my ranch, but no luck until this goat thing is settled. For God's sake lend me fifty dollars to keep me till I leave for home."

Curry unlocked a desk drawer with a key attached to his

watch chain, drew out a checkbook bound in yellow calfskin, shook down the ink in a gravity pen, and began writing. "When you say *home*," he said, rocking a blotter over his signature, "are you referring to Las Cruces or El Paso?"

"I haven't had a home since I left Alabama when I was three." Rising with the check in his breast pocket, he nodded at the governor. Neither man offered his hand. "Thanks, George. This is just a loan."

"You're good for it."

The tone of both men's speech bespoke the likelihood that the debt would ever be repaid.

The curved-dash Oldsmobile jittered out of a cloud of its own dust, bowed alarmingly but flexibly in the middle when one of its spindly wheels dipped into a chuckhole, and sputtered to a stop beside the boardwalk where Pat stood, far enough back to prevent the drifting grit from settling on his boots. The motor went on galloping a full minute after the ignition had been switched off, then died with a wheeze. Instantly a thick cloud of steam poured from the radiator. The driver, a stout young Hispanic in goggles, a duster, and a cap made from ticking, hopped down from behind the wheel, unhooked a goatskin bag from the spare tire on the back, and with a red bandanna wound around his right hand unscrewed the radiator cap. Pat felt the moisture on his skin from the geyser, whose force could not remove the broad white grin from the driver's dark face.

Emerson Hough, all eastern dignity even with dark stains on the crown of his dove-gray Stetson from the condensing vapor, stepped from the Oldsmobile's running board to the boardwalk with the easy assurance of an old seaman quitting his launch for the jetty. He wore an ankle-length duster over a tweed suit and garish yellow gaiters laced to his knees. He had a broad face, clean-shaven but for a military brush moustache flecked with gray, and pale eyes set in thickets of sun-creases, sparked with gentle good humor. He was, after Owen Wister and Zane Gray, the most popular writer of frontier stories in the United States.

"Pat, I see the life of the gentleman rancher has not made you fat." He did not smile with his mouth when he took the long man's hand in his firm grip, calloused at the finger ends from the keyboard of his Oliver typewriter, but the warmth in his eyes made the driver's grin look empty and false.

"You're fat enough for us both, Em."

Hough patted his stomach. "It's all this deep frying out here. Back home I'm content with tea and toast."

"What do you think of Lincoln?"

The writer looked around at the patched adobe and weathered clapboard, the loafers lounging in front of the general merchandise. A dog with running mange lifted a crooked hind leg against a wooden trough containing nothing but dust. "I think the county seat should be closer to the railroad than Carrizozo. Where is the famous courthouse?"

"We're standing in front of it." It was a two-story territorial style with two wooden staircases wobbling diagonally from the street to a balcony in front.

"Were there bars on the windows when the Kid made his break?"

"No. The town didn't have a jail then, so I placed him under guard in an upstairs room."

"It would be better with bars."

"He didn't make his play from inside. He shot J. W. Bell on the outside stairs and Bob Olinger from the side window with Olinger's own shotgun."

"I heard they taunted him."

"Bob did. He was a mean son of a bitch. J. W. wouldn't raise his voice to a dog."

"Did he draw on the Kid?"

"No. Billy shot him twice in the back while he was running from that smuggled gun."

"We might have to do something with that. Readers today want a Billy who's smarter than paint and kind to old ladies."

"He was a tricky little shit."

In the hotel room Pat had arranged for him, Hough unstrapped his suitcase, found a bottle of gin, and filled two glasses, handing one to Pat. He shed his boots and gaiters for a pair of worn leather slippers and sat in a straight chair at a drop-front secretary while the long man stretched out on the bed, his boots protruding over the footboard. "What is it you want from me, Pat?"

"I don't look at it like that. Last time I saw you in El Paso you said you wanted to poke around the Southwest for material. You need a guide for that."

"Are you volunteering?"

"I ain't volunteered for a single thing since I ran for sheriff in Doña Ana County. You read my book?"

"The last part. I thought the first part was a mess of cowflop. Upson must have been plenty drunk to have come up with it."

"Ash was plenty drunk most of the time. He said that's what sells books—the cowflop, not the drinking, though if that was true he'd have been rich as Croesus. Well, it was a poor job and I went along with it. I can't see as we'd do any worse telling the truth."

Hough refilled both glasses, then smacked the cork back into the bottle with finality; he was no Ash Upson. "Well, there's truth and truth. You have to cut the gin with something or no one will want to drink it. Are we talking about collaborating on a new life of Billy?"

"What do you think?"

"It's all right as far as it goes. It's not ambitious enough. Grosset and Dunlap want me to write a new and complete history of the war in Lincoln County. You know the kind of book: embossed covers, painted starbursts, prominent American flag. You'll find one in every parlor from Leadville to Union City."

"Where do I fit in?"

"Primary source. Of course you'll be paid a fee."

"Royalties?"

Hough shook his head. "It's the market, Pat. My hands are tied."

Pat took a drink, held it, then swallowed. The gin burned all the way down. "How much?"

The writer stood, took a yellow leather billfold out of the breast pocket of his tweed coat hanging on one of the bedposts, and thumbed out five twenty-dollar banknotes, which he laid on the maple nightstand. "Consider that an advance against expenses. New York takes too long. I'm still spending the royalties from *The Mississippi Bubble*."

"Thanks, Em. I'm short until I resolve this goat business."

"I heard you were in real estate."

"That went sour. The bookkeeper cleaned out the safe and lit a shuck for old Mexico."

"You should have stuck with keeping the peace."

"Better class of people," Pat agreed.

Hough finished his drink. "Where do we start?"

"Stinking Springs."

"Sounds pretty."

"It used to be. I can't answer for it now."

* * *

The horses they had hired—fat, town-kept, more accustomed to picnic rides on the flats outside Lincoln than hard gallops up standing country—found the going rougher than had the lean, experienced mounts the Garrett posse had ridden through the heavy December snows of twenty-eight years before. A late January thaw had turned the drifts on the ridges to greasy slush, the runoff standing in vast brown puddles that splattered Pat's slicker to the elbows and surprised uncharacteristic blasphemies from Emerson Hough when rooster tails splashed his face and neck, chilling him to the bone. The river was sluggish with mud and floes of dun-colored ice piled up like discarded mattresses in the bends. Hoofs slipped and scrabbled in the slime that coated the grades. The men stopped often to let the horses blow. Pat, helping himself to a slug of hot coffee from a vacuum bottle, confessed that if they'd made this kind of time in '80 and '81, the Kid would still be terrorizing the countryside.

"That's hard to picture," said Hough. "A fifty-year-old Bonney."

The shack took finding. The slant roof had fallen in, splaying out the walls, and the pine timbers and siding had rotted and settled into an orange mulch to match the carpet of sodden dead needles that surrounded them; from any distance it looked like one of a hundred treefalls lining the river. They picked their way down the slope where Pat, Lon Chambers, and the others had stretched out on their bellies in the predawn, dismounted and tethered their horses to the fallen ironwood roofpoles. Lengths of squashed and rusted stovepipe and a corner of iron bedstead stuck up out of the debris, looking like the calcified skeleton of an extinct beast.

"Not much left," Pat said. "Two more years and you won't be able to find the spot."

"Are you sure this is it? It doesn't look like the kind of place the Kid would choose to make a stand."

"He didn't. He thought we wouldn't follow him in no blizzard. Billy always did underestimate his friends."

"You mean his enemies."

"Everybody liked Billy."

Pat walked back and forth in front of the ruined house, measuring with his stride. He stopped. "Right here's where Charlie Bowdre was standing when he was shot. I got him first, through the lungs. He was carrying a nosebag. I thought it was Billy coming out to feed the horses."

"You and Bowdre knew each other."

"I knew all of them, him and Rudabaugh and Tom O'Folliard and Billie Wilson and little Tom Pickett. Billy was the only real card player in the bunch. Dead now, the lot, and not a one of them in bed, neither."

"Are you sorry?"

"I wouldn't trade, if that's where you're headed." He scraped a clot of mud and pine needles off his boot heel against the edge of a foundation stone. Then he looked at Hough. "You know Billy stood Charlie up, all shot to pieces as he was, and stuck a pistol in his hand and shoved him back out the door to draw our fire. They was fixing to go partners in a ranch when they'd rustled enough."

"He must have been crazy."

"Everybody said so."

He kicked at the loose weeds and other rubbish inside the foundation. "We left Billy's horse right here, where I dropped it to block the door. I reckon coyotes carried off whatever was left."

Hough's smile was tight beneath the brush moustache. "Maybe he came back for it. Maybe they're ghosts together."

"That ghost talk's horseshit." Pat jerked loose his horse's tether and mounted. His face felt tight.

The writer opened his mouth, then shut it. He followed suit, looking puzzled. They spurred the fat, complaining horses up the slope.

When they reached Fort Sumner they didn't even step down. It was dry there. A cold wind skinned crystals of white dust from the ground and knifed through their coats, Pat's a good one made of heavy bearskin, Hough's tailored in Chicago with a red silk lining that must have felt like ice when he first put it on. There was nothing there but a stone well heaped high with sand and a maze of broken adobe walls. The town had picked up and moved down the road when the wells went dry. The desert was busy reclaiming what was left. They had glimpsed its only apparent resident, a fat gila, waddling toward the cover of a granite shelf, when they'd drawn rein.

"Bonney hung out *here?*" Hough asked.

Pat leaned on his arms, folded on his pommel. "You could get anything you wanted in Fort Sumner: Girls, cards, tequila. Steaks as thick as your arm. The best fighting cocks west of St. Louis dropped their feathers behind Pete Maxwell's place, and that's the best in the world. If Billy ever thought about heaven, this here's what he had in mind."

"Hard to imagine, even for a writer."

"I can't hardly tell where Pete Maxwell's was."

"Approximately."

Pat pointed. "He was hunkered right there with some of the locals. I'm sure now it was him, though I didn't see the green hatband in the dark. He walked over there and let himself over the fence."

"That's when you went to see Maxwell."

"I was sitting with him in the dark when Bonney come in, asking Pete who those fellows were outside. I knew his voice. He'd walked right past Poe and McKinney. I shot him twice while he was still asking who it was."

"Where's the grave?"

The long man stirred himself and put his heels to his horse. He led the way to the ruins of the old fort wall, where a cluster of sorry weathered wooden markers lolloped about at crazy angles. After a few minutes spent picking their way among the sunken graves, most of which were no longer marked, and some of which had given up their charges, they reined in. Pat shook his head. "Floods and weather. There's no telling which one's his."

"Or if he's still here," Hough said.

Chapter Twenty-two

The March of the Torreadors

Pat was relieved to see, when he got in from the El Paso station, that Mrs. Brown was out, even though the late hour meant she was probably across the river sharing the bed of her Mexican policeman. He hadn't the energy to keep up with her chatter, which would probably have led to a fight, and he was too tired to take his boots in hand and try to sneak between the sheets without stirring her awake. Visiting the scenes of his youth only to find the features he best remembered in an advanced state of decomposition had depressed and exhausted him. It was like receiving news of the death of an old friend or elderly relative, despite whose late infirmity he could convince himself he could always go back to his earlier happiness, only to find that door slammed resoundingly and forever by fate. The thoroughness of the decay had appalled him. In his mind it was all so fresh. He felt the weight of his years.

In the dark he undressed completely, his long underwear peeling like greased paper from his armpits and crotch. He could never remember where Mrs. Brown put his nightshirt after washing it—she refused to drape it over the back of a chair beside the bed, as he was accustomed to in Las Cruces—and he didn't feel like lighting a lamp and pawing through drawers. The soles of his naked feet shrank from the surface of the wide floor planks, worn smooth and cold as polished stone. The stove had gone out, he lacked the will to start it up, and so he slid quickly beneath the heavy quilt and shivered while waiting for the heat of his body to fill the cavity where he lay. The air smelled musty and damp. There had not been a fire in the house for a week, which meant that Mrs. Brown had left immediately after seeing him off from El Paso.

He should have stayed in Las Cruces. There, Apolinaria had welcomed him as warmly as if he had been away only a few days and sat him and his guest down to a hot meal of fresh tortillas and peppers that stung their tongues, with gallons of strong coffee served hot enough to raise blisters. After dinner his children had scurried to find his favorite pipe and tobacco and lined up to report on late developments, carefully avoiding the subject of the goats at Bear Canyon. That chore fell to Dudley Poe—already out of his father's favor for allowing himself to be taken in by Cox and Brazel—who came by the next morning during breakfast. At twenty-one the young man was as lean as Pat although not nearly as tall, with his mother's dusky skin and a languid way about ranch work that belonged as much to his Garrett blood as his Mexican. On several occasions, he said, he'd been forced to herd the disagreeable creatures away from the house, where they had worried nearly all the paint off the northeastern corner rubbing it with their horns, and once they had pulled down a clothesline, dragging his mother's washing through the dust of the backyard. Pat advised him to shoot them the next time they wandered inside range.

Later, showing off for Hough while they were riding near Bear Canyon, Pat had fired his Yellow Boy Winchester at one of the animals grazing along the lip. The hammer snapped on a punk shell.

"The same goddamn thing happened the day I had Oliver

Lee square in my sights," he'd said, ramming the carbine back into its scabbard.

He should have stayed. Telling Apolinaria good-bye had set him low. She was too much the saint in their bedroom and could be shrill as a bitch coyote when he tracked mud into the parlor or scratched a chair rung when he forgot to take off his spurs, but she was worth more than all the Mrs. Browns in Texas. He could not abide looking out a window he had paid for and seeing goats.

"Quien es?"

He did not know he'd slept. He was lying there in the bed Mrs. Brown had brought with her from Fort Worth. He could see her dress form standing in the moonlight skating through the window, reminding him of the torso of a Chinese prostitute, armless, legless, headless, found behind a crib in Lincoln County when he was sheriff, a case he hadn't solved. When he'd asked Mrs. Brown to put it in some other room, she'd laughed at him and ignored the request. It was demonstrably her room. But there coming through the door from the hall was that half-naked figure he'd seen in Pete Maxwell's bedroom, and indeed every bedroom he'd slept in since that night. The knife was in the man's hand, his stockinged footfalls were silent. He smelled pungently of greasewood fires and semen, sweat and sulphur, horse and rawhide and tequila and other men's butchered cattle. Pat knew Billy Bonney's special scent as well as any stray yellow dog he fed scraps to in Fort Sumner.

"Quien es?"

He drew his big Colt's and fired; fired again, screaming over the second report. Screaming because, in the flare from the first, he saw the young man's face clearly, though not in time to stop his finger from squeezing the trigger again. It was his own face, not Billy's; his own face, yet not his own, younger than he had been in 1881, gentler, with Apolinaria's great dark eyes. The face was Dudley Poe's. He had slain his son.

He was awake a long time, and had lit a lamp and explored every room of the house, before he satisfied himself that he had only dreamt, that the dream had merely found a new path toward torment.

The next morning he went to see Deacon Jim Miller, but the woman who kept his boardinghouse, a fat Mexican and former madam who had turned out her girls and hung out a new shingle in response to a city ordinance zoning low commerce out of her neighborhood, told him he was out. The building had been a bishop's house during Spanish colonization; a separate carriage house stood in back. Pat found Miller currying his horse inside. It was a short-coupled strawberry roan, sixteen hands high. Its hooves had been waxed recently, and although its coat shone, Miller continued to work at it with his hands inside the straps of the best-looking set of matched combs Pat had seen in a long time. The Deacon was in white lawn shirtsleeves with the cuffs turned back to his elbows. His forearms were hairless and corded with muscle. Without the coat, in his squared-off hat and black vest he looked less like an undertaker and more like a preacher at a tent revival. He breathed heavily as he worked and a glassy sheen of sweat coated his face.

"You'll rub the hide right off that pretty horse if you ain't careful," Pat said.

Miller, whose back was turned to the entrance, went on combing as if he'd been aware of the other man's presence right along. "There is an order out here," he said. "Horses first, guns next. There are nesters dead in the Panhandle who forgot that."

"What's Brazel about?" He didn't want to know any more about the nesters in the Panhandle. The rumors he'd heard had involved shotguns.

"I talked to him Saturday. It seems he miscounted."

"Money or goats?"

"The price is still three-fifty a head. Only instead of twelve hundred head it's eighteen hundred."

"Who does his counting?"

"That's neither here nor there. It's an additional two thousand dollars. I haven't that much to spend."

"The deal's off, then."

"It doesn't have to be."

Pat said nothing. The scrubbing of Miller's brushes was the only sound in the stable.

"Brazel is on his way back to Las Cruces," Miller said then. "He's taking a buckboard over the Mail-Scott Road. A man on a good horse taking the Freighter's Road could overtake him easily."

"Why would he want to do that?" Pat asked.

The currying stopped. Miller clapped the combs together, placed them in a worn leather satchel on a shelf containing an old lantern and a bucket of coal oil, and used a chamois cloth to wipe his hands, paying particular attention to the nails. "I'm as good with a rifle as with a shotgun," he said. "I favor a forty-four-fourty Winchester. You can't tell from the slug whether it came from a long gun or a pistol."

Pat produced a plug of Levi Garrett's and his pocketknife. He sliced off a chew the thickness of a dollar and popped it into his mouth. When the saliva came he spat a jet at the stone foundation. "I do my own shooting. When I do it."

"A man's eye at sixty isn't what it was at thirty. It won't cost you," Miller added. "I have a brother-in-law, Carl Adamson. We'll buy your ranch for three thousand, just like you and I agreed, and pay you a dollar a head to drive those cattle up from Mexico. That makes the goat problem ours. It won't concern you how we handle it."

"It ain't the way I care to profit."

"Look on it as a courtesy. Cox holds the mortgage on your spread, and he's in with Brazel. I can go to him with the same deal."

"Go to hell."

Miller took his black coat off a nail, brushed it with the edge of his hand, and put it on. Pat noticed the special harness for his shotgun stitched to the lining. "That's a mistake," said the deacon.

"More than likely. At sixty, one more don't matter all that much." Pat left.

Tom Powers, taking the sun in a captain's chair in front of the Coney Island, listened without expression to Pat's account of his conversation with Jim Miller. He had a bottle of tequila on the window ledge beside him.

"Miller's a bad hat," he said when Pat finished. "Don't let him see your back."

"I don't believe that story about his killing no fifty men. My pa was a colonel in the Confederate Army and he didn't see that many kilt the whole time he was in. Ash Upson said Billy Bonney killed a man for every year he lived. I wouldn't go above six."

"Six or sixty, what's it matter? One's plenty if it's you. Stay away from Miller."

"I am done with him. I'm done with ranching, too, just as soon as I get rid of them damn goats."

"Go back to Las Cruces. El Paso is no place for you."

"That's just what I'm fixing to do, Tom. I come to say good-bye."

Powers got up and stuck out his hand. "You watch all around and up and down. You've got more enemies than any man I know, and I'm in the saloon business."

"You don't need a lot of enemies to have to watch yourself," Pat said.

He went to the El Capitan for the kind of breakfast he preferred when traveling, rare steak and runny eggs and fried potatoes swimming in grease, washed down with three cups of thick black coffee. Across the river a fresh group of Mexicans, or perhaps they were the same, were having a celebration, this one somewhat less morbid than the one he had witnessed the last time: A pair of boys capered down the street sharing a black crepe cover, one in front wearing a papier-mâché bull's head complete with scarlet-stained horns and a painted snarl, his partner behind, flipping a tail made from a frayed length of rope. Bawling convincingly, they undulated along, sometimes charging into the crowds that lined the street, forcing them to scatter in mock fright, while the ubiquitous band followed, playing "The March of the Torreadors." Performers dressed up as picadors darted in and out and pretended to puncture the beast's back with banderillas. At length the matador appeared, borne upon the shoulders of half a dozen brightly dressed newcomers, who set him on his feet before the bull. The boys in the black costume pawed the ground, lowered the head, and charged, enabling the bogus matador to wheel his red cloak in a passable veronica, then twirl on his heels and apply the death-stroke. As the collapsible sword seemed to sink between the shoulder blades, a girl in a frilly black dress and a mantilla came forward carrying a pot with a ladle and basted the crepe with red liquid to represent blood. The ersatz bull reeled, tossed its head, wobbled, and fell with a resounding groan, the boys inside rolling over onto their backs and kicking their feet. The matador bent over the "carcass" for a moment, then straightened with a leap, displaying a severed black papier-mâché ear in each outstretched hand. The crowd shouted "olé!"

Pat reflected that the bullfight season was starting early this year. He had been to only one fight and hadn't enjoyed it. Some people felt bad for the horses that were gored when the picadors rode too near the bull, but these were bony, spavined nags destined for the gluepot anyway. Some feared for the men, but to Pat's thinking if some damn fool was determined to get himself gutted he oughtn't to expect tears when it happened. It was the bull Pat felt bad about. The dumb brute never had the luxury of choice, and even when it managed to kill the one who was out to kill it, the picadors stepped in and slaughtered it. It was a harsh world for bulls.

Mrs. Brown was still out when he got back. He pulled his valise out of the closet and packed carelessly, not bothering to fold anything since she never bothered to iron anything anyway, though he bet she put a nice crease in her Mexican's uniform pants. When he took his shirts from the bureau he found a letter he had received recently from Emerson Hough and reread it. The Lincoln County War project had foundered in New York, but Hough's new publishers had commissioned him to write a serial entitled *The Story of the Outlaw*. They had further agreed to pay Pat two hundred dollars for his cooperation, that amount to be returned if the completed book failed to make expenses. "While its changed arrangement makes it general in application and not applicable to any one locality," Hough wrote, "it may surprise me by making money, in which case I think you can depend that I will do the right thing by you."

He crumpled the letter and tossed it into a corner. Then he strapped up his valise, flipped his key onto the bed, and went out to catch the noon train.

Chapter Twenty-three

Leap Year Day

At half-past 4 A.M. Saturday, February 29, 1908, Patrick Floyd Garrett made love to his wife.

They had been awakened an hour earlier by a ranch hand, who reported he'd glimpsed someone prowling around behind the corral. Pat tucked his nightshirt into the corduroy trousers he'd worn the previous day, pulled on a pair of boots and his bearskin, snatched up his folding Burgess shotgun from the corner near the bed, and went out with the hand to investigate.

"What did you see?" Pat asked.

"Just something moving. I'm sure it was a man. He was all dark. I think he might have had on a black coat."

The night air had a snap to it, but the ground was still soft from the last thaw. Pat struck a match and put it to a lantern. Fresh bootprints crossed a bare patch of earth and vanished into the grass beyond.

"Vagrants come to the door sometimes," reported the hand. "There's a deal of cowpunchers afoot these days since they fenced the range."

"Well, stay awake."

Pat climbed back into bed, but he was too alert now to sleep. He found the hem of Apolinaria's shift and pushed it up to her hips.

She started. "Your hands are like ice."

He withdrew them from her bare skin. "I reckon I can do this without hands," he said.

She felt hot when he entered her. Mrs. Brown was always chilled—he was forever getting up to feed the stove, even on nights when he would have been comfortable with the window open—and he had almost forgotten how much he missed Apolinaria's warm Spanish blood. Within minutes he was sweating. His release came soon after, an explosive shudder.

He was wide-awake now. He had an appointment with Wayne Brazel and Carl Adamson, Jim Miller's brother-in-law, in Las Cruces that morning, to settle the business of how many goats Brazel had to sell. Sometimes a careless shaver, he now handled the ivory-handled razor with precision, pinching his nose to get at the short coarse hairs that grew in the creases of his nostrils and trimming his moustaches with the long-bladed steel shears from his toilet kit. He dressed just as carefully in his best linen shirt, boiled blue-white and ironed by Apolinaria, the good black broadcloth suit he had worn for his first meeting with Roosevelt, stovepipe boots he'd blacked himself—a chore he trusted to no other—and a string tie, which he did over when he could not get the ends even the first time. He didn't want anyone taking the impression he wasn't familiar with the niceties of civilization.

Breakfast consisted of Apolinaria's corn bread, hot and crumbling in pools of melted butter, rashers of crisp bacon, fried eggs slightly overdone—her only failing in the kitchen—corn fritters drowned in honey, and of course coffee strong enough to float a boot, his wife being the only woman in the world who had the sand to throw in that extra handful of ground beans. Almost the entire family was gathered in one room: Dudley Poe's grave-eyed older sister Ida, married now but living on the ranch while her husband looked for work in Texas; eighteen-year-old Elizabeth, sightless since childhood, home on a visit from the Texas School for the Blind in Austin; twelve-year-old Patrick Floyd, Jr.; nine-year-old Annie; little Pauline, Pat's favorite at age eight; four-year-old Oscar; and Jarvis, the baby, at two and a half already displaying signs of growing up to look the most like his father. Dudley Poe had spent the night in town and would join Pat and the others at the meeting. The children's mother sat at the opposite end of the trestle table from Pat, watching closely for crimes of etiquette and the occasional smuggling expedition from the table to the dog. In the presence of such substantial proof of his claim upon the twentieth century, Pat felt invincible, and in uncharacteristic good humor. When Annie helped herself to a third portion of corn bread he chided her for her plumpness, then winked to remove the sting when her lower lip began to quiver. Apolinaria reminded him to go easy on Dudley Poe for his part in the Brazel mess. He told her not to worry. "Brazel promised calves. He knew goats don't throw calves. If I didn't know him for Cox's bootlick I might have went for it my own self." Relieved, she smiled brilliantly.

Apolinaria and the girls were clearing the table when the hand who had awakened Pat early that morning came to the door to announce that a two-horse buggy was coming down the ranch road. A few minutes later Carl Adamson drew the buggy up before the porch and got out. He was a good foot shorter than Pat but outweighed him by twenty pounds. The stout newcomer wore a brown bowler and a tan coat whose hem swept the tops of his Wellington boots, the coat unbuttoned to expose a vest strung with fraternal medals; he jingled when he stepped up onto the porch to shake Pat's hand. He had a pink, youthful, clean-shaven face and glass-blue eyes that reminded the long man of the insulators on telegraph poles.

"The sky looks mighty like snow," Adamson said by way of greeting. "There is no good purpose your catching your death on horseback."

Pat said, "I reckon I rode through heaps worse before you were born." But he went back to the door to tell his wife good-bye.

"I don't like him," Apolinaria whispered. "He smiles too much."

Pat showed his teeth. "You're always telling me I don't smile enough. You're powerful hard to please, old girl."

"I don't like him," she said again.

"If I only did business with men I got on with, we'd be in even worse shape than we are. I've got a good feeling about this. Our money problems are about over."

The road, narrow and rutted, wandered past the former boomtown of Gold Camp, inhabited now by prospectors motivated more by habit than hope, prostitutes too old and fat to move on, and the odd armadillo, across San Augustine Pass between the peaks of the Organ Range, through Organ, and down to Las Cruces. The sky was low enough to touch and the landscape was all the same dour shade of gray.

"Desolate country," Adamson said.

"There ain't a square inch of it not crawling with some kind of life." Pat elaborated to keep his mind off the damp chill; he had driven off without his topcoat. "When Geronimo was about you took your hair in your hands every time you went out."

"They sent that old bastard to Florida. They should have hung him in Arizona."

"He'd agree, I reckon."

A mile farther on, Adamson leaned over and craned his neck to peer back up the road. "Now who's this? Not some Apache who hasn't got the news, I hope."

Pat looked. "It's just my daughter on her mare. Let her catch up."

They stopped. Pauline, tall for her years and slender, an accomplished horsewoman at eight, slowed from a gallop to a trot, then drew rein alongside the buggy. She had her father's bearskin folded across the pommel of her saddle. "Mommy says you'll catch your death." She was panting.

Pat climbed down and lifted her off the saddle. He kissed her on the cheek, tickling her with his moustaches so that she screwed up her face and turned it away. "Gracias, azúcar. Take good care of Mommy, and I'll bring you back a pretty." He took down his coat and helped her back astraddle. She was still watching when the buggy rattled over the next hill, putting the country between them.

"I never dreamed you had so many children," Adamson said.

"Me neither. Every time I look up it seems there's another." Pat felt uncommonly good.

From the pass they could look across La Jornada del Muerto, the long man's favorite route to the border. A split in the clouds spilled red morning sunlight onto the sand, reminding him that it was soaked two feet deep with the blood of Spaniards, Indians, mountain men, prospectors, and settlers, not to mention Albert Fountain and his young son, forever to be unavenged. Pat had chased buffalo across it, Billy Bonney, too, and been chased across it by Apaches. He had thought to irrigate it and make it green, but he was glad now he had lost the chance. To do so would have been like chaining a lion. He never felt so alive as when he was crossing its hammered arid surface. For this reason he could never bring himself to refer to it by its name in English. He did not even think of it in private as the Journey of the Dead.

The jangling of Adamson's medals brought Pat out of his

reverie. The stout man had taken out his watch and snapped open its face. "We're making excellent time," he said. "There's a chance we'll overtake Brazel on his way in."

"I'm for getting this business over as soon as possible."

"All the more reason to make haste. We'll celebrate with drinks in Las Cruces." Adamson returned his watch to his vest pocket, shifted the reins to that hand, and gave them a flip. The matched grays broke into a canter.

Organ was a scattering of adobe huts that looked as they might have when Coronado came through, log buildings constructed of mountain pine that were nearly as old, and a clapboard general store that had thrived on the first push of miners and now hung on with help from the hollow-eyed men who continued to sift through the sand for the glitter of their lost youth. They would always need coffee and tobacco, the open front door seemed to say; there may yet be a strike. Bow-legged overalls and stiff suits of long johns swung like board signs from the clotheslines strung behind the buildings, reminding Pat grimly of the washing the goats had spoiled. He felt his good mood slipping away through the loose grains of sand churned up by the buggy's wheels.

Everything looks so old, he thought. *It was all so new and stinking of green wood and sawdust.* He spotted an old man sitting on a chair splattered with whitewash on the front porch of the assay office, his white beard stained yellow all around the mouth, and he thought, *I'm old, too, by God; older than all the sorry-looking horses in this town strung end to end.*

"What an ugly place," Adamson said then. "A flood here would bring nothing but improvement."

"The prettiest whores in the territory used to hang around in front of that store. Cowboys without a nickel to their names used to ride in for sixty miles just to get a look at them."

"That must be why they moved on. They couldn't have made any living off the locals either."

Pat lapsed back into silence.

South of Organ the road forked. The Mail-Scott Road, a relatively smooth route, meandered among the foothills, while the Freighter's Road bucked and jounced the short way into Las Cruces. They came together two miles north of the town, but travelers generally chose the longer Mail-Scott in deference to their fillings. Just ahead of the fork, Pat directed Adamson to haul up in front of Russel Walter's livery stable. He recognized Russel's son Willis standing in the bed of a wagon, scooping alfalfa through the open door of the stable's second-story loft.

"Have you seen Wayne Brazel?" Pat asked.

Willis pointed his tines down the Mail-Scott Road. "He just left."

As they turned down the fork, Pat saw two riders stopped with their horses nose to nose a half-mile down. At the buggy's approach one of the riders backed off, wheeled his mount, and dug in his spurs, kicking up a thick cloud of dust as he galloped down the road. The long man's eyes weren't as good at a distance as they used to be. The horse was either a sorrel or a strawberry roan.

Brazel, sitting a blaze-faced black with his blanket roll across his cantle, was a tall, loose-jointed thirty, slender rather than lean, with no hair on his face and thickish lips twisted into the kind of permanent smile that Pat in his youth had enjoyed knocking off the face of many a fellow cowhand and hider. He had on a town suit and a new gray Stetson that he nudged back with a knuckle to avoid staining the brim with sweat from his fingertips.

"You're off to a quick start," he told Adamson.

"I wanted to get to the livery before all the best vehicles were spoken for." The stout man tried out a smile, which faded in the awkward pause that followed.

Pat ended it. "Who's that you were talking to?"

"Some drifter." Brazel took up his reins and coaxed his black into the road.

"Not a lot of those around these days."

"Folks stay put now," Adamson agreed. He started the horses moving. Brazel rode alongside. Plainly Adamson was a man who disliked silence. "Yes, there is not much now of this blowing with the wind. When folks get the urge to move they motor out into the countryside for a picnic or what-have-you. I don't care for it myself."

"What, picnics?" The rider looked puckish. It was those thick lips, in a mouth too narrow for his face.

"Motoring. Automobiles in general. You can't hear the birds singing for the noise. And then there are the punctures. No, sir, I don't care for it at all."

"I don't know. I'd sooner ride on springs than bones and hay."

Pat made a noise of impatience. At that point the road narrowed. Brazel struck out ahead, and for a time there was no need for conversation. Then it widened again and the rider fell back beside the buggy. In his desperation to avoid embarrassment, Adamson chose a poor subject for jest. "Are your goats kidding yet?" He chortled.

"They must be," Pat said. "I can't feature how twelve hundred got to be eighteen hundred otherwise."

Brazel's smile changed. "I missed counting a bunch in Bear Canyon."

"I reckon you're as bad at numbers as my boy is at judging character."

Adamson jumped in. "See here. There's bad feeling between you two and Cox, and to put it right Miller and I are willing to buy the original twelve hundred goats. We don't want even that many, but it's part of the price Mr. Garrett is asking for his ranch."

"If I don't sell the whole bunch, I won't sell none."

Alameda Arroyo was coming up, a jagged-edged pool of shadow under the overcast. Adamson pulled back on the horses and handed the lines to Pat.

"Puncture?" The friction with Brazel was restoring the long man's humor. Nothing brought him down lower than a false civility. He liked things out in the open. He seemed to be one of the few left who did.

"I have a weak bladder." Adamson climbed down and hurried behind a clump of mescal, unbuttoning his fly.

Alone with Pat, Brazel smiled down at his nails. "Maybe I'll just hang on to that lease."

"It don't make any difference what you do. I'll get you off the land somehow."

"Cox is right about you, Garrett. You're a muleheaded old son of a bitch."

"Goddamn right."

When Adamson returned, Pat gave him back the reins and stepped down to the ground, taking his folding shotgun. "I believe I'll bleed the goose myself."

"Do you always bring along a weapon?" The stout man laughed nervously.

"Ever since Lincoln County."

Disdaining the cover of brush—his dingus was in proportion with the rest of him and he wasn't ashamed to haul it out into the air—Pat turned his back to the buggy and pissed into the dust, balancing the shotgun along his left forearm. The air was getting colder; his urine steamed. He smelled iron. His joints ached. That meant snow, and plenty of it. It was going to be a regular Stinking Springs winter, perhaps even as bad as '86. Maybe the damn goats would all freeze to death. Maybe God, if He did exist, would take pity on the frontier and blast down every stick of civilization, every last brick shithouse and oil derrick and cattlemen's trust, put the territory back where it was when he came to it in '77. Pretty señoritas and bandidos with gold teeth, asshole-ugly longhorn steers and Apaches as mean as bloody turds and tortillas deep-fried in buffalo lard.

He'd had to pee worse than he'd thought; he had a partial erection. It had been good that morning with Apolinaria, he remembered. Damn good, for a man bearing down on fifty-eight. He wondered if there were any cute whores left in Las Cruces. Some of them might be granddaughters of the ones he'd known, in which case he might be committing incest. Old man dreams. What was that tune the tricky little shit loved to whistle? "Darling, we are growing older."

He finished. He shook the dew off the lily and buttoned up. He was passing the last one through the eyelet when he heard a noise behind him. He started to turn his head. *Billy?*

Chapter Twenty-four

The Rock and the Desert

The cruellest jest the old gods ever played is to withhold truth until the very moment it no longer matters.

The change is coming. I feel it in the weakness of the hand that must pause, even in the midst of a word, as I write upon these sheets; in the coldness of my lower limbs despite the suffocating quilts and native blankets with which my poor pallet is heaped; moreover I feel it in my thoughts, which will not stay to their purpose as of old, but fly in all directions like startled birds and are compelled to resume their perch only through great effort on my part, which drains the little strength I still possess. The store is depleting, it shall not be restocked in this pale. I must write until I can no longer will the pen to move.

There is no formula for the transmutation of base metal, this I now know. Gold is gold, lead is lead. A hedgehog cannot soar, nor an eagle suckle its young. The Black Maria, if it ever existed, is but a fungoid growth, good only for adding flavor to one's repast, if indeed it is not deadly poison. My great-grandfather, whose memory I have placed above all others, was a puffer and a charlatan, more culpable than his father who gulled a king, for he has made the descendants of his own blood the victims of his lies. He did not create silver from quicksilver, as he recorded in his notes. He merely sought by them to live beyond his span, and in his blind arrogance had not the wits of a lowborn fool, who knows that in the infinity of time all must be revealed and every ruse made transparent. In this, he had at the last fallen prey to his own deception. The pages he had written comprised the last fuel I fed to the athanor. The brittle parchment offered itself to the flame like a disenchanted maiden stretched upon the conjugal bed and was gone up the chimney in the drawing of a breath.

There is no Philosopher's Stone. My life, long though it has been, is but an empty vessel, open at both ends, so all that was poured into it passed through the bottom and vanished into the sand, wasted. My line, more ancient than all of Europe's great dynasties, has been an extended irrelevance, a row of antique snuffboxes twinkling facetiously upon the shelf of a collector of amusing obsolescences. In our time, we had represented knowledge, and all that was awesome and holy there attendant. Kings envied us our independence. Popes feared our freedom from superstition. We knew all that was known, had read every tract, dismantled and examined every discovery from the charts of Copernicus to Galvani's coils, and declared it insufficient. We had dared to strike out into the dark part of the universe in search of yet more illumination. We were Oedipus and also the Sphinx, Columbus and Mohammed, Tamerlane and Tesla, Odin casting his eye into the Well of Wisdom and Paul addressing the Corinthians. We were the conductor and the light. Albertus the Great, demonstrating his ability to coax St. Elmo's Fire from the vane atop the cupola of his house to an iron staff in his hand, and from the staff to a silver goblet held by his son, without harm either to man or boy, kept in thrall for an afternoon an audience that outnumbered all of Caesar's legions, and dispersed them with no weapon other than that same slender staff and his own formidable will when they cried sorcery and surged forward to seize and crucify him. In those days education was looked upon as a treasure bestowed upon the chosen by divinity, like dominion. But Magnus was as deluded as the rest of us. The truth had passed us by, or we had passed it heedless, beguiled like an infant by a glimmer in a false mirror. We had sought to write the book, and been consigned to a nota bene entangled in the close print of the index.

The athanor has grown cold. No coals glow there for the first time since 1680. The remaining villagers must wonder that there is no curl of smoke from the chimney. I do not miss its light, although I lament the loss of heat. The great-grandson of the boy who first brought water to my rock now brings hot broth to warm my stomach and slow the creeping weakness, but he is eager to look for work in Mexico City, and though he is too much his father's son to express it, he is impatient for my death and his liberty.

I do not begrudge him his restlessness. Had I a son I would not have called upon him to serve an indenture that has already consumed too many lives to no purpose. Moreover, the village is dying, as I am dying. I witnessed its conception, when I was a young man of seventy and my simple hut was the only structure made by man for a hundred square miles. I had measured its slow growth in the beginning, and when the norteamericano petroleum interests came to test-drill for oil I had heard, as on a sudden, the drawing of saws and percussion of hammers, the braying Klaxons, chortling motors, whizzing cable, hydraulic sighs, and all the rest of the din of solvency in the new century. When the wells produced nothing but dust, I had seen the flatbed wagons and great rubber-tired trucks roll northward, carrying the heavy equipment home. The merchants had followed, leaving their buildings to peel and pucker and fill with jackrabbits and tumbleweed. Now when the wind blows, doors open to admit no one and shutters slam to repel nonexistent invaders. Mute signs, their painted legends worn away, creak when they swing and occasionally fall, with no more noise than is made by a leper's fingers dropping away. The wooden oil derricks are gone. The last of them collapsed from dry rot after the others were eaten by fires no one bothered to extinguish. In another year all the roofs will have fallen in; in five, even the foundations will be covered by the jealous desert, and from the vantage of my rock, all will be as it was when the Aztecs abandoned Popocatépetl for the caves of Chihuahua.

But I will not see it.

I have given the boy detailed instructions for the disposition of my remains. This I have done in person, for like all the others who are left in the village he has no knowledge of letters, the last of the padres having been recalled from this parish two years ago. I wish to be laid out upon my bench in my father's velvet robes, my hands folded upon my breast with the pages containing my notes, the complete record of my empty existence, these sheets included, between. I further direct that the hut be set ablaze, and that the flames be allowed to burn themselves out, down to the naked stone, so that nothing survives, least of all the herbs I have cultivated these hundred years. Those that remain must be left to whiten and shrivel in the pounding heat and fall to dust, which the wind will then seize and scatter along with my ashes. The rock alone will stand, the rock and the desert and those things that belong to it. It will be unchanged from the place my father saw when he came south to escape my grandfather's fate. In this at least my vision will succeed where Pat Garrett's failed.

Of the long man's fate I remained ignorant for many months. In the spring of 1909, a professor of zoology at the University of Texas paid me a visit in the course of his Mexican sabbatical, examined the stuffed armadillo hanging from my ceiling, and declared that it represented the only known specimen of its particular subspecies extant. I declined to sell it, but I gave him permission to measure it and make detailed sketches, in return for intelligence from the north. At present, he reported as he laid out his instruments and colored chalks, all of New Mexico and Southwest Texas was buzzling over the recent verdict in the Pat Garrett murder trial.

So far as was known, Pat died instantly when a bullet smashed into the back of his head, fired from either a revolver of standard manufacture or a breech-loading rifle in the identical caliber. The position of the body, lying on its back with one glove removed and its trousers partially unbuttoned, suggested clearly that the long man had been ambushed from behind while relieving his bladder alongside the Mail-Scott Road, and yet Wayne Brazel, who stood trial for the killing, claimed to have struck in defense of his own life. His testimony, supported by Carl Adamson, that the dead man had threatened to get Brazel off his land one way or another, and the fact that Pat's Burgess shotgun was found next to his body, were entered into evidence and let stand by an indifferent prosecutor, who failed to summon key witnesses in support of the territory's case or produce subpoenaed documents suggesting a conspiracy involving Brazel, Adamson, Deacon Jim Miller, and W. W. Cox before and after the killing. An apathetic jury deliberated for fifteen minutes, then delivered a bill of acquittal. Two hours later the ex-defendant attended a barbecue in his honor at Cox's ranch.

The men who gathered in Tom Powers' Coney Island Saloon to drink, play cards, and discuss politics and local events were of the general opinion that Brazel was a stalking horse, put up to draw fire for a deed for which he was not responsible. Some fixed the crime on Adamson, who had not the luxury of a plea of self-defense, while others named each of the legion of enemies Pat had made in Texas and New Mexico, including one or two of Billy Bonney's compatriots whose deaths went unrecorded and so were believed to have wandered the West for nearly thirty years, awaiting their opportunity to avenge him. One provocative theory, that Bonney was not dead at all but had come out of hiding in old Mexico to slay the man credited with slaying him, enjoyed a certain popularity until someone thought to ask what motive he might have had to take the life of one who had not, after all, taken his. Still others preferred Jim Miller. These identified Killin' Jim as the mysterious horseman with whom Brazel had been conversing on the Mail-Scott Road when the buggy carrying Adamson and Pat arrived to separate them. There were a thousand lofty places in the vicinity of Alameda Arroyo where a man armed with a Winchester could station himself and shoot the proprietor of Bear Canyon Ranch at long range.

Partly because Miller was widely hated and feared, and partly because his murderous celebrity suited the murder of so celebrated a victim, the Miller Solution, as it came to be known, spread rapidly. By now it has entered the legendary annals alongside Ash Upson's claim—based on nothing but his own imagination, colored with printer's ink and cured with alcohol—that at the time of his death at age twenty-one, Billy the Kid had slain a man for every year of his life; and there it will remain, as permanently as James Butler Hickok's last hand of cards and the old woman in Missouri whose mortgage Jesse James took it upon himself to pay off with money stolen from the same bank that issued it. But by the time the men of the Coney Island arrived at this conclusion, the point was moot. On April 19, 1909, the same day the jury in Las Cruces declared Wayne Brazel innocent of the crime with which he was charged, a masked mob pulled Jim Miller from a jail in Texas where he was awaiting trial for the brutal murder of a local man and hanged him from the rafters of a livery barn nearby. As if to ordain the event, one of the vigilantes draped Miller's sober black coat over his body where it lay among the loose hay and horseshit after it was cut down.

Whether because of outrage over the affront to justice or because of an Old Testament faith in blood cleansing blood, the manner in which Pat Garrett was beheld underwent a dramatic change in the months following his death. Old enemies waxed sentimental upon his subject, and friends vexed by his complicated personality forgot his inconsistencies and dwelt upon his more sterling characteristics. The public in general, which in response to the inundation of paperbound novels deifying Billy the Kid had been wont to consider his killer in a category with Bob Ford and Jack McCall, assassins of Jesse James and Wild Bill Hickok, respectively, now took into account his official status as a peace officer and the long months spent combing the backcountry for Bonney's trail, and awarded him a place among the great lawmen of his day. Copies of the disastrous *Authentic Life of Billy the Kid* surfaced from mercantile storage rooms where they had lain neglected for three decades, and inquiries were made to Apolinaria Garrett by a major publishing company in New York in regard to a new edition, to be edited and annotated by an established authority on the history of the Lincoln County War. A maker of moving pictures, having relocated in California to escape an injunction brought by the Edison Company to protect its patent on the filmmaking process, had announced plans to produce a two-reel feature dramatizing the young bandit's career, with equal attention paid to Bonney and Garrett. The resurrection was in full cry.

My relationship with the long man is more difficult to interpret. Although I did not hear of him for years at a time, when news did come I experienced, as in a sudden burst of illumination in a dark room, the whole of his thoughts and emotions as they occurred throughout the long silences, as if they were my own, delayed by deep preoccupation. I am a man of science; prescience lies outside my field of study. It may be that because we were both seekers by nature as well as by profession, more compelled by the search itself than by the bitter disappointment of the result, we shared a consciousness. Or it may be that I am a vassal of my imagination. Certainly the evidence of my life and my line is sufficient to prove my capacity for self-delusion. What does it matter, since this record must die with its author?

One success at least I may claim, and that is the answer to the riddle of the cyclone and the peccary. The old gods, accustomed as they are to chaos and conflict, are bored unto death by their inaction in this desert exile, and must amuse themselves with challenges, counting games and the like, to forestall decay. The great Leonardo, whose mind and energies were too adept even for the diversions of the Renaissance, recorded his observations and conclusions backwards, inscribing in his fine hand from right to left, so that he who would benefit by them must turn the pages to a mirror. So too did the pagan immortals write the object of the lesson of the natural force and the dumb beast. Thus, destruction does not follow salvation. The truth is in the reverse.

All things that come from clay go back to it in the end. Save gold.

> Francisco de la Zaragoza, Viceroy in Absentia,
> Durango, Mexico,
> 1782–1911

Chapter Twenty-five

Transmutation

W ell, Big Casino."

"Well, Little Casino."

"Come far, looks like."

"Just down the Jornada. It ain't so far when you know the way."

"I think you know all these boys: Tom O'Folliard, and little Tom Pickett, and Billie Wilson, and old Charlie Bowdre, and there's Rudabaugh."

"How do, boys."

"I sure hope you brung money, Big Casino. We been pushing around what was in our pockets when we got here for ever so long. We wore the injun's head clean off all the pennies."

"I'm fixed okay, I reckon. Only it don't look like Charlie's so glad to see me."

"You know Charlie. It took him the best part of forever to put aside my pushing him out the door at Stinking Springs. He'll come around. Look at Tom. You shot him all to pieces at Roswell and he don't bear no grudge no more."

"Tom always was a Christian."

"Take my seat, Big Casino. Could be it'll bring you more luck than it brung me."

"What's the game?"

"Five card, nothing wild. Excepting me, of course."

"Whose deal?"

"Yours. With these boys I got so I don't know what it's like to get one off the top."

"Stop that whistling."

"Sure thing, Pat. You're dealing."

Westerns available from TOR FORGE

TRAPPER'S MOON • Jory Sherman
"Jory Sherman takes us on an exhilarating journey of discovery with a colorful group of trappers and Indians. It is quite a ride."—Elmer Kelton

CASHBOX • Richard S. Wheeler
"A vivid portrait of the life and death of a frontier town."—*Kirkus Reviews*

SHORTGRASS SONG • Mike Blakely
"*Shortgrass Song* leaves me a bit stunned by its epic scope and the power of the writing. Excellent!"—Elmer Kelton

CITY OF WIDOWS • Loren Estleman
"Prose as picturesque as the painted desert…"—*The New York Times*

BIG HORN LEGACY • W. Michael Gear
Abriel Catton receives the last will and testament of his father, Web, and must reassemble his family to search for his father's legacy, all the while pursued by the murdering Braxton Bragg and desire for revenge and gold.

SAVAGE WHISPER • Earl Murray
When Austin Well's raid is foiled by beautiful Indian warrior Eagle's Shadow Woman, he cannot forget the beauty and ferocity of the woman who almost killed him or figure out a way to see her again.

Available by mail from

TOR FORGE

1812 • David Nevin
The War of 1812 would either make America a global power sweeping to the pacific or break it into small pieces bound to mighty England. Only the courage of James Madison, Andrew Jackson, and their wives could determine the nation's fate.

PRIDE OF LIONS • Morgan Llywelyn
Pride of Lions, the sequel to the immensely popular *Lion of Ireland*, is a stunningly realistic novel of the dreams and bloodshed, passion and treachery, of eleventh-century Ireland and its lusty people.

WALTZING IN RAGTIME • Eileen Charbonneau
The daughter of a lumber baron is struggling to make it as a journalist in turn-of-the-century San Francisco when she meets ranger Matthew Hart, whose passion for nature challenges her deepest held beliefs.

BUFFALO SOLDIERS • Tom Willard
Former slaves had proven they could fight valiantly for their freedom, but in the West they were to fight for the freedom and security of the white settlers who often despised them.

THIN MOON AND COLD MIST • Kathleen O'Neal Gear
Robin Heatherton, a spy for the Confederacy, flees with her son to the Colorado Territory, hoping to escape from Union Army Major Corley, obsessed with her ever since her espionage work led to the death of his brother.

SEMINOLE SONG • Vella Munn
"As the U.S. Army surrounds their reservation in the Florida Everglades, a Seminole warrior chief clings to the slave girl who once saved his life after fleeing from her master, a wife-murderer who is out for blood." —*Hot Picks*

THE OVERLAND TRAIL • Wendi Lee
Based on the authentic diaries of the women who crossed the country in the late 1840s. America, a widowed pioneer, and Dancing Feather, a young Paiute, set out to recover America's kidnapped infant daughter—and to forge a bridge between their two worlds.